Blood Memory:
Eye for an Eye

Skip Clark

Bent Key Press, Apopka, Florida

ISBN: 978-1-935720-00-3

Bent Key Press

PO Box 2184

Apopka, FL 32704

www.BentKeyPress.com

Disclaimer:

Cover Design:

Rik Feeney / **usabookcoach@gmail.com**

Photograph credits:

©Spauln / Dreamstimes.com

©Jcpjr / Dreamstime.com

Dedication

I would like to dedicate this book to my father Sherman Schuylar Clark (1927-2009). He would not have approved of some language my characters use, but he would have forgiven them their lack of manners.

Acknowledgments

I would like to acknowledge the contributions of the following groups and individuals in the development of my book.

Rik Feeney: Book Coach, Editor, Cover Designer and mentor. Without his nagging guidance, the book would never have been completed. Thanks Rik. Yes! I'm working on the next book.

Lara Zielinsky: Proofing and editing. Thanks for taking my gibberish and translating it in to English.

Joyce Bowden: Editing. Thanks for your help

Seminole County Harley Owners Group (SCHOG). Thanks for the use of some of your names. When I tell our story, I'll use names from Lake County to protect the guilty.

Thanks to all my friends and family for listening as I babbled through story lines from the sixteen people in my head.

Blood Memory

According to Irish mythology a select few people inherit not only unique memories but also curious abilities from their ancestors.

Prologue

"Keep your head down. I'm not sure how big the explosion is going to be."

"What the hell do you mean; you don't know how big the explosion is going to be!" Sam said.

"Oh, it's going to be big. I just don't know how big!" Rick said adding a shoulder shrug.

Sam mumbled, "Men!" as she slipped a 40-round magazine into the waistband of her shorts at the small of her back.

Rick asked, "Do you really think you're going to need that?"

"A girl can never have too many accessories, and besides you don't know how big the explosion is going to be."

Loading then closing the grenade launching tube on the M-16 Rick pointed at his head and said, "Hello, amnesia, I don't remember if I've ever blown up a boat before. But I'm sure it's just like riding a bicycle."

"Rick if you blow us up, I'm really going to be pissed."

CHAPTER 1

Rick Blane is the name on my passport. Somehow, it just doesn't fit. You should own your name and most people do! There can be ten other people in a room using your name. But you know they're all imposters, you're the one, the only, the original. I don't feel that way anymore. I'm the imposter and someone else is the original.

Over the intercom, I heard the final call for flight 1057 to Miami at gate 43. I looked at my boarding pass and glanced at my passport. Staring back at me was my picture. Well a close facsimile to the face that stares back each morning in the mirror. Brown hair, blue eyes, six feet two inches tall, two hundred and twenty pounds. Looks like I've lost thirty pounds, along with my memory, since this picture was taken.

The name Rick Blane does not belong to me, I merely parrot the sound. In truth, I feel like Rick's doppelganger, playing a trick on everyone by pretending to be him.

I stood up and put my backpack over my shoulder and started walking toward the gate. The woman making the announcement was in her mid-thirties. Her name tag says she's Anna and is stationed in Atlanta. We've run into each other several times over the past few months and even gone for drinks a couple of times.

"I was beginning to wonder if you were going to join us," she said in a low, sexy voice, that I'm sure she doesn't use on many other passengers.

I handed her my boarding pass. "I don't like to rush things."

She looked me in the eyes and then at my pass. "I've noticed, Mr. Blane, you seem like a man worth knowing and I suspect, worth the wait," she winked and gave me a big smile, "I hope you enjoy your trip."

She handed me my boarding pass. I smiled back at her and started down the passage, "I'm going to try and do just that."

I knew she was watching me as I walked toward the plane or at least I hoped she was. Good for the ego you know. I won't look back; it might spoil my imaginary moment.

She's a very attractive woman and there has been more than a little sexual tension between us. But it wouldn't be fair to her or anyone else to start a relationship, when I'm still healing both physically and emotionally. Besides, I'm still shocked by what I see in the mirror. When I take my shirt off, I don't know how to answer the question of how I got the bullet holes, or these hideous, angry looking scars that criss cross my upper chest. Trying to explain that to someone new in my life is a bridge I'm not ready to cross.

I walked down the dimly lit corridor and stepped onto the plane, looking around as I found my seat. The flight was not crowded, and best of all, no screaming kids. I put my backpack in the overhead compartment and sat down.

There was no one in the seat next to me, so I took the window seat. During a flight, looking at the clouds and patterns on the ground has a calming effect on me.

I have flown a lot over the past several months. My doctor has sent me to specialists in Dallas, LA, Chicago, Tampa and New York. All have told me the same thing; I have amnesia. They don't know when or if my memory will return. I've tried with questionable success to adjust to this fact over the past several months. I've filled in pieces of my life with help from friends and family.

I'm not sure if a psychologist should be called a doctor. What he does seems more like voodoo than medicine. He asks, "How does that make you feel, Mr. Blane?" I want to say, for the amount of money you're charging me, you should already know, but I hold my tongue. At times, I imagine him jumping and up running around the room chanting, shaking a voodoo doll, and hitting me on the head with a chicken's foot. If he was a real doctor, he would be able to write a prescription for something stronger than baby aspirin to help with these headaches.

Anyway, over the last several weeks, I've had a lot of Déjà vu moments or flashbacks. My brain has been trying to connect random events and places. This has made for interesting but false memories. I don't think my "Voodoo Doc" believes I'm crazy. But he suspects I'm getting to the point where I can see crazy from my front porch.

According to him, when I look at the clouds my brain knows this is a new experience and doesn't try to connect them to a memory. That's why I feel relaxed and calm. So the plan is for me to go some place I've never been and make new memories. Hopefully, it will give my brain a chance to heal and stop connecting unrelated events.

So, I'm going to finish the trip I was on when all this started. That means I've got to go back to Miami, return to the scene of the crime, as it were, and face my worst nightmare. I'm going to meet two detectives in the airport who have some new information about my case.

It seems I was big on keeping journals over the last 15 years as I traveled to different parts of the Caribbean.

After reading my journals, I came to the conclusion that all my trips revolved around solving a mystery about some pirates. I wasn't trying to find out what had turned them into ruthless sociopaths, or even where they had hidden their treasures. No, this was about a secret code I believed they developed to warn each other about danger in certain parts of the Caribbean. In the beginning, I thought they were trying to avoid the British, but the timeline was wrong. Besides, they openly laughed and talked about the pending crack down. I think this loosely connected group of cutthroats were themselves being hunted. To me, the messages were a desperate attempt to avoid something or someone.

It all started with a quote from Edward Teach, (Blackbeard) himself, "There are things in these waters. Even those in league with the Devil, himself need fear. I pray never too see their Bloody Sails or smell their stench again."

I've collected books, documents, logs, stories, rumors, and rumors of rumors. All of which had some connection to this mystery.

I've found several comments like Blackbeard's over the years, from infamous and not so infamous pirates. Each gave a warning, but never mentioned a name. I had circled one comment in my journal made by a Captain John Evans. "Heed yea warning from those with the mark. For if yea don't, yea will understand the cursed flag."

The question I asked in the journal and even now; what was out there that was so horrific it makes these men and women, who robbed and murdered for a living, stand up and take notice?

In my last journal entry, I had found some new clues and was excited. They had something to do with the Island of St. Morgan. Unfortunately, the next journal, the clue, and my memory are all missing.

CHAPTER 2

The trip from Atlanta to Miami seemed short. When the announcement came that we were next in the landing pattern, I got a knot in my stomach and noticed my knuckles were white from gripping the armrest. The plane landed and taxied to the terminal as I released my death grip on the armrest.

Everyone quickly stood up and got his or her luggage and proceeded to wait in line to disembark. I don't like standing in lines. After the line cleared, I retrieved my backpack and started down the passage toward the terminal.

When I walk into a room I sometimes get a gut feeling like something is about to happen. Colors seem brighter, smells are stronger, every sound is amplified, and everything seems to slow down. I chuckled to myself. I'm looking for the boogeyman and hopefully I'll recognize him first. Right now I am looking for two men who are going to take me from the safety of the airport back to the mean streets of Miami.

The back of my neck tingled as two men walking toward me looked at something in a folder. They wore dark suits, which may have fit each of them 40 pounds ago, but were definitely straining with the effort to hold back their excesses now.

I knew them without benefit of introduction. They were the detectives who wanted to take me back to the place where I was mugged; a place that turned me into a mental cripple; a place that turned me into a homeless person living on the streets of Miami for three years.

I locked eyes with the shorter and rounder of the two men. He handed the folder to the younger man, walked up to me, and showed me his badge. "Mr. Blane?"

I resisted the urge to say, "That's what's on my passport." Instead, I answered with as much of a southern drawl as possible, "Yassir."

I've noticed that a southern drawl puts people at ease. They think you're slow, stupid, or sometimes if you are chatting with a lady, cute. Either way, it gives you time to find out what type of a person you're dealing with.

"I'm Detective Smith and this is Detective Harris. We talked on the phone. We have some new information."

"Yes Detective, but as I told you I don't remember anything," I said.

"I understand, however, we hope that taking you back to the scene and showing you what we have will help jar your memory," Detective Smith said.

I let out a deep breath, "OK."

"I know you must be apprehensive about going back to the scene of the mugging...

"Lets get this over with; I've been dreading this for too long." I said

"I assure you, we will get you back in time to catch your plane," Smith continued despite the interruption.

"How are you doing?" Detective Harris asked. "I understand you were in bad shape when you were dropped off at the hospital."

"The wounds have just about healed, but I still can't remember shit. The good news is everything is new, the bad news is everything is new."

Detective Harris laughed, "I have a couple of ex-wives' and a girl friend I wish would forget about me, if you know what I mean."

"Did you find out anything about the people who dropped me off at the hospital? I'd like to thank them for saving my life."

"Just what the doctors and nurses told us. A man and woman brought you into emergency. They found you in the street just a couple of blocks from where we're going. The woman said she thought you were homeless because she'd seen you in the area for the last few years. After getting you stabilized, the nurses noticed the couple had left. Mr. Blane, we think you were a victim of a drive by shooting," Smith said.

13

I could feel a stranger's eyes on me as we walked down the concourse and out the doors. We walked to the detective's car, where they put me in the back seat. People look when you're put into the back of a police car, even an unmarked one. I glanced out the back window as we drove away. People were watching and wondering what was going on.

I shook my head and smiled in agreement.

While we drove through the streets of Miami, Harris told me a man had confessed to mugging me and had shown them where the crime had happened. The police had even recovered some of my possessions.

"Since I can't ID this guy and he's confessed, what's the real reason for this trip?" I asked.

"We still have some unanswered questions," Harris said.

We pulled up in front of Poco's, which according to my journals had been my favorite Cuban restaurant in Miami. I got out of the car and looked at the building, then glanced around the parking lot, the landscape, and the restaurant's sign. I tried to take it all in. The sound. The smell. The colors. It all looked vaguely familiar, but that was the problem; everyone and everything looked familiar to me lately.

Looking back at the detectives I said, "Nothing jumps out; it's just a parking lot and building."

"Ok, come over here for a minute." They lead me to the side of the building next to a street where a dumpster was sitting. We stopped near a grassy spot under some palm trees.

I looked at the building again and at the trees and grass. "Still nothing."

Harris filled in some details, "This is what we know. You came out the front of the restaurant. You walked this way toward the street." He pointed to the street and a bus stop. "Our suspect walked up behind you and pulled a gun. He forced you to walk back toward the dumpster."

"There was a struggle and he struck you on the head with his gun. The gun went off. He grabbed your wallet and backpack then ran over to that corner." Harris pointed to the side street behind the dumpster. "The suspect looked back to see if you were following him. He saw you get up and stumble toward the building."

I shook my head "I don't remember ever being here even though I know it was my favorite place to eat in Miami."

"Are you sure?" Harris asked.

I asked, "How many times did the gun go off?"

"Once," Harris answered.

I walked around to look at the building from different angles. The windows and doors were boarded up. I walked back toward the detectives.

"What happened?" I asked pointing to the building.

"Gangs and drive by shootings. After 50 years, the owner decided to close the restaurant. The area has become too dangerous," Smith said.

I looked at the area outside the parking lot and saw trash and gang tags everywhere. This had been a nice place at one time. Now, I wouldn't want to be here after dark.

Returning to the site of my mugging did not jog my memory even a little.

I walked back to the detectives and asked them to give me a minute. I looked all around and took some mental notes, then I took a deep breath, closed my eyes, and tried to relax.

After a minute or so, I felt a sharp pain on the side of my head and could hear the sound of fireworks off in the distance. The pain passed and the sound stopped. I opened my eyes, looked at Harris and said, "Headache and fireworks."

"What do you mean by headache and fireworks?" Smith asked.

"My shrink told me when I'm trying to remember something I should close my eyes and lean my head back a little to clear my mind, and then hum. The humming helps drown out other noises. After a while, something usually pops into my mind. I'm supposed to say it out loud no matter how off the wall it sounds." Sometimes, I think my shrink is some kind of sadist or just getting a good laugh at my expense.

"Sometimes I cheat. If I smell his receptionist's perfume, things come into my mind that are definitely not from my past; more like the present moment."

Harris and Smith both chuckled.

15

"Okay, back to reality and clearing my mind. What I get is that my head hurts and I hear fireworks."

Smith repeated, "Your head hurts and you hear fireworks."

"That's what came to mind, a headache and fireworks. Well the receptionist too, but I assure you she has nothing to do with my getting mugged."

Smith said, "That makes more sense than you may realize."

"Is there anything else you can tell us?" asked Harris.

"I don't remember anything until I woke up in the hospital," I said looking at both detectives. "So what's going on? I know you've got more to do than solve a 4-year old mugging case."

Smith said, "Our informant, your mugger, gave us some info on another case that happened around the time of your mugging. We hoped you could confirm his story."

"What other case?" I asked.

"Tell him, it may help," Smith said to Harris.

Harris nodded and got out his notebook. "We have four unsolved murders. Your mugger gave us information on these murders.

"Little Wee, the scumbag that mugged you, is in jail. He's a low level street thug with no real street creds, so he's telling us everything he knows to get our protection."

Smith chuckled, "We know he's lying because his lips are moving, but we have to verify everything he tells us before taking any kind of action."

Harris continued, "Little Wee said he was hiding at the corner of the building as you walked by. He came up behind you and after a struggle hit you on the head with his pistol and it went off. You fell to the ground. He grabbed your wallet, passport, and backpack, and then ran to that corner and ducked behind the bushes to see if you were chasing him. He saw you get up and stumble toward the restaurant."

"He heard gunfire from inside the restaurant and then all hell broke loose. People ran out of the restaurant into the parking lot shooting at each other."

Smith said, "We think there may have been a meeting going on between rival gang leaders inside the restaurant."

Harris continued, "Little Wee told us he saw Franco Juarez, one of the gang leaders, using you as a shield while shooting at a black Escalades."

Smith added, "That was the first time we knew of your mugging or involvement in the shootings."

Harris spoke up, "Little Wee ducked behind the bushes and got rid of your backpack and wallet. When he looked up, you and Juarez were lying on the ground. He ran off knowing the police would show up at any minute. When the police arrived they found Juarez dead with a gunshot to the head."

Smith said. "Someone got off a good shot and caught him dead center between the eyes. They also found three other dead gang members. There were some 200 rounds fired from inside and outside the restaurant. We think you somehow got lucky and ran off, because when the officers got here, there was no one left, no one that was alive anyway."

Harris said, "Little Wee gave us the names of several people we think were involved in the shooting. Most of the people on the list are dead from other shootings or are not talking."

"Two hundred rounds and four people killed. That was a small war not a shootout," I said.

"Drive by shootings and murders have become the norm for this area," Smith replied.

I looked at the restaurant and the parking lot again. It all looked familiar but no memories came flashing back. "I'm sorry gentlemen, I don't remember."

Smith said, "There's one more thing. We recovered your backpack. It was still under the bushes. It's been out in the weather since the mugging so everything is trashed, but who knows, the contents may spark some memory."

He got a box out of the trunk set it on the hood of the car and opened it. I looked inside.

I said, "I've got the same taste in backpacks. This is like the one I'm carrying now."

The old backpack fell apart as I tried to get it open. Inside were the remains of some sandals, a shirt, and a pair of shorts. Some papers that water and bugs had turned to mud. Under all that, I saw the cover of the missing journal, but it too fell apart as I tried to pick it up. As it dissolved in my fingers, I saw a piece of plastic buried in the journal's remains. It was a zip-lock bag with what looked to be a folded envelope inside. The bag had somehow kept moisture from its contents.

The baggie tore as it opened. There was nothing written on the outside of the envelope. On the inside, I found two photos, one in black and white, which looked to have been taken several years before the other photo, which was in color.

The pictures were almost exactly the same. A man was kneeling on a cliff beside a dark rock. He was pointing at something carved on the rock. In the background, you could see a sailboat. These must be the pictures I mentioned in my journal and was so excited about. The black and white photo showed the sails to be dark; they looked black. But in the colored photo, the sails were red!

"Red! Red sails!" I shouted.

"Did you remember something?" Harris and Smith asked at the same time.

I felt myself start to blush. "No, not really, and it has nothing to do with the case. I'm sorry, I still don't remember anything that can help you."

"Okay." Harris said, "Let's get back to the airport so you can get on with your vacation."

I put the photos back in the envelope and stuck them in my back pocket. Doc had been correct about this trip helping me. I've got several bullet holes in me that fit the time frame of my mugging, which may explain how I got them but did nothing to jog my memory of the incident.

We pulled up in front of the airport departure terminal. Detective Harris turned around and handed me his card. I said, "I know, if any thing comes to mind give you a call." He smiled.

I opened the door and got out of the car. I wanted to run back inside to the safety of the airport, but made a conscious effort to remain calm and walked as normal as possible. After going through the security checks, I walked cautiously toward my gate, every nerve on edge.

I had faced my demons by going back to the place where it all started. The bad memories I had feared did not come crashing back. I stopped two gates from where I was to board my plane and leaned against a support column. Something didn't feel right. The hair on the back of my neck tingled. I scanned the room. It was full of the same generic people as earlier today; nothing out of the ordinary.

Then something caught my attention; two men standing at the next column up the concourse from me. I was behind them, so they had not seen me walk up. I stepped behind the column and watched. They were looking for someone and not in a, "Hi I'm happy to see you way."

They could have been twins, 6'1" tall, shaved heads, about 190 pounds. They were both wearing khaki colored slacks and tee shirts. Narrow waists with wide shoulders and arms the size of hams. The only way to tell them apart was one wore a green shirt, the other one a blue shirt. They were serious gym rats. The one in the blue shirt turned, glanced in my direction looking past me taking in the room. He looked back in the direction his partner had been staring. I watched as they both started walking further down the concourse still looking for something.

I walked closer to my gate and as usual sat across from it with my back to the wall. I made myself comfortable; there was still a half-hour to wait before boarding. I had grabbed a burger on the way back with the detectives and was feeling full, comfortable, and safe. I was on my way to sailing the Caribbean for as long as I liked. Life is good.

CHAPTER 3

I heard my name called over the intercom asking me to report to the check-in counter at my gate. I cautiously walked over to the counter. "I'm Rick Blane. Is something wrong?"

The blonde behind the counter was just over five-feet with gorgeous green eyes. All her other attributes were hidden by the counter. She spoke with a girlish voice, "We have a little problem and wondered if you would help us."

I raised one eyebrow, "I'll try, but I'm a private pilot, single engine only. I can't fly this heavy equipment."

She looked confused. It may be true what they say about blondes.

"That's not the problem Mr. Blane," she said still looking a little dazed. "We seem to be overbooked."

Being more than a foot taller, I stared down at her with my best disapproving glare. "I'm going to get bumped?"

She continued without seeming to notice my glare or losing her smile, "We wondered if we could move you to first class. It would help us a lot."

My scowl vanished, replaced with a smile from ear to ear. In my best consoling voice I said, "Of course, anything I can do to help my fellow passengers."

"Thank you so much Mr. Blane. It's very nice of you to do this for us." She took my ticket and marked out the old seat number and replaced it with the new first class one, and then handed back my new and improved ticket while still wearing that charming smile.

I took the ticket, thanked her, turned, and walked back to my seat. Just before I sat down, I had to give one little arm pump.

This trip just keeps getting better and better, I marveled. A friend of mine got me a boat rental on St. Morgan that was almost a steal. I got a great deal on the airfare, now bumped to first class. The gods are smiling on me today, I thought. Could Publisher's Clearinghouse be next?

Finally, the announcement came to start boarding. I waited until the line disappeared down the ramp, then strolled over with my first class ticket in hand, handed it to the woman with the great smile and girlish voice. I gave her a great big smile and walked jauntily down the ramp to the plane. Looking at my new hand written seat number, I saw row 3, seat "B". An aisle seat. I didn't care; first-class travelers don't need no stinking window seats.

There was a woman in the seat next to me staring intently out the window. She seemed oblivious to everything except what she was watching outside the plane. After putting my backpack in the overhead compartment and sitting down, I noticed she was still looking out the window. I took a closer look at her. She had chestnut colored hair pulled back in a ponytail, a white tank top, and beige shorts that nicely accented her tanned skin. She was not an anorexic looking little girl, but a well-toned and shapely woman.

While I fumbled for my seat belt, she turned toward me. Her full lips formed a smile. She was stunning. I could see flakes of gold and green in her hazel eyes. They were also red and bloodshot. I thought she might have been crying.

"Hello."

I replied, "Hello."

She was still staring at me. She stuck her hand out, "I'm Samantha."

"I'm Rick."

She blinked but kept staring at me.

My libido went into overdrive. This gorgeous woman is staring at me. There must be something on my face or in my teeth.

She asked, "Don't I know you?"

My brain was spinning out of control as multiple thoughts collided. There's no way the gods are cruel enough to make me forget someone like her.

"I don't think so," I mumbled.

"Are you all right?"

I stammered, "Yes, why?"

"You've been staring at me with the strangest look. I thought you might be having a seizure or something," she answered.

"No, I just… *Ahhhhh!*" My brain was still spinning.

"Did you say your name was Rick?" she asked again.

I nodded, still trying to regain a conscious thought.

"May I ask your last name?"

"Ba, Blane," I stammered.

"Rick Ba Blane?" The way she said it, it seemed more like a question than my name. "No that doesn't sound right. But if we met, it will come to me. I've a good memory for names and faces." She smiled and turned back to look out the window.

She must think I'm a complete idiot I thought. Now she thinks my name is Ba Blane. I felt someone brush against my shoulder. I looked up and saw one of the two muscled men who had been looking for someone in the concourse. He was staring at Samantha who was still looking out the window. He noticed me and averted his gaze.

As he walked by, I saw a tattoo on his forearm that gave me one of my dreaded memory flashes. All of my flashes are unsettling, because they remind me of how much I don't remember about myself. But this one made the hair rise on the back of my neck. I got a strong fight or flight feeling. Like I had just been trapped in a cave by something large that wanted to eat me.

A few weeks ago, I'd have been trying to find the connection by walking to the back of the plane and asking the two men several questions they most likely wouldn't be able to answer. At that point, I'd have gotten frustrated and without meaning to probably caused a scene.

Chasing the flashes is what got me to the point where my shrink was questioning my sanity and why he suggested I take this trip. I believe he expected to find me wandering around in the woods talking to furry little animals. Damn shrink.

"Déjà vu all over again," I mumbled.

Samantha turned from the window, "So you're a Yogi Berra fan."

"I guess." I was still feeling uneasy but was no longer stammering when I answered her question.

She looked puzzled and asked me, "Are you all right? You look way too serious for someone just starting his vacation."

"I'm sorry. I was just trying to remember something that's probably of no importance."

"So, you do that often; try to remember things and then quote Yogi?" she asked.

"More often than I'd like," I said, turning to see where the men had gone and resisting the urge to go talk to them. They were both seated toward the back of the plane. When I turned back, she was looking over her seat in their direction.

"So, are Hanz and Franz friends of yours?" she asked.

Hanz and Franz, I got another memory flash and asked quickly, "Who?"

"Hanz and Franz, you know Saturday Night Live. It was a spoof on Arnold Schwarzenegger. 'I want to pump you up, girly-man.'" She chuckled.

"Oh! I don't think so," I said, as a wave of relief flowed over me.

"You don't think so! I believe it would be hard to forget meeting those bruisers," she said.

"It's a long story," I said.

"Intriguing. It is a long flight," she answered, "and something tells me it will be interesting. If I get bored, I'll just fall asleep."

Here I am sitting next to a perfect stranger. Someone I've known less than 15-minutes and she wants to know about my little problem. I don't know if it was the way she asked the question or the tone in her voice, but something about this request put me at ease.

The flight attendant walked by, checking our seat belts and that our seats were in the upright position, which gave me time to consider whether to tell her, and if I did, how much.

I turned to her, took a deep breath, and said, "I have amnesia."

She looked startled, "Really!"

"Yes, really."

"How did it happen?"

"I got mugged in Miami."

"So, if you don't mind me asking, how much do you remember?"

"In the beginning, nothing, not even my name; now, after talking to family and friends, I've put some bits and pieces together."

"So, do you remember those two men?" she said, looking over the back of her seat to the rear of the plane.

"No! I'm not sure what I was trying to remember. It could have been the tattoo, a color, or any of a dozen things. I try not to chase memories anymore because it drove me crazy. Now, when something like this happens, I just file it away and hope if the memory is important, I will recall why later.

"How does that make you feel?"

"Geez, you sound like my shrink."

"I'm sorry! I find this very interesting and wonder what it must be like," she said.

"Well, it's like I'm trying to live a stranger's life while reading and hearing about it for the first time! I had to be introduced to my mother, father, brother, and sister! Every day I meet people for the first time that I've known all my life. Everyone wants to help and tells me endless stories, both funny and sad, about my life hoping to jar a memory loose."

"I know where I went to high school and my first girlfriend's name. I can tell you stories about my college roommate, the first time I got drunk, even when I got chicken pox. I know most all the facts of my life. But to this point I have no personal connection to any of the stories."

She said, "That's sad and even a little scary. There are things I'd love to forget, but there are things I really want and need to remember."

I shook my head in agreement.

"I'm sure it hasn't been easy, being unable to remember people you love. It must be devastating for those who love you to know they've been forgotten."

I thought her voice cracked a little before she turned back toward the window.

Just then the flight attendant started to give her well-rehearsed speech about seat belts and airline safety.

I glanced at Samantha. She was still staring out the window as we taxied toward our runway.

A tone in her voice, made me think there were things she wanted to forget. My Spidey senses told me she'd been hurt. Probably by some hairy-legged man, the memory of whom came crashing through just now so she'd turned toward the window to get control of her emotions.

The flight attendant continued her well-rehearsed speech. I saw Samantha furtively wipe something from the corner of her eye. She'd been crying.

CHAPTER 4

It had been quite a day, first meeting the detectives and finding out about the mugging, a memory flash, and now a damsel in distress with a possible past she wanted to forget. Ok, so maybe that's wishful thinking. She doesn't look like the damsel in distress type. Even if she was, I'm far from a knight in shining armor.

After we were airborne she turned to me and asked, "So where are you going?"

"I rented a boat in St. Morgan and I'll be sailing around the area for a few weeks."

"I'm going to St. Morgan and will be doing some sailing myself. Have you ever been there?"

"No, I started there four years ago and you know the rest," I said.

"So this is the trip you were on when you lost your memory?"

"Yes it is."

"Are you going to finish some old business and start your new life?"

I nodded my head, "Are you going there on vacation?"

"No, I was raised in the area but haven't been back for a while. Are you going to sail from place to place or do you've a destination in mind?" she asked.

"Well, I have a destination, but I don't know where it is."

"Oh really!" She paused trying to remember my name. With some hesitation, she said, "Rick, you're getting more and more interesting. How can you have a destination and not know where you're going?"

"I've got two pictures of a place I'm trying to find."

"Are they pictures of a building, a port, or an island? I've lived in the area most of my life, so I may be able to help."

I reached for my backpack from the overhead for the photographs, then remembered while with the detectives I had put them in my pocket. I pulled out the photos and stared at them side by side for a long moment. I had read about them in my journal, but this was only the second time I could remember seeing them.

She studied the photos, looked me in the eyes with a strange little smile and asked. "Where did you get these?"

"According to my journal, I found them in a little diver's bar on Treasure Island near St. Pete, Florida. I got the color one almost ten years to the day after finding the black and white one. They were both pinned to the same spot on the wall. No one in the bar could tell me where they came from or when they were placed there. Why, do you know where these pictures were taken?"

"It looks like any one of a hundred places around the area. The man has his hand over his face in both photos. So you can't make out his features. The boat in the background is nothing special. So what are you looking for?"

"It's what he's pointing at." I replied.

"The rock."

"Actually, the carving on the rock."

"I can't make it out."

26

"I think it's a skull with swords or daggers through its eye sockets so they form an X," I answered.

"Like X marks the spot! Please tell me you're not looking for pirate treasure. The people in the islands hate treasure hunters."

"There's no pirate treasure except in Hollywood. Those boys and girls spent it as fast as they got it."

"Then why is this rock so important?"

"I'm trying to solve a mystery I think may be about pirates. The carving may help me prove it."

"It's no mystery, they did exist, and some were very nasty characters."

"I believe there was something in the Caribbean even Pirates feared."

"Why would you want to look for something so dangerous even pirates tried to avoid it?

"Oddly enough, I know more about the people in my journal than I know about myself. I hope by finding them and proving they existed I will somehow find part of my past. If I find some forgotten treasure along the way, that's okay too."

She gave me a silly little grin before saying, "Sounds spooky to me! Woo!! You know you're going into The Devils Triangle looking for people that struck fear in the hearts of mere mortal, bloodthirsty pirates.

"I know it sounds crazy."

"How do the pictures connect to St. Morgan and the scary people?" Samantha asked.

I felt silly and a little uncomfortable. "Ok, my notes and last journal were destroyed, however, based on my notes in the journal before that one, I was excited about going to St. Morgan. I mentioned a list and two photos that may be clues to finding my people.

"What was on the list?"

I laughed and read the list, "Valhalla, Black, moon, Foul Smell, Demons, Bleeding Eyes, and Red Sail

She was silent for a moment, and then asked if she could see the photo again. After studying the pictures for several minutes she said,

"Rick, several things on your list are in these pictures. The Rock is dark, maybe even black. The carving has knives through the eyes, which could be the bleeding eyes. The boat in the background does have red sails. The man does have his hand to his face and could be holding his nose for the foul smell. I don't see Valhalla, moon or a Demon but four out of seven is not bad."

I stared at the pictures. She was right. The list was there. "I still don't know what it means, but it seems like I was on to something."

"How long have you been looking for these people or things too frightening to mention?" Samantha asked.

"Based on my journals, several years at least," I said.

"It sounds like karma to me."

"Karma."

"Yes karma, you're a man who has lost his past, trying to prove that these people or things had a past; by proving their past existed, you hope to find yours."

There was something comforting about what she said. It gave me a sense of belonging. At the moment, I didn't feel like part of my family. My old friends were people I had just met. My house, my car, and things I owned were just possessions that could have belonged to someone else.

Samantha's simple statement changed that. I owned something. I don't know if it is karma, but it is a quest, my quest to find who or what had been so terrifying to the pirates. The very people who struck fear in the hearts of many a seafaring sailor, were themselves afraid of something in the Caribbean Sea and in a strange way provided a sense of connection for me.

The flight attendant started down the aisle serving drinks. I turned and asked, "Samantha, may I buy you a drink?"

She looked at me and said, "Yes, that would be nice, but please, my friends call me Sam." Sadness had crept back into her voice and she turned toward the window.

The flight attendant asked what we would like. I answered, "Two Captain Morgan and diet Coke's please."

She poured the drinks and handed them to me. I passed one to Sam and said "Thank you for my destiny."

"That was yours, Rick. I had nothing to do with it," she said as she held the glass up and gave me a glance, "but this I'll have to think about," she paused, then said, "Cheers."

I took a sip of my drink and sat my glass down. I could see Sam still had her glass to her lips. After a second, she held the glass in front of her and swirled the ice around, and then in one swallow drained the glass of all remaining color. I tried to hide the look of surprise on my face. But when your jaw drops that far, it takes a while to close your mouth.

With a little smile she said, "I must have been thirstier than I thought and that was just what the doctor ordered."

Still looking at Sam, I raised my hand toward the flight attendant, who I thought was still serving the seats across from us. I felt something being placed in my hand. In a glance, I saw two more of those cute little bottles of Captain Morgan rum. The flight attendant was also handing me the can of diet Coke. Have I told you how much I love first-class?

Sam watched while I added the rum and diet Coke without saying a word.

"Ok, it's your turn," I said.

She gave me that I don't follow you look.

"How did you put it? It's a long flight and if I get bored I'll just go to sleep," I said.

She cracked a smile. "Well to start with I don't have amnesia. Although, as I said there are some things I'd like to forget, but there are also things I need to remember, even if they hurt."

"I've lived in Florida all my life. My parents have a place in the islands around St. Morgan where I spent every summer while I was growing up. I work for an Import/Export Company that deals with all the Caribbean Islands. I'm old enough to be an adult and young enough to not want to act like one. Now you've a thumbnail version of Samantha Van's life."

My Spidey senses tingled and then some. Ok, so my tingling radar has made me a paranoid freak over the past few months, but I could tell by the look in her eyes and hear in the tone of voice there was more she wanted to tell me.

I took a drink from my glass. "You said you left the area for a while. I guess that wasn't because of work?"

She gave me a startled look and answered, "No it wasn't."

"Would you like to talk about it?" I asked.

She took another big drink, then let out a deep breath and said, "I had a friend we were very close."

Suddenly, I wasn't sure I wanted to hear anymore, but it was too late, the genie was out of the bottle.

"He got involved with some questionable people who were doing some importing and exporting of their own. These are not the type of people you want to mess with or cross. Something happened and he disappeared. I felt it would be in my best interests if I left the area myself for a while."

"Do you know what happened?" I asked.

She took another big drink and shook her head, "I'm not sure. I haven't heard from him since before I left. I called my friends in the area yesterday. No one has seen or heard from him since the night he vanished. I also asked about the people he was dealing with. That information is less reliable but no one has seen them either."

"You're ok with going back?" I asked.

"Yes, I've to go on with my life. I wasn't involved with those people and wherever he is, I wish him well. We have a saying in the islands; 'People they come, people they go, and yesterday was a long, long time ago.'"

As she talked, I noticed there was something comforting in the sound of her voice. We laughed and talked for the rest of the trip like two old friends. I didn't want the flight to end.

The flight attendant came by and told us we would be landing in Puerto Rico in a few minutes.

Sam said, "I want to thank you for an enjoyable flight. I've not laughed that much in quite some time. You're easy to talk to. I feel like I've known you for a long time, much longer than this flight anyway."

"I feel the same way," I said.

"So when does your flight leave for St. Morgan?" she asked.

I checked my ticket and said, "There's about thirty-minutes between flights."

"Really, that's the same flight I'm on," she said.

A big smile spread across my face. I get to spend a little more time with her I thought.

She looked at me with a strange grin. "So you've never flown into St. Morgan?" she asked.

"My first time," I answered.

She still had that strange grin.

"Why?" I asked.

"Oh, no reason. What's your seat number?" We found the seats were beside each other and her grin grew bigger. She wants to be next to me so we can talk some more I thought. This has turned into a very good day.

We landed and taxied to our gate with Sam still smiling. When we were told to disembark, I stood up to let Sam out. We first-class people get to leave first you know.

Sam stood up. It was the first time I got to see her standing. She was tall; 5'9' maybe 5'10; not a little girl. She was a woman with curves in all the right places.

CHAPTER 5

Since Sam had made this flight several times, she lead the way to our gate. While walking she played tour guide and told me some of the island history. She gave me her evaluation of its better restaurants and nightclubs.

We got to our gate and handed the lady behind the counter our tickets. She told us the plane was already boarding. Before leaving the counter, I realized this was the first time in a long time I had walked through an airport without looking under each seat for boogiemen. I followed Sam down the steps, through the door, and out on to the tarmac.

As we waited to board, Sam let out a deep breath, looked at me and said, "I had hoped this trip back would be under a different set of circumstances. As someone once said, "Fasten your seat belt, it's going to be a bumpy life.""

She didn't get the quote exactly right but, I gave her an "A" for effort. I think she feels the same way I did when I saw the detectives. The demons in my mind were a lot worse than the ones waiting for me.

We boarded a 12-seat wing over Island Hopper, which would give us a great view of the water and islands, but it would not be good for having a conversation. The cabin noise is a lot louder than the bigger planes, so I decided to enjoy the view and hope to talk to her later. The only thing dividing the passengers from the pilots was a set of curtains. The pilot left them open to give us a good forward view.

The flight would seem long not being able to talk with Sam. I glanced at her several times, each time she was staring straight ahead. I noticed she was gripping the armrest and seemed to be pushing herself back into the seat. She must be a white-knuckle flyer when it comes to small planes.

The view was incredible. The different colors of the water from deep blue to turquoise and the white sand around most of the island reminded me of jewels in a necklace.

I heard the landing gear come down and the pilot cut back on the power. I glanced at Sam, she had not moved. I looked at the man sitting in front of her. He was gripping his armrest and pushing himself back in his seat as well.

Sam took hold of my arm and said with a huge smile, "Wave good-bye to the nice people." I smiled and thought of the Jungle Cruise at Disney World. The guide tells everyone to wave good-bye to civilization, because you may never see it again.

I saw the jagged edge of the island jutting out of the waters forming a steep cliff, but no people. Suddenly, people appeared standing not fifty-feet from the end of the wing! We were less than twenty-feet from the ground. This was unlike any airport I had ever seen. They let people on the runway with their cars? There was no fence between them and the plane. The people were all waving and laughing.

I glanced at Sam who was looking straight ahead. The smile was still there, but more tense than happy. I started to ask why the people on the island were laughing.

She said without looking in my direction, "Get ready!" Her hands were clamped tightly on the armrest.

The pilot said over the intercom, "Everyone hold on tight! I've never done this kind of landing before, but I did sleep at a Holiday Inn last night." There were several nervous laughs.

I felt the pilot add power to the engines, a lot of power. He's going to do a go around because of a missed landing, I thought. The plane nosed down, the engines at full throttle; I was pushed back in my seat from the forward thrust of the engines.

"What the Hell," I said.

As a pilot, I thought this couldn't be happening. We're in a power dive on the runway. The curtains were open so I could see out of the windshield. The runway was below us and we were in a steep descent with power on screaming toward it. The runway was covered in black skid marks and looked extremely short and getting shorter by the second. Those big white numbers that indicated the start, or maybe in this case, the end of the runway filled the windshield.

I felt the nose of the plane pull up abruptly, heard the engine cut power, saw the flaps fully-extended and our air speed dropped dramatically. We found the runway with authority, as my instructor would say when I thumped a landing.

This was not a landing; it could only be called a controlled crash. The sound of screeching tires and smell of burning rubber filled the cabin. Gravity was pulling me down into my seat and pushing me forward against my seat belt. The plane came to an aggressive stop.

There was water at the end of the runway and at another time I'd have enjoyed the view, but now I was trying to get my head around what had just happened.

The pilot said, "Welcome to the Aircraft Carrier St. Morgan." There were some chuckles from around the plane.

The pilot and co-pilot turned around smiling and said, "For those of you who have done this landing before; thank you for your silence. For the new-bees, check your underwear and imagine how much fun it will be next time."

Sam was trying not to laugh, but not succeeding and said, "Rick, you need to get some sun, you look pale."

I glanced at her unable to speak, still processing what had just happened, mostly glad I had survived. "So as far as landings go, how was this one?" she asked.

"Any landing you can walk away from is a great one," I answered.

You could tell the first-timers by their lack of color and the let me the hell off this thing look in their eyes. That same look was in some of the experienced travelers eyes as well. I don't think this is a landing anyone ever looks forward to.

The pilots turned the plane and taxied back to the terminal. I noticed all that separated the parking lot from the airstrip was a 3-foot high chain link fence. There were openings every thirty-feet or so leading to the parking lot. People could come and go as they pleased without security checks.

The plane stopped and the co-pilot opened the door. The door folded out turning into the steps allowing us to disembark from this death-defying joyride.

Sam's laughter had slowed to a chuckle by now. I stood up and stepped back so she could go in front of me. Everyone took their turn and waited in the doorway until the person in front of them was safely on the ground.

Sam started down the steps while I stood in the doorway. Several people had gathered around the bottom of the steps, waiting for someone they knew to get off the plane.

There was one man selling necklaces made of shells and other island souvenirs. When Sam got to the bottom of the steps, he pushed his hand full of trinkets up toward her. He froze, staring at Sam, quickly looked at me then back at her. His mouth and eyes opened wide; he dropped everything in his hands and mumbled something while making the sign of the cross, then he turned and ran toward the parking lot, looking back every few steps until he disappeared behind some palm trees.

I heard a collective voice from the crowd, "Look." They were all pointing in my direction. I came down the steps and stood beside Sam. The people were still looking at where I had been standing. "What just happened?" I asked.

"I'm not sure," she answered.

"He looked like he saw a ghost."

A man standing beside me, who had been waiting for someone said, "A bad omen," and pointed to the plane.

Sam and I turned to look at the plane. There was a black bird on the plane, and someone in the crowd murmured, "It is bad luck, very bad."

Sam said, "I don't see it"

"It just vanished," a man said.

The people moved back from the plane and became very quiet. As we looked for the bird I said, "That was creepy. I thought that man was looking at us."

Sam answered, "So did I."

"What's the deal with the black bird?"

She answered, "Just one of the many island superstitions, I'm sure."

CHAPTER 6

I collected my luggage and Sam suggested we share a cab into town. She told me her hotel was next to the dock where I had rented my boat.

The ride from the airport to the hotel was breathtaking. The island is a big rock with houses stuck any place a flat spot could be found or made large enough to place a foundation. The road twisted, through, around and between rocks and houses.

Our cab driver obviously felt he should be on an Indy circuit, but he got us to the hotel in one piece, more or less, in what I'm sure was record time. I got out to help Sam with her luggage. She only had one small bag so my intended gesture went unrewarded. She threw the bag over her shoulder and said, "I'd like to see the boat you rented, if you don't mind."

"Sure."

Ok, I'll go check in, get cleaned up, and find you at the dock in a little bit.

"That would be great,"

She turned and walked toward the hotel. Her white tank top and tan shorts with all those pockets really worked for her. Ok, with those long tan legs, she would look good in most anything.

I told the driver I had rented a boat and gave him the name of the dock as I got into the back seat

He gave me a strange look and said, "Ok," and drove me approximately 100 feet to the end of the building and stopped.

He said, "Here we are. Nick is the man to see. He may be in the office. He pointed to a little building with signs for ice, cold drinks, bait and boat rentals. I'll wait till you find your boat and help with your luggage; you have more than the lovely lady."

I walked to the office; it was empty. I asked the two men walking toward me if they had seen Nick. They pointed down the dock and one said he is at the far end.

I looked at the boats or should I say yachts; each one seemed nicer than the one before. As I walked, I could see the big ones were out in the bay. The boats here at the dock were only big enough for the rich. The mega-rich were out there on those floating castles.

The dock was crowded with people, some were tourists like me, and I am sure some were owners. Farther down the dock, I heard screaming and saw a large man, extremely agitated, waving his arms. He was pointing his finger in the face of a much smaller man. The small man was apologizing and saying "I'm sorry, I'm sorry". I couldn't make out what the big man was saying. He held the small man by his tee shirt and struck him in the face several times.

Then the big man drew back and hit the smaller man in the stomach so hard it lifted the little man off the dock. The small man's knees buckled. He fell to the dock and lay on his side. That's when the big man kicked him and cursed.

He turned and started down the dock in my direction, pushing everyone as he walked past. He was purposely walking from one side of the dock to the other trying to push people in the water.

Ok! A new thing I now know about myself. I don't like bullies.

I stepped toward the man, so I would be next to one of the pilings that supported the dock. It was about waist high and would be at my back. As the man got closer, I spread my feet for better balance.

He was a huge hunk of beef, not as tall but twice a broad across the shoulder as I. He stepped toward me and stiff-armed me in the shoulder. Unlike the others, I was ready for him. Being taller, it made him have to push me at an awkward angle.

When he meet more resistance than he expected he put more weight behind his push. My resistance was just enough to put him a little off balance. When I felt the extra force applied to my shoulder. I took hold of his wrist pulled him toward me. His force and mass did the rest.

Well I did stick my foot out to keep him from regaining his balance. He tumbled forward off the dock into the lovely clear water of the

Caribbean with a loud splash. I looked to see him disappear under the water. The bigger they are the more the splash I thought. Yes, I did get a certain feeling of satisfaction from that, but I'm not sure why.

I heard whistles and someone shouting from the direction of the office, there were also shouts from the other end of the dock. Everyone he had pushed was running toward me screaming cheers and laughing.

Looking in the direction of the whistles, I saw two police officers also running toward me. The big man had come back to the surface and was thrashing, snorting, and coughing in the water like some kind of a wild animal.

The first officer was a tall slender dark-skinned man. He was holding a nightstick to his side. He slowed to a walk when he got closer to me and never once took his eyes from mine.

His partner was quite a bit shorter and just as slim. He was a nervous, twitchy type and reminded me of a black Barney Fife. I wondered if he kept his single bullet in his shirt pocket. He was trying to look at everyone at the same time and seeing nothing as a result.

Barney tripped over a loose board and fell against the tall officer who glanced up at the sky and shook his head in disgust. He turned slightly toward Barney who was trying to regain his balance and gave Barney a swift jab with his elbow, pushing him back to an up right position. He did that all the while maintaining a certain air, not of dignity, more like self-importance.

When he got closer to me, he looked at the man in the water and asked in a demanding voice, "What happened here?"

I shrugged my shoulders and said, "I think he tripped."

There was total chaos as everyone started complaining about the man, pointing at him as he continued to thrash and flounder in the water. He tried to push me off the dock, He was beating up Nick. They went on and on with their complaints.

The officer in charge, and it wasn't Barney, said, "Hold on, hold on. First, we need to get this man out of the water." He motioned to his partner indicating that he wanted him to help the man out of the water.

"Where is Nick?" Several people pointed to the end of the dock. Before the officer walked off, he told everyone to wait until he got back.

"I need to take statements, especially from you," and he looked in my direction. Shouts and curses filled the air. "I'll get your statements after I check on Nick."

The big man, with guidance from Barney, found the ladder. He was climbing up to the dock just past where the crowd had gathered. He started toward me when Barney stepped in front of him and said, "Bulza, you know you shouldn't cause any more trouble."

The man stopped, put his hand on Barneys shoulder, and pushed him off the dock into the water.

Oh shit, I didn't have the advantage of surprise this time. Things could get interesting. Barney hit the water with a big splash and everyone started screaming. The big man just stood there. He clinched his fist and let out a primal roar.

A strange thing happened then, my thoughts became calm and clear. I saw humor in the situation. Except for the lack of green skin and the torn shirt, he reminded me of the Hulk.

Instead of being scared, I heard David Banner saying, "You wouldn't like me if you were to make me angry." After seeing what he had done to Nick, I realized I didn't like him even before I had pissed him off. I faced him with resolve and the intent to cause as much pain as I could before he beat me like a junkyard dog.

After the scream, he just stood there like he was trying to get more than one brain cell working at a time. He snorted water out of his nose, turned, and ran off the dock. He jumped into a waiting car that quickly disappeared behind a building.

By the time the lead officer got back to us, after hearing the shouts from the crowd, Barney was standing on the dock dripping.

"What happened?" The tall officer asked with more than a little disgust in his voice.

"Bulza shoved me off the dock," Barney said.

The tall Officer said, "That son-of-a-bitch is going to push me too far one of these days!" He turned to the crowd and said, "Ok, we have a good idea of what happened and we will take care of it. Please continue with your vacation and enjoy our lovely Island. Nick is going to be fine. It was just a little misunderstanding. My deputy will take your statements at the end of the dock by the office." Barney led the way, dripping water as he walked.

The tall officer pointed toward me and said, "Stay here. I need to have a word with you." The officer turned away and helped escort everyone off the dock.

After getting things calmed down, he walked back to where I had been waiting and watching the big yachts.

In a demanding, overbearing voice he asked, "What's your name?"

For the third time that day, I went to my deepest southern drawl and answered, "Rick Blane, sir."

"Give me your passport!" He demanded

As I handed it to him, he stared at me and asked, "Don't I know you?"

I wish people would stop asking that, because I don't know if they do or not. "I don't think so sir, to the best of my recollection, I have never been in this area before," I answered.

"You look very familiar," he said staring at the photo on my passport. Then with disgust he mumbled, "An American I should have known," as he handed me back my passport,

"What does that mean, suh?" I asked imitating the Looney Tunes character Foghorn Leghorn.

"American's, you all act like a bunch of cowboys. If there is trouble on my island you will find an American close by." he said.

"I've rented a boat from Mr. Nick. When he tells me everything is good to go. I'll be off your island, Mr. Morgan," I said.

There was a brief flash in his eyes, so he got the sarcasm. "That is good; the shorter the better for both of us. Stay close to the dock and avoid that man if you see him again. I am Officer La Nau," he said.

After taking my statement, which was more like an interrogation, Officer La Nau gave me a list of does and don'ts while on St Morgan. Before leaving, he told me to have a nice trip. If there was anything he could do to speed up my departure just let him know. I felt like I needed to take a bath. There was something greasy and slimy about him. The way he told me to be very careful and not cause any more trouble.

Looking toward the end of the dock, I saw Nick had been put on a boat next to where he had been assaulted. There were several people attending to him.

I heard a female voice call my name and turned to see Sam walking toward me with a big smile. "So where's your boat?" she asked.

"I haven't got it yet and it may be a while," I said thinking Nick might need some time to recover before conducting business. "If you don't mind, could we go get one of those tropical drinks and I'll tell you all about what just happened."

Sam said, "I thought you would be more of a Scotch drinker than Rum and Fruity drinks."

"I don't know if I like Scotch, but islands and tropical drinks just seem to go together."

We walked off the dock. I paid the cab driver and put my stuff in the office and gave the cabbies cousin ten dollars to watch my bags. I've read my journals and believe me you always tip the cousin.

I followed Sam past the front of the hotel, across the street and up a winding path to a bar. The view of the harbor was breathtaking. There was something about the surroundings that seemed out of place.

The waitress flashed us a big smile and with a heavy island accent asked. "And what you lovely people have today?"

I asked. "What do you have that will put me in the island mood?"

She answered. "Oh honey I will make you something special, certain to put you and the lovely lady in the mood."

We sat there enjoying the view till she returned with two frosty mugs. Sam said with a little disappointment in her voice. "Beer"

"Oh no honey this be a Horney Captain. It's Hornsby Hard Cider and Captain Morgan Spice Rum. It be the island drink for St. Morgan and the effects last all night long." And she gave me a wink.

We both took a sip and Sam said. "This is good; a few of these and your vacation will be well under way."

The waitress laughed and said. "Baby a few of these and there will be more than his, vacation under way."

Sam took another drink. "Now tell me what happened on the dock." She laughed as I told her about the big man tripping and falling off the dock, splashing in the water like some wild animal; the look on Barney's face as he flew off the dock, and how the big man snorting and clenching his fist reminded me of the Hulk.

We enjoyed the view and our drinks, after a while Sam said,

"I see Nick is walking back toward the office.

I took a long look at the harbor. The water, boats, and palm trees; it was beautiful, but something was not right and it had been nagging at me since we sat down. Something was missing.

Sam said, "The view here is beautiful, there are not many places that compare."

That was it, nothing looked remotely familiar. That voodoo shrink of mine was right; it is all new.

We walked down the hill toward the dock passing shops, several of which were high-end jewelry stores all selling Rolexes and other name brand watches at big discounts. Of course, diamonds, rubies, emeralds and gold are a pirate's dream I thought.

We walked by the hotel, rounded the corner, and saw Nick holding a piece of ice to the side of his face. There were scrapes and red bumps on his face and arms. When he moved the ice, you could see his left eye was swollen shut.

"Hello, I'm Rick Blane I was here earlier. I'm sorry I couldn't stop him."

"Are you the man who threw him off the dock?" Nick asked.

"Well, he sort of tripped," I answered.

"Thanks mister, but you shouldn't have; that man is bad. He will cause you trouble. You had better stay out of his way. Please, just stay out of his way," Nick said.

Sam went to the hotel for some medical supplies. I said, "A little too late for that. What was he so mad about?"

"Please mister, don't get involved. They'll kill you, so just don't," Nick said.

"It's ok; I've rented a boat from you and will be out of here in a little while anyway, so you can tell me. Besides, I told Officer La Nau. He knows who the man is and I'm sure will be arrested," I said.

"La Nau arrest him? That is funny." He looked around to see if anyone was listening. "What was your name? I'll see if your boat is ready so you can get the hell out of here.

"Rick Blane," I said.

Sorry, Mr. Blane, I still need to clean the boat. That's what I was doing when…" he stopped and put the ice on his eye and looked at the floor.

Sam came back with a first aid kit and set to work on Nick's eye. Just as she finished with the bandages, her cell phone rang. Nick waved her away with a smile of thanks and Sam walked out of the office to answer the call.

I told Nick to take his time with the boat. I would go to town and check back with him later.

CHAPTER 7

After ending the call, Sam walked back to the office with an urgency in her step. "Come with me, it's almost time," she said.

Nick looked at her, pointed toward the sky and smiled.

Sam saw his hand, smiled, and shook her head in agreement. She took me by the hand and all but pulled me off the dock toward the hotel. After letting go of my hand, she ran across the street and jumped into a car. Well, it was what was left of a Volkswagen Thing.

The paint job was a vintage Island motif. Complete with peace signs, pot leaves, happy faces and every bright color of the rainbow. Since my door did not open, and had not for some time, I threw my leg over the door to stand in the seat. Before sitting down, I saw what tied all the art together. On the hood was a painting of Bob Marley. They say pot slows you down, or it may have just stopped time somewhere in the late 70's.

Sam hit the starter and the beast rattled to life. We started up the hill and passed the bar where we had sat looking at the bay.

"So what do you think of my ride," Sam asked.

"I think I may get a contact high just sitting it," I laughingly answered.

"Oh come on…" she stumbled on my name.

It is always awkward when you start to call someone by another name or forget the name all together. Maybe I hadn't made as big an impression on her as she had me.

"Ahh Rick, sorry I'm just feeling the effect of a Hard Captain. I do remember your name but it just doesn't fit you somehow," she said.

Her driving was just as fast and crazy as the cab driver. I wanted to put a seat belt on but it was broken. I tried to brace myself by gripping the dash and pushing my feet against the floorboards. Soon, I could see we were getting close to the top of the mountain. She came to a screeching stop, just as we came into a clearing and the road leveled out. There in front of us was something you will probably see no place else in the world. A sign that simply said stop and look for planes. Sam looked both ways and drove to other side of the clearing.

The clearing was no more than fifty feet wide. On both sides of the road were shear cliffs and no guardrails. The road crossed the two-hundred foot clearing and continued on to the other side of the island. We stopped and parked at a wide spot in the road with some other cars.

"Ok, it's almost time." she said

I stood up in the seat to get a better view. To the left was a cliff, about two-hundred feet below us was the landing strip covered in black skid marks. To the right was a sudden drop into the beautiful Caribbean Sea. The clearing we were in had been made by removing the top of the mountain. This is where I had seen the people waving and thought they were on the runway.

Looking at the people lined up, it was obvious this was a big tourist attraction on the island. They lined up behind a white line painted on the asphalt that simply read safety zone.

I heard someone say, "De plane, de plane!" in a bad French accent. Looking out over the water, I saw a light in the sky. It was a plane coming in for a landing.

Sam stood beside me and said, "Wave and smile to the unsuspecting people."

The plane came in slow and was so low I thought the wheels were going to touch the road. I could see the people looking out and some were waving; others were looking straight ahead, and one woman was waving and laughing. The plane nosed down and dove toward the runway. In that instant, the laughing woman froze in place and turned white.

Everyone on the ground stared in silence as the pilot defied all the rules of a normal landing. The plane's nose was pushed down, engines roared as power was added, and its speed increased. The plane hurled itself toward the postage stamp runway. We all held our collective breath and watched. A split second before crashing, the pilot jerked the plane's nose skyward; smoke exploded from it tires. Smoke from the tires obscured our view of the plane and the runway for agonizing moments.

There was not a sound from the crowd untill the smoke cleared and we saw the plane sitting safely on the runway. Then everyone started laughing and cheering. It was funny, but only after we knew everyone was safe.

I was watching the plane taxi back to the terminal when I noticed Sam glaring at a car as it drove by. I tried to get a look at the driver and passenger. Sam stepped in front of me blocking my view and with tension in her voice said. "Now you know what you looked like."

"Now that I've seen it from up here, it's even scarier," I said.

"Most of the people who live on the island won't land here. Nobody minds the takeoff, but they usually land on an island close by and get to St. Morgan by water taxi," Sam said.

"I don't blame them. If possible, I never want to land here again," I said.

Still looking down at the airstrip, I thought about the car. Something unexpected had happened, and at this point she didn't want to share it. I asked, "Do you think my boat is ready?"

"Well, I was going to take you to a nude beach on the back side of the island, but you're right, you need to get on your way," she said.

"A nude beach!" I said.

"This is a French Island," she answered.

"I've been to nude beaches before. The excess number of old bodies compared to the very few somewhat young hard bodies usually makes the experience not worth the effort," I said.

She gave me one of those cute girlish grins and said, "I agree there are some things that just shouldn't be shown in public," and gave an uncontrollable shiver.

The trip back to the hotel seemed shorter. Gravity pulled us down the mountain, brakes growling and screeching the entire way. Sam parked the pot mobile back in the same spot. I got out of the death trap and realized since being on this Island, I had fallen out of the sky in an airplane, given the Hulk a swimming lesson and plummeted down a mountainside in a car with little or no brakes. It would be nice to get on my boat and sail off into the sunset.

Starting back to the dock Sam asked, "Did I tell you that I love sailing?"

Before I could say anything, her phone rang. She looked at me and mouthed *I have to take this*, answered, and started back toward the car.

I walked to the office and saw Nick at the far end of the dock. He motioned for me and pointed to the boat. Sam was still talking on her phone. I pointed to Nick and she shook her head. I walked to where he was standing next to a 32' sailboat. It was nothing fancy, but everything I needed; big enough to sail from island to island providing the weather was not too bad. It was small enough for me to maneuver around small uninhabited islands; ones without harbors, places where the carvings may be hidden.

Sam came on board and helped me check it out. She definitely knew her way around a boat I thought.

I heard someone call to Nick from the office and saw two men. He said "I'll be back in a minute, it's the dock master." He ran toward the office holding his side where he had been kicked.

I started to ask Sam if she would like to take a shakedown cruise around the island when I heard loud voices coming from Nick's office.

I could see the men were upset, walking back and forth, shaking their heads while having a vigorous discussion. One man walked over and stood by Nick. The other one pointed his finger at each of them in turn, shouted something I couldn't make out, then turned and walked off the dock. Nick and the dock master turned and disappeared into the office.

Sam was interested in the boat and had checked every part of her; paying little or no attention to what was going on with Nick.

I started to ask her again about the shakedown cruise when I saw Nick coming out of the office. He walked toward us still holding his side, but shaking his head as if in disagreement with something.

When he got to us, he wouldn't look at me, he said in a quiet voice, "I'm sorry Mr. Rick, but that was the owner of this boat. He said he was planning on using the boat and did not want it rented. The dock master is trying to find you another boat. He thinks he will have you one in the morning."

I said, "That's ok, a boat is a boat, but I'll need a place to stay. Can I sleep here tonight?"

Sam said, "Don't be silly the hotel has plenty of rooms. I'll even show you a nice restaurant; you're buying of course. That way you can enjoy your last night on dry land."

The hotel was made of coquina with walls at least three-feet thick. There were small slits in the walls for windows on the street side making the place seem dark as you walked in from the bright sunlight. You were cooled instantly as the breeze rushed in from the ocean.

Sam walked over to the man standing at the registration counter. She said, "Max, this is my friend Rick. He would like a room for the night."

Max looked at me with one eyebrow raised, then with a heavy French accent pronounced my name slowly, "Monsieur Rick." He bowed his head slightly, looked back at Sam and said, "Will the room next to yours be sufficient."

47

"That's perfect," she answered.

He handed her the key and she said, "Come on, I'll show you the room."

"Don't I have to check in?" I asked.

"Don't worry, Max trusts you. He trusts everyone. We can take care of it in the morning," she replied.

Max disappeared through a door behind the counter. Sam lead the way up the steps to a small hallway, walked to the second door, opened it and said, "Your room awaits, my liege."

Sunlight and breeze filled the hallway. I looked in the room; it was sparsely furnished. The décor reminded me of an Errol Flynn pirate movie. There was a heavily carved four-poster bed complete with mosquito net. The dresser, table, and chairs were made from thick pieces of dark wood, also heavily carved. The floor was made of planks and looked like the deck of an Old Spanish Galleon. I walked through the room and out onto the balcony, which gave a fantastic view of the harbor. I heard a cough from behind me and turned to see Sam standing in the doorway.

"Yes," I said.

"Aren't you going to invite me in?" she asked.

"Well milady, I will if you promise to behave yourself."

She looked at me and with a wry smile and said, "Just what fun would that be?

Sam quickly continued, "So where are you going to start looking tomorrow? It's a big ocean and all you have are two pictures of a rock and no clue of where that rock is located."

According to my journals, I had run into a lot of skeptics during my first search. Even though I was not as committed to the search this time as in my previous life, the sarcasm still bothered me.

"I'd like to make you a proposition that may help both of us. First, let's get something to eat. I'm starved."

There's something about a sexy woman in a hotel room and the word proposition. I am a man after all.

I must have been grinning, because she punched me on the arm and said, "Pig! Let's go before I really hit you."

"Ouch, that hurt," I said rubbing my arm.

"Good, I meant for it to hurt," she said cracking a smile as she started to the door.

CHAPTER 8

A car sped by just before we stepped out of the hotel. Sam paused for a second watching then stepped out of the doorway onto the sidewalk and walked past the dock. She was clearly agitated.

"If I buy you a drink, will you tell me what's going on?" I asked.

"I guess, but right now I need something to eat and a drink," she answered.

We followed the road up a steep incline past more shops that catered to the tourists who arrived on the weekly cruise ships. The crest of the hill was a dividing point from the gaudy painted buildings selling cheap trinkets and over priced island memorabilia, to a clean well-maintained area where the people who called the island home lived and worked.

I could see a small marina full of boats. They were not the fancy yachts like the ones at Nick's place, but were well-maintained working boats. These boats had a purpose other than demonstrating to the world that "mine is bigger than yours". Commercial fishing boats, live-on sailboats, and regular Joe six-pack runabouts populated the marina.

We walked down the winding narrow road toward a two-story building that looked like it belonged on the coast of Maine not a tropical island. The building sat on a corner facing a street that lead down to the marina while the main road continued around the island.

I saw tables and chairs sitting in a courtyard. Sam opened the wrought iron gate leading to the front of the restaurant. The fence was all that separated the tables from the street. She walked toward a table for two, next to the building, and sat down with her back to the wall. The place was cool from the shade of all the trees and the breeze coming off the water.

The walk had been brisk and without conversation. Sam seemed intent on getting to the restaurant. The few times we stopped to look at the view or for window-shopping were brief.

On our walk, my old need to check for boogieman reasserted itself. There were even a couple of occasions I thought we were being followed. I would catch something moving out of the corner of my eye. Each time I looked, the street was empty.

Sam looked at me and asked, "So what do you think of my little hideout?"

I looked around, "This is nice."

Sam continued, "This building was built in the twenty's by a gentleman from the Northeast, United States. He had been a lobster fisherman and got tired of the cold. He moved here and opened this as a fish house, but it has been a restaurant for as long as I can remember. This is also where Jimmy Buffett wrote *Cheeseburger in Paradise*, but there are several other restaurants on other islands that claim the same thing."

The waitress came over and dropped off a menu, then placed drinks on the table of two men sitting next to us.

"So what is this proposition?" I asked.

"We can help each other. I borrowed a boat from a friend. It will be hard for me to sail her by myself. I planned to do some island hopping, visit old friends, and relax. You're planning to island hop anyway. I want you to sign on as my crew and I'll be your guide."

My thoughts were racing out of control. She actually wants me to sail with her? The gods have truly smiled on me. This is turning out to be a great trip.

"I know I'm asking a lot of you, so to sweeten the pot I'll introduce you to a man who is a legend in the area and knows more about the history of the Caribbean than anyone. He has helped many people find lost ships. He even helped Mel Fisher find the Atocha.

"I thought you said the people around here didn't like treasure hunters?" I asked.

"He's not a treasure hunter, he's a historian. If there's anyone who knows about your rock; he's your man. He can and will tell you in short order if what you are looking for is real or not," Sam replied.

"So how do I know you're a good guide?" I asked with a smile.

"To paraphrase Mr. Buffett, I have sailed upon these waters since I was three-feet tall," she replied.

"Can you cook and clean?" I asked, turning my head to hide my smile.

"When I have to, but you're the crew, I'm the captain," she answered.

"Ok, but after a long day of sailing my neck and shoulders get really tense. How are you with massages?" I asked.

"Massaging you say; did you know it only takes 14 pounds of pressure to snap the human neck?"

I don't know if she was correct on the amount of pressure it would take and didn't really want to find out. "So massages are definitely out. Okay, deal."

She laughed and said, "Deal!"

This was great, I had been dreading leaving tomorrow because I didn't think I would ever see her again. "So, where is this historian?"

"His name is Mads Andersen, but everyone calls him the Mad Viking or just Mad. He has a home on Sabee, which is about two to three days southeast of here, depending on the wind and weather. There are several places along the way we'll need to stop at and look for your rock. They're small uninhabited islands; not visited much. Who knows? The rock may be hidden on one of them," Sam added.

She stretched her hand over the table toward me and said, "Then, if we have an accord, we must shake on it."

I took hold of her hand. She had a surprisingly strong grip. I said, "Arrr matey, we set sail tomorrow in search of the mysterious hidden rock."

Sam picked up the menu and started looking it over and said, "No matter what Jimmy Buffett said, don't order the cheeseburger."

"Why?" I asked.

It's a French thing; they can't leave well enough alone. They have to put some kind of a sauce or add tropical fruit. I love French food, but they just can't cook a plain good old American cheeseburger. It must be something in their DNA.

As Sam continued to look over the menu, I overheard the two men at the next table talking. One of the men was telling a joke about some man catching his best friend in bed with his wife. The punch line was, John Paul why, you're my best friend. She's my wife, I have to have sex with her, but you don't.

I started laughing and Sam asked what was so funny

I leaned forward and told her that I had overheard a joke from the next table.

Sam asked, "So you speak French?"

"No, not a word," I said.

"Then you just understand French. I had a friend like that once. Her parents spoke Polish and she could understand everything they were saying, but couldn't speak a word," she said while continuing to look at the menu.

I answered, "Keine."

"That's German," she replied.

"See, I told you I don't speak French. Why do you ask?"

Sam gave me a puzzled look and said, "The men telling the joke were definitely speaking French."

"It was an old joke," I said, "there must have been just enough English thrown in for me to make out what they were saying.

After we placed our orders, I noticed that Sam seemed uneasy. She had been that way since we left the hotel. I thought it was something to do with asking me to sail with her. She excused herself and went to the restroom. While she was gone, I decided to walk to the wall and look at the marina. Being on the water, or even looking at it, makes me feel like I belong.

While I was looking at the boats and the water, I noticed two men standing on the dock talking. It took a while but I recognized them; it was the two men I had seen at the airport and on the plane. What had Sam called them; Hanz and Franz?

They looked around for a while, then walked out of sight behind some fishing boats. I heard Sam call to me. When I got back to the table, I told her about seeing Hanz and Franz.

She laughed and said, "They must have caught the next flight. I know they must have loved the landing as much as you did."

CHAPTER 9

After we finished our meal Sam said, "Come with me so I can show you how good a guide I am. This will be something you've never seen before."

She seemed to be more relaxed and was eager to tell me about more of the local cuisine; like the best place to get fish head soup, freshest conch salad, and even where to get lobster in or out of season.

We walked from the restaurant toward the marina and followed the boardwalk around the island passing more local stores and shops. The boardwalk ended at a huge boulder.

I could see steps carved into the rock and Sam started up the path. I followed her to the top, where I was surprised to find several other people. They were standing and sitting on every spot possible. Sam turned and followed a narrow path around the edge of the rock. The steps and path kept getting smaller until we found ourselves on a rock that stuck out over the water high above the others.

"What are we doing?" I asked.

"Just wait, you'll see this is the best place on the island to see the sun set. Did you know it only takes 59 seconds from the time the sun touches the edge of the mountain until it sinks totally out of sight? There's something unique about this spot because at this time of year you get to see two sunsets; once when it touches the top of the mountain and a second.

The sun touched the top of the mountain and I could see everyone below us count as the sun disappeared, then to my surprise they started counting in reverse 10, 9, 8, and when they got to one, a ray of bright sunlight shot through a hole. The light was so intense it looked like the sun was burning through the mountain. Sixty seconds after it started, it too vanished.

I looked at Sam and said, "I have seen some beautiful sunsets, but that one was spectacular."

She gave me a little I told you so grin. "I know."

We waited till the people left the rock below us before starting down. I was surprised how fast it got dark. The trip down the rock in the dimming light was not as much fun as it had been going up. By the time we got back to the boardwalk, it was almost dark.

Sam smiled and said, "When you have the island between you and the sunset, things happen fast." We started walking back toward the hotel as the dusk to dawn lights started to come on.

We came to a street I hadn't noticed on our way to view the sunset. Sam said, "Let's go this way; it takes us to the section of town where the locals live and shop." She pointed out places she had mentioned before; with the best jerk chicken, best cooked this and that. It was obvious this was her small hometown and she was proud of it and the people. I did find it a little strange that she didn't take me inside any of the places.

This section of town was not like the tourist part where everyone was in a hurry trying to see and do as much as they could in their short stay. That section of town was all but deserted now. Here, there were lots of happy people in the stores and streets coming home from work or just out for a drink, before going home and getting ready to do it all over again tomorrow

"Just like in the real world," I said.

Sam smiled and said, "No! Tomorrow we'll be out there on the water. That is the real world."

We walked through part of town and turned down a dimly lit street leading back toward the boardwalk and the marina. Something didn't feel right and the hair tingled on the back of my neck.

Sam could tell I was on edge, so she laughed and said in a little girl voice, "Don't worry. I'll protect you from the dark." She turned and took hold of both of my hands, and then facing me started walking backwards; pulling me toward the well-lit street only two blocks away.

As usual, I thought I saw something out of the corner of my eye. When I looked this time, there was a small man standing between the buildings in the shadow.

I started to speak but Sam tripped and screamed, "Oh no!"

The small man stepped from the shadows and screamed something. I saw a gun in his hand as he lifted his arm toward us. Sam was pulling on me trying to keep herself from falling. I jerked my hands free, threw both arms around her in a bear hug, and pushed her to the ground covering her body with mine. I heard a bang and saw a flash of light before we started falling, followed by two more gunshots in rapid succession. Glass broke some place close to where we were falling.

I heard the sound of footsteps growing fainter as someone ran away from us down the alley. I turned my head and looked at where the shooter had been standing. He was no longer there. "Sam, are you hit?"

"No, I'm fine. How are you?"

I got to my feet and helped Sam up. "I'm okay, no new bullet holes today." We heard a noise and flattened ourselves' against the wall.

The sound of someone running suddenly stopped. Several muffled noises drifted toward us from far down the alley, just before total silence.

This is one of those things I probably already knew about myself but can now verify with certainty; I don't like being shot at. As a matter of fact, it pisses me off.

I started sliding along the wall toward the alley and got to the corner. I took a quick glance down the alley, looked back at Sam and whispered, "Someone's down there." I glanced again and realized something was wrong.

Someone was there, sitting on the ground not moving with his back against the wall of the building with his legs sticking straight out into the alley.

I kept looking at the man and said to Sam in a whisper, "He's just sitting there."

I looked at Sam who gave me a puzzled look. "Something doesn't seem right. Stay here. I'm going to check it out." I gave her a wink. "I've never done this kind of thing before, but I have seen it on TV."

I stayed close to the wall watching for any sign of movement. When I got about thirty-feet from the man I saw a gun lying in the middle of the alley. Someone touched me on the shoulder and I almost jumped out of my skin. Sam snorted, "I'm sorry."

"I told you to stay back there!"

"Yeah, like that was going to happen. Trust me; I can take care of myself. That is a little pistol," Sam said pointing toward it like it was something disgusting.

I said "Looks like a cheap Saturday Night Special. It sounded like maybe a .32 caliber, must be his."

We were close enough to see his eyes were open; his gaze was blank and unfocused. His arms were hanging limp against his sides. Blood was covering his chest and his head was resting on his shoulder at a weird angle.

I started looking for any movement or sound from the other bad guy.

Sam said in a calm voice, "Well we won't have to worry about him anymore."

"What do you think happened?" I asked.

Sam answered, "I don't know, but it's not good for us. We need to get out of here now!"

"What! We didn't do anything, we're the victims. He shot at us!" I said.

She replied. "You don't understand, right now that doesn't matter. We have to get out of here!"

"He shot at us."

"Rick, trust me on this, we have to go, and we have to go now!"

She stepped past the dead man and walked to the end of the ally and looked up and down the street.

I stood there trying to make sense of what had happened and said, "Sam this is the little man that was selling trinkets at the plane, the one who ran off!"

Sam was standing at the street frantically motioning to me, she said, "I know, I'll explain it later."

I said, "Someone cut his throat! Where did all this water come from? He's soaked."

Sam said, "Rick! We've got to go now!"

We left the alley in a fast walk passing the rear doorways of several shops. Sam stopped, looked up and down the street, and knocked on a door. She waited a couple of seconds and knocked again. The door opened, a girl in her teens casually looked out. Sam said, "Thank God, Eva it's you, I was hoping it would be either you or your mother.

She looked at Sam and gave me a glance and asked, "What's up Sam, I thought you…?"

Sam interrupted, "We need to pass through and pulled the door open. Tell your mom, hello. No matter what, if anyone asks you haven't seen us, understand?" The girl shook her head in agreement.

We repeated the process several times, entering through the rear door and out the front door or in the front and out the back, with Sam placing her finger to her lips indicating the need to be quiet. Around the second or third shop, rear doors were oddly unlocked and the clerks didn't even look up as we passed through.

Sam reminded me of a street urchin, running through the alleys of some town in a third world country, after picking the pockets of a rich traveler.

We came out another back door. Sam crossed the street, jumped a small wrought iron fence, walked across the yard of what looked to be a house, then up a set of steps and through a door that opened into a kitchen; surprising the workers as they cleaned.

Sam said, "Hi boys, just passing through." and kept walking. I shrugged my shoulders and smiled as I passed them.

A set of swinging doors opened into a restaurant with a long wooden bar. As she walked by, Sam said, "Two large margaritas with salt, please.

Give them to Sharon. I followed her through the front door and realized we were at the restaurant where we had eaten earlier.

CHAPTER 10

Sharon, the waitress, was bussing tables and looked at us in surprise. Sam picked up two used plates and set them at the table we had used before. I picked up two empty margarita glasses and placed them on the table. Sharon turned and went inside without saying a word.

Just then we heard a siren blaring in the distance and getting louder by the moment.

Sharon returned in what seemed to be less than a second with the drinks. She set them down, listening to the sound of the sirens and said, "I knew when I saw the two of you things were going to get interesting before the night was over." Sharon left and went back to cleaning the tables.

"Take a drink you're going to need it. All hell is about to break loose," Sam said.

A police car with lights flashing and sirens blaring topped the crest of the hill almost going airborne. It continued down the hill and through the curves. I watched as it went by, Officer La Nau was driving, and his sidekick Barney was holding on for dear life. Our eyes locked as the car moved past the restaurant.

The tires screamed as he locked the brakes and skidded to a stop. He threw the car in reverse and backed toward us.

Sam picked up her glass tapped it to mine, "Hail, hail the gang's all here." We both took a sip. The car screeched to a stop.

La Nau glared at us and said, "I should've known, I should've known. Stay here; don't leave I'll need to talk to the both of you." All the time he talked he had been pointing and shaking his finger. He put the car in gear and left in a cloud of dust and screaming tires.

Sam gave a little smile and said, "That Clarence is such a kidder."

I said "Sam before he gets back and starts the fifty questions. Would you like to tell me what's going on?

She took a big drink of the margarita and said, "I'll tell you everything, but not just now. What I can tell you is Officer Le Nau is a crooked cop. He came to this area about 10-years ago. Some around here think he came from some place in Northern Africa, where he had been a cop. His brother Joey showed up a year or so later.

Clarence moved his way up the chain of command very fast. Rumors started about him having a lot of money. He used to bribe his way to higher and higher positions. For a while, everyone thought it was just sour grapes. Besides, why would anyone pay to be chief of police on a small island like St Morgan? Nobody cared until the man making most of the noise and filing the complaints about La Nau was found murdered.

There hadn't been a murder on the island in years. Clarence ran the investigation and called in all the usual suspects. After one week, he announced it was a random act of violence and closed the case. His investigative skills are questionable, especially when it comes to someone he doesn't like.

Now, for his brother and part of my problem with the La Nau family; Joey is the biggest drug dealer on this and several surrounding small islands. Joey is who my friend was dealing with when he disappeared. Today, I saw him pass us while watching the plane land. I had hoped he had not recognized me, but I suspect the shooter was one of his thugs. I'm sorry I got you involved."

We heard a car speeding toward us from the direction of the dead man. It was Officer Le Nau. He slammed on the brakes and slid to a stop in front of the restaurant. La Nau got out of the car, leaving the lights flashing and engine running. As he walked toward us, he was shaking his head in disgust. "I told you every time there is a problem on my island, one of you damn American's is close by. How long have you been here?"

"Rick, don't take it personal. Clarence here is a transplant himself. Now what country is it you're from?"

I spoke up, "We've been here for quite some time. I had a fish dish that was out of this world and those margaritas are just to die for. What seems to be the problem Officer?"

59

He pulled a notebook out of his shirt pocket, opened it up and read my name "Rick Blane. I haven't placed you yet, but I will."

"Have you tried the Post Office?" I asked.

Sam snorted her drink out her nose and started to cough.

Le Nau glared at me before turning his attention to Sam and said, "Now, as for you Miss Samantha Van Helsing." Sam stopped coughing and got stone cold serious. She stared at him with anger in her eyes. "When did you get back into town?"

Sam replied, "Today, and when did you get reassigned."

"Not that it is a concern of yours, but today. I guess you haven't had the chance to see your father, Dr. Moreau?" Le Nau answered with a chuckle.

"No Clarence, I haven't seen him yet. I hear he is doing great, however I need to call him because one of his mutants has escaped, but I could be mistaken, it might just have been that piece of shit brother of yours, Joey!" Sam said. The way she pronounced Clarence name somehow pushed his buttons.

"What are you talking about Van Helsing?" The way he said her name was venomous. "Are you saying you saw Joseph, Where?" Le Nau demanded.

"Yes, I saw that murderer Joey."

"I told you before he had nothing to do with those murders. If he had, you and your friend would've been able to prove something by now." Le Nau screeched.

"Right, we proved it, but the officer in charge botched the case and the witnesses were also murdered. Incompetent police work, but you know about that since it was your case, Clarence!"

"Van Helsing, I don't care what you think about me or my brother. You're back on my island and there is already trouble. You are involved somehow and I will prove it."

I spoke up to stop the discussion before it really got out of hand. "Officer Le Nau, what trouble are you talking about?"

"A man has been killed."

"How?"

"His throat was cut."

"Well sir, as you can plainly see we've been here enjoying good food and adult beverages," I said.

Sam defiantly glared at Officer Le Nau, "There's another way of looking at this tragedy. You and your brother are back in town and people have started dying again. So was this person a friend or an enemy of Joey's?"

Le Nau took a step toward Sam.

I spoke in a loud voice to get his focus off her. "Officer, we've been here enjoying a meal." Making sure to point at the glasses on the table again. "You came by and ordered us to stay put and then return making wild accusations insulting me and my country. I am insulted and appalled by the way I have been treated, perhaps I should talk to your boss."

"Get off my island; both of you get off my fucking island," Le Nau screamed.

"Now see, that's something you need to tell tourists about. I knew you had topless beaches and nude beaches, but now I find out it's a fucking island. You do need to get with the local chamber of commerce and let people know." The French language is so elegant they can tell you to go to hell and it sounds like a poem. Officer Le Nau was not reciting a poem, but he did question my parentage and told me to do something that for me was physically impossible.

He thankfully ended his rant, by issuing a warning, something about if he could find any connection to this or anything on that and so on... He got in the car, slammed the door, and left.

Sam said, "You didn't have to piss him off. I was doing just fine on my own."

"Why should I let you have all the fun?"

The doors swung open and Sharon walked out with two more drinks. "These are on the house. The owner said anyone who can get Clarence that upset deserves a drink."

We thanked her and she hurried back inside. "So this verbal feud has been going on for some time."

"You could say that."

Sharon came back and started cleaning the table next to us and said, "Sam, the two of you need to get off the island fast."

Sam asked, "Sharon, what's going on?"

"Joey got into some kind of trouble off the island. His boys think someone narked on Joey. They have been terrorizing the island, assaulting people and destroying property.

People started complaining to the Governor. Not understanding the problem, he requested Clarence be brought back to the island because he was soooo good at controlling crime."

Sam said, "I saw Joey today. He is back and he looked like hell."

Just then we heard the police siren and saw La Nau and Barney speed past, around the curves, and over the crest of a hill and out of sight.

"I wonder what that's about. I've never seen him drive that fast," Sam said. Sharon left and went inside. "Well, whatever it was he can't blame us. He's our alibi."

Sharon returned, "The owner is going to make some calls and try to find out what's going on. People close to Joey, the ones that will still talk say whatever meds or drugs he's on has made him crazy."

The owner stuck his head out of the door, "It's Joey; he's shooting up Big John's place right now."

Sam and Sharon just stared at each other. Sam said, "He must be crazy if he's going after Big John. That's one scary man."

"Big John, what's he four feet tall?"

Sam and Sharon laughed and Sam said, "Big John is a cleaner and handles problems for a price. No one is sure if he works for Joey or Clarence.

Sharon walked off to finish cleaning the tables. Sam looked at me and said, "If you don't mind, let's go back to the hotel. I feel a little exposed out here."

I shook my head in agreement and we waived bye to Sharon. While we walked, I thought about the events of the day. There was more to this than Sam had told me, but this was not the time to press the matter. After all, we would be on a boat together for the next several days. I was sure the subject would come up again.

To say we were on edge as we walked, would be an understatement. We checked each shadow, doorway and alley as we passed while staying out of the light and close to whatever structure we could find that might provide cover.

When the hotel was in sight Sam said, "What you did in the alley was brave, thanks."

"I wasn't brave; I was just trying to get out of the way of the bullet. Tripped and fell on you. I'm such a klutz," I said. Sam just gave me a little smile.

We passed by the dock. The lights were still on in the office, but I didn't see Nick. I noticed the boat I was going to rent had been moved and none had taken its place.

We entered the hotel and there was no one in the lobby. Sam tiptoed behind the counter where she picked up a key, then motioned for me to follow her up the steps.

At the top of the stairs, she opened the door to a room that was neither of ours and motioned me in.

Sam closed the door, locked it, and whispered. "Two things, one, if someone is looking for us they'll look in the other rooms first. Two, you're not getting lucky tonight, so don't even think about it; just get in bed so we can get some sleep.

CHAPTER 11

After a restless night, I awoke the next morning acutely aware of every creak and moan of the old building. Sam had curled up next to me. More accurately, I should say she had curled over me. Her head rested on my arm, her arm lay across my chest, and her leg straddled my waist. She was one of those clingy-cuddlers. It felt nice except my arm was asleep and I couldn't feel my fingers. I also really needed to use the bathroom.

I tried to slip out of her grip. Opening her eyes she smiled at me. "Good morning. Looks like we made it through the night."

"Good morning. Looks like we did. How did you sleep?"

Sam said, "Like a baby. I'll go to my room, clean up a little, and come back, then we can have Max fix us breakfast."

I went to my room quickly showered and was pulling on a clean tee shirt when I heard a knock at the door. I froze, wondering if they had found us.

Sam said, "Come on, I'm hungry."

I opened the door. She was standing there, bag on her shoulder. My first thought was something had to be wrong. I have never seen a woman change clothes, put on shoes and makeup, and repack in that short an amount of time.

"So how do I look?" she asked.

That put my mind at ease. She is an earth woman and not an alien from another planet.

"You look great. So, where are we going, Miss Guide?"

"That be Captain to you, matey. We're on a quest to find your rock and I will show you the first stop when we get out of the harbor."

Sam led the way down the steps, past the desk, through the lobby, and out to the patio. Max appeared with juice and two plates of tropical fruit. "Sorry, Max doesn't do bacon and eggs."

After eating our breakfast, we went in search of Max who, after serving breakfast, was nowhere to be found.

Sam said, "We'll settle up with him when we get back. He doesn't like getting up early and may have gone back to bed."

I was glad the walk to the dock from the hotel was short. Something about being shot at the night before had made me a tad apprehensive. I saw Nick walking toward us from the far end of the dock, his eye was swollen shut.

As he walked closer, he said, "I'm sorry, Mr. Rick, but no one wants to rent their boat."

Sam said, "That's okay, Nick, he's signed on as my crew." Looking down the dock Sam continued, "Good, I see she has been delivered."

Nick gave her a strange look. "Yes, they dropped her off early this morning."

Sam winked at Nick and walked down the dock. "Rick, let me show you my friend's boat."

If a boat can be called beautiful, she was. The hull was royal blue, and her deck was off-white. There was just enough color to cut the sun's reflection but not enough to make it too hot to step on. Clean, well-oiled teak. I couldn't see so much as a water spot on any piece of stainless steel.

I walked down her length and saw her name. "*Alchemist*." The owner, whoever he or she is, could be a chemist or even a druggist, I thought. Alchemists were the original chemists, more or less. They put basic elements together in hopes of creating something new or different. Making gold from lead was one of their quests, their Holy Grail. Gold was also the Holy Grail of pirates who sailed these waters.

I smiled at Sam and said, "She is a true *Alchemist*. She takes the basic elements like water and wind and she binds them together and gives us travel, freedom, adventure, and fun." *Okay, so fiberglass is not a basic element. Sue me.*

"A little bit of a stretch, but I get your point," Sam answered.

Stepping on the boat I felt a rush of excitement. I saw the instrument panel in front of the captain's wheel with every state of the art high-tech electronic device you could put on a boat. It looked like the panel for a 747. The owner of this boat is a man, and he loves his toys. Why a man? Because a woman would never spend this kind of money on electronics.

I turned to Sam. "I'm in love and never leaving this boat again."

Sam replied, "That's not love; it's lust. As for never leaving, the owner may have something to say about that."

We spent the next forty-five minutes putting our stuff away and making sure the *Alchemist* was seaworthy. After Sam and I agreed the boat was ready, I said, "Arrr, matey. Ye be ready to find me rock?"

Nick just shook his head and started to walk off. Abruptly, he turned back. "Please be careful. There are real pirates out there, and you've got something they want, this boat."

Sam said, "We'll be careful, no open water excursions. Rick, can you get us out of the harbor without hitting anything?"

"Aye, Captain." I started the motor as Sam and Nick untied us.

Sam went below deck while I motored us out of the harbor. The motor on this boat was a pod. Suffice to say, it's very fast, very expensive, and way cool.

When we cleared the last buoy marker, the hair tingled on the back of my neck. I reached over, opened the cabinet, and pulled out the binoculars. I focused the lenses to where the top of the mountain had been blown away to help planes land. There he was: Officer Clarence Le Nau with his binoculars watching us. I waved to him and put the binoculars back in the cabinet

Sam came up the steps and said, "Arr, matey. Coffee?"

I answered, "Arr, yes. Now turn, wave goodbye to civilization, and your friend Officer Le Nau. He's on the cliff making sure we get off his island."

Sam turned so fast she spilled her coffee. "I'll wave to him, all right."

With vigor, she presented the one-finger salute and stood there for a long while. I finally cleared my throat. Keeping her hand and finger raised, she glanced at me over her shoulder.

"Good coffee," I said.

"Yes it is," she answered, still keeping her hand and finger raised.

"Now that we're off the island, and enjoying good coffee, would you mind telling me what's going on between you and the Le Nau clan?"

She dropped her arm and let out a breath. "Well, since I got you involved, I should tell you what has happened. I've known Joey for a good part of my life. Joey was always trying to be someone important, without success until he found people were afraid of him because of his brother. He started dealing drugs, using his brother to eliminate his competition. Now, he's the biggest drug dealer in the local islands."

Sam moved to the railing. I watched the wind pull at her hair as she continued her tale. "About a year ago, Joey heard a rumor that Angie a mutual friend, was selling drugs on his turf. He narked on her to his brother. Clarence checked Angie out and said she wasn't dealing. The rumors continued and Joey sent some of his boys to pay her a visit. They went too far and killed her."

An alarm beeped on the electronic panel. Sam jumped, "Is something wrong?"

Removing my finger from the pushed button I smiled and said, "Oops, just playing with some of the toys. So what happened after Angie was killed?"

"You mean murdered! Her family went to Clarence and told him what had happened. He said he couldn't do anything without evidence. Angie's mother moved to St. Morgan and started asking questions. Joey must have thought she was getting too close, loaded up his boys and did a drive by."

Sam swallowed some of her coffee so fast I was sure it had burned her throat. There were tears in her eyes.

"There were four thugs in the car. Joey was the shooter. Stan, an old friend, was in the car. He was upset by what Joey had done and wanted to know what to do. I told him to go to the police and tell them Joey was the triggerman. Clarence arrested Joey and put him in jail. Before the trial could take place, Stan committed suicide. He hanged himself." She didn't sound like she believed it even as she said it. "Without a witness, they had to let Joey go. The other two men who were in the car that night were found dead the next day."

Sam slapped the side of the boat. "Joey killed my friend and her mother and the three people who could finger him. Joey knows it. Clarence knows it. I know it. But, every dog has his day, and Joey will have his. Okay, let's get this show on the road. First mate, hoists those sails. I'll take the helm since I'm the guide, and know where to find ye rock."

"Aye, aye, Captain."

I hoisted the sail and, after completing the rest of my duties, sat on the bow. Even with the slight breeze, I could tell the *Alchemist* was fast. She cut through the water like a knife and, for a moment, I wondered if we were even leaving a wake.

The doctor was right. This is what I needed. There had not been a single memory flash or even a thought of my amnesia. On the other hand, there had been several things to keep my mind occupied.

Like Sam. She was a very attractive woman with a great personality. The type of person you called on when you needed help. It bothered her deeply that she hadn't been able to help her friends.

She was also very much in love with a man who may or may not be dead. I was going to ask her if she thought Joey had killed him, but this was not the right time. Sailboats are not the fastest way to travel, and there would be lots of time to talk.

After a few minutes of thinking about nothing, I looked back at Sam. She had a big smile, enjoying the wind in her face.

"I was wondering if you were going to come up for air?"

"Tough to say, Captain, I've only been here a couple of minutes."

"Look behind us. Tall islands like St. Morgan don't disappear from the horizon in a couple of minutes," she said.

"How long was I up there?" I asked.

"That's not the question. The question is, was it long enough?"

I smiled. "For now."

"We're about fifteen miles from the first rock," Sam reported.

"Let's hope it's the right rock," I answered.

"I don't know if it's the right one or not, but it's a big rock. Well, it's really a mountaintop."

I went below and started to fix us something to eat. Sam called to me and suggested I take the wheel instead because all I was going to do was make a mess. After we ate, I saw a spot on the horizon.

Pointing off in the distance, Sam said, "That's our rock."

It was just a jagged rock maybe seventy-five feet high and a hundred feet across. Exploring it didn't take long. I had brought the binoculars because while I was at the wheel playing with the radar there had been something at the very edge of the screen. I looked toward St. Morgan and to where the blip on the screen had been. If the boat was following us, he had stopped at the edge of the horizon. I watched for the boat with the binoculars for a while, but he didn't move. He was just sitting out there, not getting any closer.

"Sam, how far is Sabee?"

"We won't be able to make it today. There are some islands up ahead. We should make them before dark. I thought we would anchor there for the night. Getting into Sabee is tricky in daylight. You don't want to try it in the dark. I don't care how many electronics you have," Sam said.

I didn't say anything about thinking we were being followed. I completed my scan of the horizon and we started back to the boat. As we got underway, so did our blip. Whoever was following us was trying to stay out of sight.

CHAPTER 12

Sunlight reflected off a necklace I had noticed Sam wearing earlier. I asked, "That necklace is unusual. Is it some kind of cross?"

"No." She paused before continuing, "It's a piece of something very dear to my heart. My father designed it for me. Take a close look and tell me what you see."

"It's a little silver hammer."

"Yes and –" she said this like I was missing something.

"A pointy thing with red on the sharp end," I continued.

"The sharp pointy thing, as you so eloquently put it, is a stake of sorts." She paused and looked me in the eyes. "Hammer, wooden stake…?"

Okay. In my defense, I was distracted by her cleavage. The answer did eventually bubble to the surface. I said, "Of course. Hammer, wooden stake. Van Helsing, vampire slayer."

"Yes, the company I work for is Van Helsing Import-Export. My father decided since our name was tied to Bram Stoker's character to use the name recognition. If you can't hide it, use it, he always says."

"Does he live in a castle?" I asked.

"Of course not, Dracula lived in a castle. My father lives in a monastery."

"Monastery?"

"Well, it has been abandoned for some time, but at one time it was a monastery. I told my father once vampires were better than slayers because they were stronger, got to wear cool clothes, and lived in a castle. He laughed and told me that slayers were better. They were the ultimate underdog. All they had was faith and with that faith they took on the biggest, baddest thing on the block armed with only a hammer and wooden stake."

She pointed to the radar screen and said, "There ahead of us, just over the horizon, is the first island. It's small and uninhabited, so it won't take long to look around."

She continued looking at the screen. "Okay, there's the island. This is us. What's that little dot?"

"It's a boat. It has been following us since we left St. Morgan. It may be another tourist, or even a fishing boat."

Sam looked at the little green dot and with some skepticism said, "If that boat is after us, they'll start moving in as it gets dark."

We made best speed toward the island and the sun kept making its best speed toward the horizon. The pursuing little green dot stayed just on the edge of our screen. As if on cue, when the sun won our race, the green dot quickly moved closer.

We would not make the island until well after sunset. A plan started to crystallize and I said, "They're going to make their move soon, so we're going to hide in plain sight. We'll steer just off the tip of the island, like we're going to sail past." I went to the bow where I prepared the anchor for a quick and easy drop. Then I pulled out three hundred feet of anchor line and tied it off. With everything set, I went back to the helm.

I said, "Okay, when the island is between us, I'm going to turn hard and go behind the island. You go to the bow and kick over the anchor when, and only when, I tell you, then help me drop the sail. Please keep an eye on the anchor line. When it gets to the last coil, tell me and hold on tight."

Sam asked, "What are you going to do?"

I gave a little chuckle. "What was it you said? You just have to trust me on this."

Sam shook her head and said, "Touché."

The sun had set, making the shallows around the island hard to see. I coached myself silently, *Stay close and wait for it. Wait for it.* The island blanked out the screen. *Wait, wait, make sure.*

Then I turned the wheel hard and the boom swung about and we lost the wind. I didn't wait; I turned the pod on and went to full power. I turned off all the lights, too; you can't vanish if you're lit up like a Christmas tree. The sail filled with air and with the pod we were screaming toward the backside of the island.

After a few seconds Sam said, "Rick?"

"Not yet." I replied in as calm a voice as I could muster.

After another second, Sam sounded more urgent. "Rick?"

"No! Not yet!"

"Rick, you are going to run us aground!" Sam screamed

Wait for it, wait, wait, I said to myself, *wait for it.*

Sam said again, in a voice filled with tension, "OOOOOH, Rickkkkk!"

I said, "Wait, wait. Okay. Kick the anchor over." We started dropping the sails. With her help they were down in a flash.

I looked at Sam; she gave me a concerned smile and said, "If you kill me, I'm going to be really pissed."

"How is the line?" I asked.

"Not yet, get ready. Okay, starting the last one!"

I turned the boat toward the beach with the pod still at full power.

Sam said, "Half left! What are you doing?"

I cut power and said, "Hold on!"

The sand anchor did what I hoped. It dragged a bit before grabbing hard. The three hundred feet of braided nylon line acted like a rubber band. There was an aggressive slowing, but not a sudden jerk that would have torn the cleat out of the boat.

The *Alchemist's* bow dipped deep in the water as we turned back in the direction we had come. On the beach, I saw a dark spot I had not expected. Running to the bow as the boat stopped, I took my pocketknife and cut the anchor line. I smiled at Sam and asked, "Havin' fun yet?"

Sam just stared with her mouth open.

"You know, I've never really done this kind of thing before, but –"

Sam interrupted, "Yada, yada, yada!"

I went back to the wheel, powered up the pod, and headed toward the dark spot. It grew a little bigger as the beach got closer and closer.

Sam stood beside me and asked, "Are you planning to beach us?"

"I hope not!"

I knew the dark spot was a bay or inlet of some kind. I just hoped it was big enough and deep enough. I powered back and the boat slipped through the opening into a small bay. Surrounded by palm trees and the boat came to a stop with her bow resting on a sandy beach.

Just then we heard the motors from a boat behind us. We froze in place as the boat idled by, going further down the beach.

Sam whispered, "How did you know this was here?"

"I didn't. I took a chance."

Sam whispered, "You just docked a boat at night in the middle of a freaking island."

I answered, "I would rather be lucky than good any day."

Our pursuer came back, passing even closer. Muffled voices drifted over the water, but I could not make out what they were saying. They shut the motors off and sat there, probably wondering how we had disappeared.

"This could be a long night," I whispered.

Sam slipped below deck and returned with some blankets. "Let's stay up here. If they find us, I don't want to be trapped below deck."

We sat there in the dark listening to every sound. Waves lapped against the hull. On the beach, creatures scurried in the rocks.

Again we heard voices; they had drifted toward our hiding place. Suddenly bright light lit up the water. After my eyes adjusted, I saw the silhouette of two people on the boat. The motor started and moved away. This time they added power and turned in the direction of St. Morgan.

We sat there for a long while until the sound of the motor faded in the distance. I started breathing again as the sound got further away and my heart no longer pounded in my ears.

Sam said, "Looks like we're safe for the night, and we're close enough to Sabee to keep them from trying anything tomorrow."

"So what do you think? Were they Joey's people or pirates after the boat?"

"They gave up too easy if they were pirates wanting the boat, and it doesn't seem like Joey's style."

We sat there trying to relax. Sam finally said, "Okay. Tell me why you're looking for the rock, if there is no treasure?"

I laughed and answered, "Well it's a mystery – or more like a puzzle – I have been trying to find the pieces to. The carving, the boat, and the man in the picture are all pieces to that puzzle."

"What was so special about the boat?" Sam asked.

"It wasn't the boat, it was the sails. In the black and white picture, the sails were darker. Then I found the color picture. It confirmed what I had hoped. The sails were red or maroon."

"Okay. Hold it for a minute," Sam interrupted with a hand up.

She got up and went below. I heard some cabinet doors opening and closing, things being moved around. She came back on deck, handed me a drink. She got her own pillow and glass then sat down beside me.

"Okay, if I'm going to be this confused, I need a reason. Cheers," she said, "So now is it really all about red sails?"

"No, well, yes."

Sam took a big drink from her glass and just looked at me. "Is it the amnesia?"

"No. Well," I admitted, "that may be part of it."

"You need to know, I checked and there are no padded rooms on this boat." Sam chuckled.

I raised one eyebrow and stared at her. "Now, if I could continue without further comments from the peanut gallery? I told you about the statement made by Blackbeard. Well, I found other statements and reports that described a boat with red sails."

I heard a rustling sound, then thunder cracked, followed by a huge thud. We both jumped to our feet, ready to fight off the unwelcome attackers. A coconut lay unconscious and motionless on the deck.

"Never a dull moment," Sam laughed nervously, then kicked the coconut overboard. "Tell me more of your ghost story. I'm not going to be able to sleep anyway."

We sat down. After catching my breath, I continued, "Next, while on a trip to Jamaica I found a report filed by one Captain Ugly Jack. In that report, he stated a small boat had followed his ship for three days and nights. Late on the third night, demons boarded his ship. The next thing he remembered was waking up on a small deserted island with his crew and his ship was missing. He stated just before the demons appeared a foul smell filled the air."

"Are you just telling a ghost story because we're on a deserted island?" Sam asked.

"No! It's not a ghost story and I don't think demons boarded his ships, but every eyewitness account like this one describes demons. Buried someplace in these stories is a grain of truth. I think someone was using superstition to hide their identity."

"Why?" Sam asked.

"That piece of the puzzle is still missing."

CHAPTER 13

Sunlight burning through my closed eyelids and the aroma of fresh brewed coffee made a good alarm clock. The fiberglass deck of a boat and being suspicious of each sound, real or imagined, didn't make for a good night's sleep.

Sam had been up long enough to make coffee and was taking a stroll on the beach. I sat up and found a hot cup of coffee next to me. I saluted her with it and gave her a big smile. She waved and kept talking on the phone.

I sat there enjoying the coffee when I noticed a straight line running from the mouth of the inlet. It ran along the side the boat all the way to the bow. It formed a right angle and continued in front of the boat toward the other side. Our hiding place was man-made. I had found someone's boat slip. I also noticed a foot or so to either side of the narrow channel would've been a disaster. The cut rocks were just under the surface and would've made a mess of the hull.

Sam walked back to the boat. I told her we needed to thank whoever built this slip.

She looked in the water and said. "That's strange; no one's ever lived on this island, it's too small."

"This is definitely man made," I said.

"Speaking of man-made, did man make his Captain breakfast?"

"Aye, aye, Captain."

Ducking below deck I grabbed two sausage biscuits and threw them in the microwave. One minute and thirty seconds later breakfast was served. Handing her the biscuit on a paper plate, I said with a little sarcasm, "Bon appétit."

Sam gave the plate one of those looks and said, "Gordon Ramsay's career is safe. Since we're here, let's look for your rock after we eat this gourmet breakfast. Then there's one more place between here and Sabee.

We want to watch our time. The channel into Sabee is tricky. The last time I was there a lot of the channel markers were missing. Good help being on island time, they're probably still missing, so I want plenty of light to get into the harbor safely."

We started climbing through the island's rough terrain. Our haphazard path lead us to another man-made structure. The cistern designed to catch rainwater was still working. "So, this was a fresh water stop for someone," I said.

"Fresh water is at a premium. Most all the small islands are dry. You collect water where you can," Sam answered.

When we got close to the crest, I heard the sound of boat motors starting in the distance. We got down and crawled to where we could see the boat. Our pursuers hadn't left, they'd just anchored on the other side of the island for the night. For whatever reason, they had now given up the chase and seemed to be heading toward St. Morgan.

I said. Those look like the two men from the plane, you called them Hanz and Franz.

Sam sat up, "I don't think I could have slept a wink last night, if I'd known they were over here." She paused, pointed, and asked, "What are those things?"

I looked. She was pointing at a ledge just below her feet. There was a 20-foot square, level area of ground definitely man-made, probably the only level area of ground on the entire island. In the center of the square, lined up next to each other, were three rectangular slabs of dark rock.

"Let's take a look!" I said and gave our friends one final glance to make sure they were definitely leaving this time.

We climbed down and started removing some of the debris which, over time, had partly covered the flat area.

"I think this is a graveyard. The small rectangular stones would mark the head and foot of each grave."

"Wiping off the stone slab that lay in the center of each grave, each slab was smooth as glass, about 18 to 20 inches wide and three feet long.

Sam rubbed the stone with the palm of her hand, "Whatever this rock is, it's not native to these islands."

"They may have been military. There are crossed swords carved in the center of each slab. But there are no dates or names."

"Why would you go to the trouble of burying someone? Bringing these stones up here, then not put their names?" Sam asked.

"The tips of the swords are pointed down. That may be a sign of surrender. If that's what happened, maybe they brought disgrace to the group and were buried without honor," I said.

Sam said, "Many different cultures and people have lived on these islands over the centuries. This is just another mystery you can try to solve after we've found your rock."

After taking several pictures, we worked our way back to the boat. I backed the boat out of the slip and started looking in the crystal clear water for our anchor line.

Sam asked, "Have you looked at the beach?"

"No, why?" I asked.

"We've plenty of sunlight. I know there's a place over there where we spent the night, but I don't see it. So how did you find it in the dark?" she asked.

I checked the beach; there was no dark spot like I had seen last night. There wasn't anything to indicate the slip existed. I looked for the graveyard. That, too, had vanished. "Just like a woman. She only shows you what she wants you to see, and only when she wants it seen!" I said.

"As it should be," Sam chuckled.

I found the anchor line and had it back on board in short order. "What's me course, Captain?"

Our next stop has a bluff overlooking the water which resembles your pictures. Since it's on the way, I guess we should take a look. Your rock might be there," she said.

There was a tone in her voice that made me ask, "And now for the rest of the story?"

She looked away from me, like she didn't want me to see the expression on her face, and in a quiet voice said, "It's haunted!"

"Did you say haunted?" I snickered. "I've heard of houses, castles, planes, trains, and automobiles being haunted, but never an island. Is this another Devil's Triangle story?"

"Oh, it has nothing to do with the Triangle. Our parents told us spooky stories to keep us off this island for one reason or another. This place gives me the creeps and people have vanished from there."

"Vanished?"

"Well, the story goes – and some of it's even backed up by history – there were three different religious groups settled on the island in the sixteen and seventeen hundreds and they all vanished without a trace."

I asked, "You mean the people were gone like on the Mary Celeste?"

"I don't know about the Mary Celeste."

"It was a ship found in the late eighteen hundreds adrift just north of here. She showed no signs of damage or any kind of a struggle. The ship was well stocked with food and water. The table was set for a meal, which was prepared and in the galley. Their money and worldly possessions were on board, but no people, they had just vanished!"

"That's the story of this place. The last people who lived here in the early seventeen hundreds were isolationists. They had supplies delivered every few months. On one delivery no one came to the boat. The captain making the delivery got concerned and went on the island against their strict orders. He found the houses well stocked, with plates on the table, but no people. Every living thing had vanished."

"So did the stories keep you from going to the island?" I asked.

"No way! We dared each other to see who could stay the longest. I haven't been there in years, but I bet the place will still give me the creeps."

We sailed for a couple more hours and our hiding place for last night disappeared beyond the horizon. One look at the radar screen showed we were closing in on the haunted island and that our pursuers were nowhere in sight.

"So why did Clarence call your father Dr. Moreau?" I asked.

"He was just being a jerk and trying to make me mad. Hoping I would do something stupid so he could arrest me," Sam answered.

"Is he a doctor?" I asked.

"No, he's not even a doctor. I'll give you a short version of what Clarence was talking about, but to do that I've got to give you a little history lesson on the area. My family owns an island. It's not as good as it sounds," she added, when my eyes widened. "The Portuguese built a monastery on the island in the early fifteen hundreds. The Spanish took it over in the early sixteen hundreds and turned it into a military outpost. They soon found it was too far off the shipping lanes to be of use.

"Then someone came up with a use for the island in the middle of nowhere. They used it as a dumping ground for all the sick and diseased people in the area.

"Slave ships stopped, cleaned their ships, removed the sick and dying before getting into port elsewhere. Then, they sailed off without a thought of ever returning. As you can imagine, the island acquired a bad reputation.

"At some point, one of my ancestors did something for a royal family. As a reward they gave him the island. By that point, the practice of dumping sick people had stopped, but the island's reputation was set."

"My Father inherited the family treasure and to his surprise found the monastery and buildings were in good shape. He found a doctor had treated the people on the island using home remedies from many different countries. The doctor kept extensive records of the plants and herbs and the success and failures of his efforts. Father was surprised to find many of the plants were still growing on the island."

"Now comes the part about Doctor Moreau. Father read about all the different diseases that had been on the island and wanted to know if it was safe. So he hired a hazmat team to see if any of the nasty stuff was still alive on the island.

"That started rumors about everything from a secret military base running creepy experiments to the creation of mutants, like on the movie version of *Doctor Moreau's Island*.

"Scientists do come and go on occasion, but they only study the rare plants and trees, and read over the doctor's records. I think Father brings them in just to keep the rumors alive."

CHAPTER 14

Sam finished her story just as we arrived at the haunted island. While she talked, I had been keeping an eye on the horizon and radar. This time no one was following us.

She pointed to a small section of white sand scattered between the rocks and said, "Welcome to Baneterra." There was no place to dock, so we had to anchor so we could swim to shore. After making sure the boat would be there when we got back, I took my shirt off and prepared to jump in the crystal clear water.

Sam looked at my chest and said, "Oh my God, are you okay?"

I felt self-conscious and a little embarrassed, realizing this was the first time I had taken my shirt off in front of anyone other than my doctors.

I saw Sam looking. I looked down at myself and saw the multiple scars crisscrossing my upper body. The doctors told me the cuts were not deep enough to cause muscle damage, but deep enough to cause a lot of bleeding and pain.

I answered with a nervous laugh as I rubbed my hand over the long scars. "Souvenirs from the streets of Miami, I guess. I'm not sure where they came from."

She walked over placed her hand on my chest. "Some souvenir. Most people just get a snow globe. What about these bullet holes?" Sam continued. I detected sadness in her voice.

"I'm impressed you know what a bullet hole looks like. I didn't untill the doctors told me. The ones in my shoulder and on the side of my head; they're what I was being treated for when I woke up in the hospital. They're healing nicely, or so I'm told."

I pointed to a few more. "These others are about three to four years old. None of them hit anything important. This one took out a little piece of my rib. The one on the side of my head grazed my skull. It happened at the same time as the shoulder. But they think I may have been shot there before. There's a mark on my skull at almost the same place."

Sam smiled and said, "I guess the streets of Miami are a rough place to be homeless."

"There's an advantage to having amnesia," I said.

"What's that?"

"I don't remember any of these; not the pain, or how they happened. It's all a story to me, like it happened to someone else. So let's go find a ghost or maybe my rock," I said as I started to jump into the water.

Two things happened before I jumped. Sam took off her shirt, and then unzipped her shorts and let them drop to the deck. I hadn't seen her in a bathing suit before. When a woman unzips anything and lets it drop to the floor men pay attention. What had Sam said when I took off my shirt? "Oh My God!" Ditto for me. All I could think of was those poor ugly girls in *Sports Illustrated*.

The water felt great as I swam toward the little strip of white beach. I walked out of the water and turned to see that Sam was still swimming and had come only halfway. I looked up and down the beach at a narrow strip of sand with jagged rocks every few feet and thought; this wouldn't make a good tourist brochure.

Sam walked out of the water and handed me a pair of sandals. "I don't know what you were thinking when you jumped in the water. It's quite a walk, most of it uphill. No sand, just crushed rocks."

"I know what you're thinking so don't say it."

She slipped on her sandals and started up a steep narrow path through the sand dunes. At the top of the path, she turned left and followed the shoreline around the island. The path led up steep sections, then leveled out for a few steps then went up again, repeating the pattern. A giant's staircase led to a peak on the island. For the entire trip you couldn't see the island because of thick undergrowth, but I did have several great views of the ocean and a shapely posterior.

I don't know if it was the stories Sam told me, but the place did feel creepy, like our every move was being watched. Sandals are not made for climbing, so the last part of our hike was challenging. When we got to the top there was a view very much like the one in my picture. We checked every rock and looked at the water from every possible angle. It wasn't the place.

"Close, but no cigar," I said.

"I didn't remember seeing the carving but thought it was worth a shot," Sam replied.

"I can tell you we're getting closer. The journals never mentioned a place that remotely resembled the pictures."

"There are a few other places. But first let's see if the Mad Viking can help," Sam said.

I turned and looked out over the island for the first time. I'm not sure what I was expecting to see, but I'm sure this wasn't it. I pointed.

"Sam what is that?"

"An old airstrip built by the U.S. during World War II. There's an old hangar over there and a couple of old crashed planes next to it."

"I thought you said no one has lived here since the seventeen hundreds?"

"No one has. This place was never manned. Two planes crash landed here and that was the only time the strip was used."

"Do we have time to take a look?"

"Yes, it's on the way back."

We started down from the peak, left what little path there was and weaved our way through the brush toward the airstrip. While we walked, I could see remains of old houses and stone fences scattered about. Sam passed a well worn path. I asked, "Where does this lead?"

She stopped, "What?"

Pointing, I said, "This path," and started following it. After two hundred feet or so, I came to a well-preserved house that looked almost new. I got a sharp pain like someone was jamming an ice pick in my left temple. I closed my eyes and placed my hand on the spot till the pain passed.

A voice in the distance asked, "Rick, are you all right?"

Looking toward the voice, the path was now covered in undergrowth and I could barely see Sam through the brush. Glancing back at the house it too had changed to the overgrown remains of a house. After making my way back to Sam through the undergrowth I said, "That was weird. This place is spooky."

I explained what had happened. Sam shook her head and said, "I told you this place is strange. It still gives me the creeps."

I knew what she meant by creepy; an uneasy feeling had been increasing the closer we got to the runway. My Spidey senses were trying to tell me something.

We stepped out of the undergrowth onto a surprisingly smooth surface. The crushed rock had become as hard as concrete and made a very good landing strip. We walked on the runway toward the hangar and around several pieces of scattered brush.

I stopped and looked around. I felt like I was missing something.

Sam said, "The planes, or what is left of them, are just around to the side of that old hangar."

Sam froze in her tracks and I almost walked into her.

To our surprise, a plane sat parked in the hangar. Not the old wrecked ones Sam had told me about, but a new King Air. Their range and hauling abilities made them the aircraft of choice for drug dealers everywhere. We both stood there in shock. Sam because she hadn't expected to find anything other than crashed junk. Me because I realized I was depriving some village of its idiot. The strip was in too good a shape for it not to have been used since the 1940s. The brush on the runway was cut, not growing.

I looked down at the runway and said, "Sam don't move, the place is booby trapped. There's a trip wire by your left foot."

She looked down at her foot and said, "That's not good."

I said, "I don't think you've triggered it. Slide your foot back slowly."

We carefully took two steps back looking at every twig and piece of gravel. Abruptly everything became crystal clear and details jumped out at me. I saw one more trip wire closer to the hangar. A wire ran up the side of a tree. I couldn't see the camera, but I knew one was there.

"Sam, there's a camera watching the hangar," I said without moving.

Sam answered, "I hope you've enjoyed the tour of Baneterra, the haunted island. Please gather your belongings, take small children by the hand, and get the hell out of this spooky place."

"Wait. I'm going to take a little peek in the hangar. Please stay here. I've seen another booby trap."

"What are you looking for?"

"I'm not sure." I crept carefully up close to the hangar wall and saw the next trip wire was attached to a claymore personal mine, anchored to the hangar, pointing toward the runway. Glancing through a small rust hole I saw a camera watching the plane. There was another camera pointing toward a small path leading away from the hangar back into the island's interior. I leaned against the hangar wall and thought *whoever this is, he's trying to protect something and doesn't care who he hurts or kills.*

I carefully walked back to Sam. "Someone is keeping a close eye on this place. There's a path over there. Do you know where that path leads?"

"The only thing back on that part of the island is an old bomb shelter."

"We should go. Someone besides the ghost doesn't want us here."

Sam agreed, took two steps back, turned, and started walking toward the boat. I noticed the brush had been used to wipe out the tire marks and hide the runway. Whoever was using this place was putting great effort into keeping it hidden.

As we got close to the end of the runway, Sam said, "This place always made me feel like I was being watched. I guess there may have been more than ghosts giving me that feeling."

We got to the path that led down to the beach. I took a quick glance to see if we were being followed, then I followed her down to the beach and into the water for the swim back to the boat. We wasted no time in putting up the sails, wanting to put some distance between potential trouble and us.

There may not have been armed guards on the island, but you can bet no one would spend the money to maintain that plane and airstrip without it being watched. The owner probably knew we were there by the time we anchored. I kept looking over my shoulder and glancing at the radar screen for little green blips.

"Sam, are all your guided trips this exciting?"

"I thought you knew. I've never done this kind of thing before, but I did see it once on TV."

It was nice to travel with someone who had as twisted a sense of humor as mine. The wind was light and we were not making good time.

"As your guide, I should tell you about our next stop. Sabee looks more like a Hawaiian Island. Deep water and constantly changing currents surround it. The island is an extinct volcano and is covered by a tropical rain forest.

There are no sandy beaches, just lots of rocks and steep cliffs. There's only one harbor, if you can call it that, and one so-called town. The population of the entire island is four hundred, more or less."

CHAPTER 15

We had been sailing for the better part of the day. Checking the radar screen had become a habit. On this glance, I saw a little green dot on the edge of the screen. I didn't say anything until I was sure it was headed toward us. I turned the pod on and added power, not full, but close.

Sam looked at me and asked, "Why are you using the motor now?"

"We've got company coming, and they seem to be in a hurry."

"I wonder if it's the boys from last night."

I looked at the screen and said, "If it is, they're trying to catch us before we get to safe waters."

Sam picked up the binoculars setting next to the hatch and looked at the mouth of the harbor, then looked for the boat coming in our direction. "I don't see them yet." She kept looking as I tried to get every ounce of power from the wind and motor.

She turned and looked back toward the harbor. "There's a boat coming out from Sabee. This could get interesting." She turned and watched for the boat coming up behind us.

I looked at the radar and said, "The boat coming out from Sabee is not coming our way."

"I still can't see the one behind us."

"He's still back several miles."

We kept moving toward the island with as much speed as I could coax.

We reached the channel leading into the harbor. The boat coming toward was still not in sight. Sam glanced at me with a big smile, "Looks like we're going to make it."

Since there were still missing markers, she stood on the bow and directed me through the narrow channel that turned and weaved around rocks. We rounded the last bend and I saw the town. Well, there were four or five buildings along the shore and several houses peeking through the trees; some I couldn't see until we were alongside. Once in the harbor, I picked an empty slip next to a large sport fishing boat and slowly pulled in.

I saw a boy about 11 or 12 years old running down the dock toward us. Sam said, "That's Bobby. His dad is from Louisiana and owns the best Cajun restaurant in the Caribbean."

We docked and started tying off when we heard Bobby screaming, "Help, please help! Miss Sam, My daddy's hurt, please help!"

Sam gave me a concerned glance over her shoulder, and I said, "Go. I've got it." She jumped out of the boat and the two of them ran toward the restaurant.

After securing *Alchemist*, I stepped on the dock and noticed the coolers on the boat next to us had been turned over, their contents scattered on deck. The door to the cabin was ajar, and it too seemed to be a mess.

I ran down the dock to the restaurant and opened the door. That old feeling something is about to eat me came back as I stepped into the room. The restaurant was small, six mismatched tables and chairs. The table and chairs to my left were overturned. Blood pooled on the floor. Blood had also been splattered on the window and several chairs.

Sam was wiping blood from the face of a man sitting at the counter and Bobby was holding his hand and sobbing. She looked at me. "He's still out of it. Someone beat the shit out of him."

I walked toward them and saw more blood splattered on the next table. Kneeling down I looked at Bobby and asked, "Can you tell us what happened?"

Bobby shook his head and sobbed, "I wasn't here."

The man being tended by Sam spoke. "I'm fine and can hear both of you! It has been a long time since a lovely woman has been this close to me. I'm trying to enjoy it."

Bobby let go of his hand and gave him a big hug. Bob groaned, Bobby let go and jumped back. "It's okay, boy. My ribs are a little sore, that's all."

Sam felt his side and said, "I think you've got some cracked or even broken ribs."

I heard the door open behind me. Turning, I saw a tall, husky, dark-skinned man in a police uniform looking very serious standing in the doorway. He said, "Bob, what's going on? Did these people do this?" He pulled a pistol, flipped off the safety, and pointed it at me.

Bob said, "It's okay, Hennery, they're trying to help me."

The officer looked at Bob and slowly put the pistol back in its holster and asked, "What the hell happened, Bob?"

"Damned if I know. Two men came in, sat at that table," he pointed to the overturned table. "A little while later, two more men came in; a huge ugly son of-a-bitch and the other normal size with a scar on his cheek. The big ugly guy just stood in the middle of the room while 'Scar' went over and talked to the men at the table.

"After a little while, 'Scar' walked back to the big man and said something. The big man walked to the counter, picked up Bobby's baseball bat, and started beating the shit out of the two men at the table. I came from behind the counter and tried to stop him. He turned and hit me with the bat. That's all I remember till I saw Miss Sam wiping my face."

Hennery looked at Bobby and asked, "Did you see anything?"

Bobby answered, "No sir, I was up on the mountain, but those two men sitting at the table came in on that big boat next to Miss Sam's."

Hennery said, "I'll check it out." He walked out and down the dock. Three men got out of the police boat and followed him toward the fishing boat.

Bob said "Hennery is another coon ass, but I don't know what he's doing here. This is Clarence Le Nau's district."

Sam said, "Clarence has been reassigned to St. Morgan."

Bob said, "Good. I'm glad to get that crooked asshole out of here."

Sam turned to Bob and asked, "Is our friend Mad around?"

"No, Mad is on another one of his treasure hunts."

"Where to this time?"

"Bobby may know, he's been taking care of that mountain lion, he calls a cat."

Bobby said, "He's a nice cat and if you would let me bring him down here, you would like him, too. Mad isn't a treasure hunter. He helps people find lost stuff. He doesn't even like treasure."

Bob gave us a wink and winced from the pain.

Sam said, "Well, that explains why he hasn't been answering his phone."

Bob asked, "Why were you looking for Mad?"

Sam said, "Oh. Sorry. I haven't introduced you to my friend Rick Blane. Rick, this is Bob, the best Cajun chef in the Caribbean, and his topnotch assistant Bobby." We nodded at one another. Sam continued, "Rick is looking for a rock."

Bob said, "The channel is full of them. Take all you want." He tried to laugh.

Sam smiled and said, "This rock has a carving on it of a skull with two daggers through its eyes."

I added, "It could be a clue to something I've been looking for."

Bob said, "Too bad Mad's not here. I think you both would have a lot in common. It sounds like you are both shadow chasers."

Hennery opened the door and walked back in, "The men are not there and the boat has been ransacked. Can you tell me what kind of boat the big man and the one with the scar were in?"

Bob said, "No I didn't see it."

Bobby said, "I saw a red 'go fast' boat with a dragon on the side leaving as I came down the mountain."

Hennery smiled and said, "That fits."

Bob asked, "Do you know something about that red boat?"

Hennery shook his head and said, "Oh, I know the Dragon and the thugs that run her."

Bob asked, "Who the hell are they?"

Hennery said, "No one you want to mess with. I'll take care of it."

He looked at me and asked, "Don't I know you?"

"Don't think so. This is my first time in these parts."

Hennery said, "I've heard a better fake southern accent form a New Yorker."

Bob said, "This is Sam and that's Rick. They're friends of mine."

Hennery gave me a grin and said, "A friend of Bob's is a friend of mine."

Bob asked, "Hennery, who are those guys?"

"I'll be able to tell you more in the morning. They were probably after the two men and you got in the way. Just in case, I'm going to leave a couple of my men here for the night. Find them a place to stay. I'll see you for breakfast."

He stared at me for a long moment then back at Bob and said, "Tell everyone to be careful. There have been reports about missing boats in the area, so we're going to be stationed here for a while. I don't think it's a big deal. Sounds like a couple of men decided to take a long trip and didn't tell their wives."

Bob said, "Tell them to take the room over the restaurant."

Hennery left and Bobby warmed us up some Gumbo under Bob's supervision while Sam taped his ribs.

CHAPTER 16

That was the first night we had slept in the cabins and the first time on the trip I had not slept beside Sam. It was strange not hearing her breathing next to me. I woke up, found my way through the hatch and out onto the deck. Daylight was just breaking.

Another sailboat bobbed on the water next to us. They must have been pretty shook up to run that channel at night.

The last few days had been hectic so I sat there enjoying the sounds of waves gently caressing the hull and a songbird off in the distance. Last night it felt good to sleep without listening for every little noise. The boat rocked and I knew Sam was awake.

She stuck her head out and said, "Good morning."

"Good morning. Look, honey, we have new neighbors. Let's hope they're decent folk and not the type that listens to that evil Rock 'n' Roll. I've heard it rots your brain."

"Oh dear, don't worry. I'm sure they're just your run of the mill Mother Stabbers and Daddy Rapers," she laughed.

"Yeah, nothing unusual about those folk," I chuckled.

She turned and went back below deck. Then it started, "Boy, you got up early and didn't make coffee or breakfast. Some first mate you turned out to be."

"Excuse me, Captain. I have your coffee sitting here, and Bobby said breakfast would be ready in about fifteen minutes."

Her open hand shot up through the hatch. I handed her the coffee and felt the boat move. I wondered if she would do that get-ready-and-look-fabulous in ten-minutes or less routine, she had done in the hotel. I sat there enjoying the sunrise. Finally, I heard her starting up the steps. Just then I noticed movement from our new neighbors. A tall thin man came out on deck next door.

"Déjà vu all over again," I said.

Sam asked, "What?"

"Nothing. The man next door looked familiar for a moment.

She came up on deck, looked over at him, paused for a moment, and then said, "Mad, is that you?"

He turned and looked back at her and said, "Samantha, you good-looking hunk of femininity. What are you doing in my little piece of paradise?"

They jumped to the dock, ran toward each other, and exchanged hugs. After several pleasantries, she turned to me and said, "Rick, this is Mad Andersen, aka 'The Mad Viking.' He's the man I brought you here to meet. Mad, this is Rick. He's a friend of mine on a quest you may find interesting."

"Oh God, not another lost treasure. Those asshole pirates spent it all. They never buried or saved so much as a doubloon," he said.

Sam shook her head. "He is not looking for treasure; he is looking for a rock."

Mad looked at Sam clearly surprised. Sam just smiled.

"Did I hear someone say Bob was fixing breakfast? I have a feeling I'm going to need a lot of coffee," Mad said. He turned to me and said, "Don't I know –?"

I said, "I don't think so. It's my first time in the area."

Sam spoke up, "He was trying to ask if you want to come to breakfast with us."

I said, "I'm sorry."

"That's okay," Mad said. Then he put his arm around Sam and they started off toward Bob's.

I went below, grabbed the pictures and some of my notes, just in case he wanted to talk about my quest. It would also give Sam time to catch up with an old friend.

I caught up to them just as they walked through the door into Bob's. The smell of cooked bacon wafted out the door as it opened.

"Bob, what the hell happened to you?" Mad asked.

Bobby answered, "Some men hurt my daddy, but Miss Sam fixed him up."

Mad shook his head and said, "He sounds like his mother."

Bob caught Mad up on all the latest island gossip. Bobby, not to be outdone, told us about Mad's cat, Tiny, and how much he could eat.

Mad told us about his latest treasure hunt off the coast of Florida.

He was in his mid-sixties, thin with shoulder length gray hair, and stood about six-two or three. He reminded me of Ricardo Montalban not from Fantasy Island, but the one from Star Trek's Wrath of Khan. He was a charming older alpha male, who kept his status through style and finesse rather than brute force but you could still see mystery and danger lurking just behind his blue eyes. His interesting stories and engaging personality made him the man most men want to be and the man most women want to be with.

CHAPTER 17

Mad turned to me, "So, Sam tells me you are looking for a rock. I've helped people look for some strange things. This is my first rock request."

Glancing around the table, I saw strange expressions from everyone but Sam. I smiled and said, "It's not the rock so much as a clue that will help me find some answers to a question about demons."

Eyebrows raised, Bobby stopped what he was doing, came over and sat down. He looked like he hoped to hear a good ghost story.

"I know everyone here has heard stories about the Devil's Triangle. Have you ever stopped to think where these stories came from or how they got started? I think there was a group of people in the late sixteen and early seventeen hundreds using, and maybe even creating, some of these stories to hide their existence. Admittedly, this theory is based on evidence accumulated over several years and logged in chronological order in a journal." I pulled my journal out of the folder sitting on the chair next to me.

Mad said, "Interesting, may I see?" I handed it to him. He continued, "Rick, I don't want to burst your bubble, but I have read dozens and dozens of Triangle stories. Never once have I seen any indications of someone using them to hide their existence. Besides, why were these people hiding?"

"That's one of the questions I'm trying to answer."

"Okay, take me through your discovery process. Let's see if you can make me a believer."

This was the first time I can remember presenting my evidence to anyone. Suddenly, it became very important this group of strangers agree with my findings.

I took a deep breath, and then started from the beginning of what I knew. "I've been coming to the islands for several years. Each year, I went to a different area of the Caribbean and researched its people. Not the famous ones that everyone knows, but the average person: storekeepers, blacksmiths, drunks, housewives, and prostitutes. Like now, there were some unique characters living in and around the Caribbean.

"On one of my trips, I came across a statement from Blackbeard that struck me as strange. He mentions bloody sails and a foul stench."

Mad looked up thoughtfully then said, "There are things in these waters even those in league with the Devil himself need fear. I pray never to see their Bloody Sails or smell their stench again."

"That's the one."

Mad went on, "I remember it because it seemed out of character. He made that statement at the height of his career, a ruthless pirate afraid of no one. Put gunpowder in his rum, liked the smell of burning sulfur, and placed lit cannon fuses in his beard before he went into battle."

I said, "That quote came from a diary kept by Alexander Stevens, who claimed to have sailed with Blackbeard. The diary was interesting because it gave a look into the life on board a pirate ship.

"He mentions spotting two ships in the Triangle, wherever that was, a Spanish galleon and a smaller vessel with red sails. When they closed on the galleon, the smaller vessel turned and ran. Thankfully, the galleon's fight was not equal to her cargo.

"Two days later, he wrote the ship with red sails started following them. 'We gave chase twice but she is much too fast. She closed in for the third time and the captain gave her a broadside, and she left for good.'

"The last entry that concerns my quest came days later. He wrote 'Monstrous things appeared out of the fog that smelled of rotten flesh. They came for the bounty we had taken from the Spanish. In strange hisses and clicks, they warned us never to interfere with them again. For if we did, we would face a curse worse than death. I pray never to see those bloody sails or smell their breath again."

Bobby said, "I knew it was going to be a ghost story."

Bob said, "Bobby, let the man finish."

I smiled at Bobby and went on with my story. "Reading his statement reminded me of something I had found on a previous trip. There was a report filed by one Captain Ugly Jack. I knew the report was worth reading after seeing his name."

I could tell by looking around the table no one had ever heard of him.

"According to the report, he was a cruel man of questionable character; a known drunk, smuggler, pirate, and general all around scum bag. Ugly Jack reported foul smelling demons in black robes had stolen his ship. They appeared on board out of a foul smelling mist. Everyone from the ship woke up on a deserted island and their ship was gone."

I saw Bob flinch as he adjusted himself in the chair. Bobby moved beside him, sat on the floor, and took hold of his hand.

"After being rescued from a small island, Ugly Jack told the authorities that demons had placed him and his crew there. He was sure they would never be able to catch his boat because it was the fastest in the Caribbean, but the boat would be easy to spot because it had red sails. Ugly Jack was quite a drinker and had over-indulged on several previous occasions. The authorities laughed at Ugly Jack because his crew said they were all drunk and didn't remember anything."

The door opened and one of the two men Officer Hennery had left for security stuck his head in and said, "We're going to let the other residents know we'll be here for a while. I'll check back with you later." Bob nodded and the man closed the door.

A quick glance around the room told me everyone was waiting for me to continue. "I told you about Captain Ugly Jack because I believe the taking of his ship was a turning point. Something had happened forcing my demons to change their behavior." I gave Bobby a quick glance to see that he was hanging on every word.

"I then started looking for reports that mentioned a ship with red sails, demons, or foul smells. I found several, but one caught my interest. A ship named The Urca De Lima had resupplied in Jamaica and was sailing to Spain. In their log was an entry about being followed for several days by a boat with red sails. Thinking their pursuers could be pirates; the captain placed everyone on alert and manned the decks. The midnight watch reported encountering a foul smelling mist. The next entry in the log was that the boat with red sails was no longer following, and not on the horizon. They soon discovered most of their supplies and a large portion of their cargo had vanished. No one knew what had happened or where it could have gone.

"They returned to Jamaica to resupply. After getting back to port, a crewmember they thought was missing along with the cargo came out of hiding. He got off the ship and told the captain demons in black robes had boarded the ship with the mist. They spoke in hisses and had claws for hands. He was terrified and swore never to leave land again."

I took a sip of my coffee. Bobby's mouth was open; he was hanging on every word.

"Now, I have two eyewitnesses from different parts of the Caribbean who reported seeing something strange happen on board their ship. Granted one or both were drunks and probably neither was a reliable source."

Mad asked, "What kind of stuff was taken?"

"From the Urca De Lima, no one knows. The manifest is missing. On a side note her claim to fame is –"

Mad interrupted, "She was part of the treasure fleet lost off the coast of Florida in 1715."

"Correct. Before her, the demons took mostly supplies like flour, sugar, livestock, etc. It was like they were trying to feed a small army. There was never a report of anyone trying to sell or trade the stuff that was taken. It just vanished. That changed after Captain Ugly Jack's boat was taken. The amount of stuff being taken grew. I found several ships' logs mentioned seeing red sails on the horizon. A day or so later, they came across a bad smell then found themselves in a completely different part of the ocean. Several days had passed unnoticed and their cargo was missing."

Mad turned a page in the journal, leaned back in his chair and looked like he was trying to remember something.

Sam touched Bobby's shoulder, "Bobby, honey, could you make us some fresh coffee please?" Bobby got up reluctantly after getting an affirmative nod from Bob and moved toward the kitchen.

"The next big change started a year later, when a Captain named Ivan McBride reported that foul-smelling demons in black robes had put him into a waking sleep and stolen his cargo. His crew remembered nothing and the authorities made fun of him. Captain Ivan was humiliated and made it his goal to prove these demons did exist. He hunted for them in every corner of the Caribbean. People started calling him Captain Crazy Ivan. I found a copy of his log in Cuba. That's where I connected even more dots.

"Captain Ivan told his men that when they came across the boat with red sails, they were to put a damp cloth over their nose and mouth because the smell of the demons breath would put them to sleep or could even kill them. He found the ship with red sails off the coast of South America. The red sails followed them for most of a day then disappeared over the horizon. The captain told his crew the demons would come for them that night. His men prepared and waited. They reported sailing into a bad smelling mist but nothing happened. The next morning the crew found Captain Ivan asleep in his cabin. Their cargo and supplies were still on board.

"Captain Ivan told everyone he had fought and killed all the demons, before he was overcome by their evil breath. He called himself a Demon Slayer and declared the waters safe."

Bobby brought the fresh coffee, refilled all the cups, and sat back beside Bob smiling.

I continued, "The official report stated there were no signs of a struggle. The crew had not seen anything and nothing was taken. They suggested the captain might have been suffering from bad food or drink.

"The next report of the boat with red sails, demons, missing cargo, and bad smell was months later. Captain Ivan had continued to brag about killing the demons in the Caribbean Sea. His next meeting with the demons would be his last. One night in unusually calm waters his crew said they encountered a foul smelling mist. The smell outraged the captain. He started swinging his cutlass at unseen attackers. The next day they found Captain Ivan tied to the main mast. There was a dagger through each eye. His first mate said even though he was dead, blood still ran from the tips of the blades. The crew verified his story. The daggers were said to be cursed because they burned the crewmembers hands when they tried to remove the daggers from his eyes. They cut him free from the mast and the Captain's body walked to the rail and fell into the ocean."

I looked around the table. Sam and Bob were listening intently. Mad was reading my notes and I couldn't tell if he was paying attention or not. Bobby was biting his lip and his eyes were opened wide. I guess it's a ghost story after all.

"This was the first time my demons killed someone, but not the last. The reported sighting of the ship with red sails all but stopped. I believe from this point on they changed from taking only what they needed and became full-fledged pirates.

Bobby's eyes were opened even larger and I thought from the way he bit his lip it might start bleeding at any moment.

"Finding solid leads after Captain Ivan McBride's death has become difficult. The tales of lost time, strange fog, and missing ships are becoming more like ghost stories."

Mad finally spoke. "Like everyone, I've heard my share of Triangle stories and wrote them off as just that, stories. I had never considered them as a tool used to hide something.

Different countries have claimed the Caribbean Islands over the years. Some of these countries were sometimes at war with each other, or, not on good speaking terms. Small, seemingly unrelated thefts by pirates would have gone unnoticed for years."

Mad tapped the journal cover. "Over the years, I also have read most everything you have in your journal. Reading it in order and then looking at it from the angle of someone using the Devil's Triangle stories to conceal their piracy makes a compelling case. I agree there seemed to be something going on. From my years of exploring these islands, and countless hours reading dusty old documents looking for clues left by pirates, I will need to look at all this information from a new angle."

He closed the journal and glanced quickly around the table. He fixed his gaze on me and asked, "So why are you looking in this area?"

I laughed. "I forgot!" Eyebrows raised around the table. "Three, now almost four years ago, I was on my way here to the St. Morgan area. There was a layover in Miami where I was mugged and lost all my notes. The mugging caused me to have a slight case of total amnesia. All that has been recovered of my belongings are two photos of my rock and a list of things that might be clues."

I pulled out the list and handed it to Mad. He read it aloud: "Valhalla, Black, Moon, Foul Smell, Demons, Bleeding Eyes, and Red Sails." Everyone looked puzzled when he finished.

I handed Mad the photos. He glanced at them and gave me a weird look. Holding a photo in each hand, he gently started waving them back and forth. "So these are the pictures, and you don't remember anything about them?"

I answered, "Nothing. Just that I was to bring them here."

Mad turned to Sam, placed the photos on the table, slid them to her and asked, "Did you see these?"

Sam said, "Yes, the man's face was covered. There was nothing outstanding about the boat and I've never seen the carving."

He then slid the photos to Bob and asked, "What about you? Recognize anything?"

Bobby was looking over Bob's shoulder. They looked at Mad with a puzzled expression, and Bob said, "Yes!"

My mind raced. Finally, I thought. The question blurted out of my mouth, "Do you know this place?"

Bob answered, "No. I know the boat and the man."

The excitement of finding someone who knew this man was almost overwhelming. "Really? Do you know where I can find him?"

Bob answered, "Yes. He's sitting next to you."

Mad spoke, feigning indignation. "Sam, you've known me all your life."

Sam started apologizing, "Mad, you were covering your face. I was looking at the rock."

Mad said, as he put his arm around her, "It's okay, but I must say it's not good for an old man's ego when a lovely young lady doesn't recognize him."

Sam gave him a big kiss, smiled, and said, "I know how hurt you are."

Mad looked at me and said, "It's no wonder you haven't found these people or demons. You couldn't find me and I'm sitting beside you."

By this time Bob and Bobby were bent over laughing. I lifted my hands over my head and bowed toward him saying over and over, "I'm not worthy, I'm not worthy."

Mad let out in a huge laugh. "Bob, it's five o'clock somewhere. We need a drink."

We sat and chuckled for quite a while and I was surprised how good a cold beer could be at ten in the morning.

Mad said, "You were wrong earlier. We have met, over the phone. We had a brief conversation. You were vague in what you wanted to talk to me about. You gave me the date you were to arrive and never showed. Now I know why."

He looked back at the list again. "Other than Bobby's feet, I can't help you with the foul smell." Bobby looked at the bottom of his shoes. That gave everyone a chuckle.

"Bleeding Eyes. When you told us about Captain Ivan it reminded me of something. It will come back to me, give it time. My boat is named Valhalla. The red sails are my spares. I only use them when my others are in for repair. It's just a coincidence I was using them each time the picture was taken. The carving is on a black rock. Demon and Moon need to be put together. The picture of your rock was taken on Demon's Moon."

I saw Bob shiver when he said the name. "There are no redeeming characteristics to that island. The larger side has dark, dirty sand with very little vegetation. The complete island is ten acres, more or less. Most of it's a ridge of old black lava from a long extinct volcano. The ocean has eroded one side of the volcano rim, making an opening to the small crater floor. The floor of the crater is maybe five hundred feet across, divided equally between water and land. Someone has carved rooms into the hard lava walls of the crater. There is one big room in the center. It looks like a dining hall with stone tables and small rooms in the back. There are three or four separate carved rooms on each side of the big one, like sleeping quarters. The mystery is who built it and when. There is no record of anyone ever living there and the locals won't even go close to the place."

I looked at Bob and asked, "Why do people avoid that island?"

Bobby said, "People say it's not a nice place. People say the place is haunted and the rocks walk at night. Sabee is a nice place, we like it here, why leave, huh, Daddy?" Bob shrugged his shoulders.

I smiled and said, "You can't argue with that logic."

I looked at Mad and asked, "So my rock is there?"

He answered, "Your rock is on the northeast point of Demon's Moon. It's fifty or sixty feet almost straight up the jagged cliff face. Once you get to the place, there is no place to anchor. The passage to the crater is full of rocks and there is no way to get there from the other side of the island."

Bobby said, "I know why you can't find those demon people!"

Sam smiled and asked, "Why Bobby?"

"They all turned into demon's rocks and walk the floor of the ocean." Bobby said. With everyone laughing, Bob said, "Guess what movie he just watched?" Mad said "Let's go to my boat and I can give you the coordinates of Demon's Moon. There's also something I want to look up on that Captain Ivan."

CHAPTER 18

When we got to Mad's boat, he turned and said, "I don't know if you'll find what you're looking for on Demon's Moon. If it's not there, don't give up. I have been chasing a phantom ship for years. Sometimes, it's just about finding the end of the rainbow, but I can tell you, finding the Leprechaun's pot of gold isn't bad either."

I asked, "What ship?"

Mad looked a little embarrassed and said, "Everyone has heard of the eleven ships in the Spanish treasure fleet that sank in 1715. I believe there was a twelfth ship and, like you, all I have to base my belief on are a few scattered clues, but for now that's all I need. You're looking for missing demons. I'm looking for a ghost ship that never existed. Aren't we quite the pair?"

We stepped on board his boat; she didn't have the luster of the *Alchemist*. Her fiberglass decks were dingy; the teak was weathered and gray. She was a well-used, lived on, working boat. You could still see the majesty in her lines. Like her master, she too carried herself with pride and dignity.

Mad went down the steps, followed by Sam and myself. The cabin was surprisingly large. Stacked on most every surface were books, papers and folders. Scattered among the papers were remains of old cannonballs, swords, and flintlock pistols. A pirate flag hung on the wall behind what might be a desk.

Mad smiled and said, "Welcome to my floating museum and research library. This is organized chaos. I can put my hand on whatever I am looking for given enough time."

He sat down behind stacks of papers and said, "I've been thinking about your lost people, because we both know they were not demons." I nodded in agreement. "They may somehow be connected to a question I've had for years. Who built the water cisterns on all these uninhabited

102

islands? Even more in line with you, could they have built Demon's Moon?"

I said, "We found a cistern about the size of a small swimming pool on our way to find you."

Sam supplied, "It was close to Baneterra."

Mad asked, "Did you see a small shelter? It would have been built out of rock or cut into the hillside, well camouflaged."

Sam answered, "No, but we did find three graves covered with slabs of black rock. There were crossed swords on each slab. I took pictures, but you can't make out the details."

A voice came from the doorway behind Mad. "If you need to find anything in this place, you had better ask me."

I looked to see a buxom brunette, in her early twenties, step out of the bedroom and close the door. I am not sure there was enough fabric in what she was wearing to call it a swimsuit.

Sam poked me with her elbow, "Down, boy."

Mad said, "This is Dee, my computer geek and finder of lost things in this place. She tells me all this stuff is recorded in a computer. Dee, this is Sam, and Rick here is looking for some lost people."

"Nice to meet you. Have these people been missing for long?"

I answered, "About three or four hundred years."

Dee said, "Shouldn't be a problem."

Mad put his hand on Dee's butt and said in a low voice. "You look stunning. I'm ready for dessert."

She bent over and gave him a kiss and gave me a naughty school girl grin then said, "You are always ready for dessert."

I looked at her and said, *"Sir, you are a very lucky man to have such a young, vivacious, and talented lady as a traveling companion."*

She gave me a sexy grin and responded, "I'm the lucky one to have met such a man. He has such a lust for life, travel, and adventure." She gave him another kiss.

Sam said, "I thought you didn't speak French."

I said, *"I don't speak French or any language other than English."*

Dee was clearly puzzled. "But you're speaking French to me now and not the slang French Mad and I were speaking. You speak a very old, proper dialect."

I looked around the room at each of them and said, *"I promise you, to my knowledge, I don't speak French."*

Dee pointed out, "You're speaking French now."

I stood there for a long moment as everyone gave me a bewildered look. "This must be what my grandmother meant by Blood Memory."

Sam asked, "Blood Memory, what's that?"

Dee and Mad still looked puzzled. Sam was massaging her little finger on her left hand and seemed to be quite intrigued.

I answered, "My Irish grandmother said Blood Memory is when you discover a talent or ability you can't explain. She claimed we all inherit things through the bloodline. Sometimes they go unnoticed, or never get triggered. She will be really upset to find there's French blood in her veins," I answered.

"Is it like your déjà vu feelings?" Sam asked.

"No, that's a feeling like I have done something or been some place before. Believe me, I know déjà vu. This was different, I didn't know I was speaking French and in some ways not aware of what I was saying."

We heard the sound of a multiple engine boat passing as it rumbled into a slip further down the dock closer to Bob's place.

I glanced at Sam who was standing next to the stairs that led out on deck. "Friend or foe?"

She turned and slowly put her head up through the hatch and reported. "It's Officer Hennery and his boys. He sent one of his men toward Bob's place at a trot. Now, he's running back from Bob's pointing in this direction. Hennery just signaled for them to stay there and is walking this way. He's not smiling." Sam got off the steps walked over and stood next to me.

Soon we heard Officer Hennery say, "Ahoy! Is anyone on board?"

Mad replied. "Yes, Hennery, how may I help you?"

He answered, "Mad, you old dog, may I come aboard?"

"It would be my pleasure to have you join us, Hennery. Come on down we were just talking about pirates," Mad replied.

Officer Hennery came down the steps. Though it was a large room for a boat, with all Mad's stuff and now five people, it was getting a little crowded. He just sat down on the steps.

"It's nice to see you again, Mad and Dee." He paused and let out a sigh, "Dee, you're looking as spectacular as ever."

Dee replied, "Thank you, Hennery, and you are as charming as ever."

Hennery said, "How are my new friends, Miss Samantha Van Helsing and Arnold? I'm sorry I didn't get your last name."

"My name is Rick, Rick Blane."

Sam spoke up, "This is very embarrassing. Arnold was an old friend. This is Rick; I just met him a couple of days ago."

Officer Hennery spoke, "I thought you told me your name was Rick. That means you have a big problem. Someone has mistakenly identified you as this Arnold."

I asked, "Why is that a problem? I can show you my passport, Georgia driver's license, and even some charge cards."

Officer Hennery continued, "That won't help a resident of another island out of my jurisdiction."

Mad said, "Hennery, stop beating around the bush and tell us what this little visit is about."

Hennery stood up looked out of the hatch toward his men and then around the dock. He sat back down, stared at Mad, and said, "You know Clarence Le Nau's brother Joey is considered unstable at times."

Sam practically yelled, "I'll tell you what I know! I know he's a murderer and a drug dealer. I know the cops won't do a damn thing about it because of his almighty brother, Clarence."

Hennery waved his hands and said, "Keep it down, keep it down!" He stood up and looked toward his men again. "I understand all that. Again, he is not in my jurisdiction."

Sam let out a deep breath and looked at Mad. It was clear from his expression Mad also had a history with Joey.

Hennery went on, "Joey has been out of the area for a while. He just came back to St. Morgan and from what I've heard, he's worse than ever."

We both shook our heads and Sam said, "We were on St. Morgan the night he went on his rampage."

"I don't have a lot of information, but the word is that he wants the two of you eliminated and will pay big money to have it done."

Mad jumped up and said, "That son of a bitch has ordered a hit? Who does he think he is? John Gotti?"

I can't remember if anyone has threatened to kill me much less pay to have me killed so I don't know what my reaction would have been in the past. Right then I felt surprisingly calm.

Hennery said, "Whether you are this 'Arnold' or not doesn't matter. He thinks you are and so will everyone looking to collect."

He stood up and looked out the hatch again. In a low voice, almost a whisper, he said, "I'm not sure about some of my men. They worked with Officer Le Nau and had to know some of what he was doing. With that kind of money on the line, I can't guarantee your safety. You need to get far away from this area fast."

Sam started to cry and said, "Rick, I'm so sorry. I truly thought this was over."

I put my arm around her and said, "It's okay."

Hennery said, "Tomorrow morning at first light, I will leave my men here to guard the island, then escort you toward St. Morgan. Once we are out of sight you can go to one of the bigger islands and get back to the U.S. His boys will not follow you there. Joey should come out of his drugged paranoia after he thinks you are gone."

He looked at Mad. "I know you and Joey have some kind of a history. Once he knows you're back in the area, he may come after you as well."

Mad said, "I should have taken that little bastard out a long time ago."

Officer Hennery said, "Mad, whatever it was, let it go. He's crazy."

He walked up the steps and I could feel him step off the boat. Mad whispered to Sam, "Make sure he has left."

She tiptoed over and peeped out of the hatch and reported, "He's gone."

Mad said, "I don't trust him. I think there's something he's not telling us."

Sam said, "Mad, please don't get involved, this could get bad."

"Sam, honey, this is bad, and I am involved. You and your family have helped me out of some tough spots over the years. We have the advantage because they don't know what they're up against. Do you think your dad knows yet?"

Sam stared at him and I got a feeling he had said more than he was supposed to. Especially the way she said "Mad!" and he stopped talking instantly. "There is nothing to tell him yet."

Mad waited for a moment and spoke again. "I wasn't afraid of that little piece of shit back then, and I sure as hell am not afraid of him now!" He took hold of the pirate flag behind him and pulled it up a little. There was an assortment of pistols, rifles, and boxes of ammo. "This time, I'm ready."

Dee looked at Sam and smiled, gave her a wink, and then said, "We're ready."

Sam glanced at me. "Rick, we need to get you to an airport."

I shook my head. "Hold on! To paraphrase a friend of mine from yesterday, how did she put it? Oh yeah. Like Hell, you have to trust me; I can take care of myself. Besides, he thinks I'm Arnold and from what I remember Arnold was a very smart pig." I glanced at everyone looking puzzled, and continued, "Boy, tough room. Green Acres? Arnold the pig? Still nothing? Ahh, never mind."

I shifted back to the topic at hand. "Sam, I don't know, and may never know, the complete story between you, Mad, Arnold, and Joey. Frankly, my dear, I don't give a damn. I am home. This is where I am supposed to be. I've felt this way since we landed. Well, after I got my stomach back and knew I wasn't going to die in a fiery plane crash."

Sam winked at Mad and whispered, "First landing in St. Morgan."
Big smiles spread on Mad and Dee's faces.

CHAPTER 19

I said, "After reading my journals, I wanted to come here to hopefully
find some more clues. I was also looking for a place where I belonged;
something tells me I may have found both."

Mad said, "I know what you mean. I felt the same way when I first
came here. Sam, he's been bitten by this place, and I think he's too
stubborn to leave."

Dee spoke up, "He's cute, good eye candy, so we should keep him
around for that reason alone."

Sam shrugged and said, "I have a feeling we don't have a choice."

Mad said, "Okay, it's settled. Let's get out of here in the morning and
hide for a while until we come up with a plan."

Sam said, "I thought hiding was the plan."

"We'll let him escort us until we get to that little island where the
graves are. I want to see them anyway. We play tourist while he leaves,
then cut between the islands, so you can't be seen or picked up on radar,
and go to Demon's Moon."

I spoke up, "In a way, Joey has declared war on Sam and me. I will
play the role of Arnold." Sam smiled. "Mad, even though you and Joey
have a past, you and Dee are in the clear for now." Everyone nodded in
agreement. I continued, "He thinks we're going to run and probably we
should. But what if we go on the offensive?"

Sam jumped up and said, "Are you nuts, he has a small army! We
can't take him on."

I said, "I don't mean hand to hand combat. We find out everything there is to know about Joey. His likes and dislikes, what triggers his paranoia, and use it against him."

Mad said, "Sun Tzu, *The Art of War*. To know your enemy, you must become your enemy."

I placed my finger to the side of my nose like you do when playing charades. "Exactly. I have been thinking of something since we found that plane and the airport."

Mad asked, "What plane?"

Sam said, "We stopped at Baneterra to look for Rick's rock and found a very nice plane hidden in the old hangars."

I continued, "I think it's Joey's. My guess is he's acting small and using his brother for protection. The rumors you heard and the plane we found tell me he is a lot bigger than he wants Clarence to know. That makes the money an even bigger problem. If he's as paranoid as we think, what does he do with it? He can't put it in the bank. It would be reported to his brother. He's too suspicious to let someone launder it for him. So what do you do with all that money?"

Back when Dee first walked out of the bedroom and before closing the door. Something other than her larger than life neural beauty had caught my attention. It had been bothering me, and I was sure it would come back soon as enough blood returned to my brain.

Dee said, "That's easy. He jumps into his plane, flies to the Cayman Islands, opens up a numbered account with a fake ID with no questions asked."

Bingo, the blood was back. Before Dee closed the door to the bedroom and my blood got diverted, I had seen the glow from numerous computer monitors. "Dee, how good are you with your computer?"

Mad said, "She's very good."

I kept looking at Dee and asked, "I don't mean entering data or doing a Google search. I mean can you hack a security system?" She dropped her eyes.

Mad asked, "Why do you need to know?"

"When we found the plane there were security cameras. I was wondering if she could tap into the signal and find out where it goes."

Mad took hold of Dee's hand and they looked at each other.

I turned to Sam and said, "Joey has hurt a lot of people. I bet if you made a few calls to your friends, they could tell you his schedule and any rumors about drug deals. They may even know who handles his money or where he takes it."

"Why do you need his schedule? And why do you need to know where his money is?"

"People are creatures of habit and tend to do the same thing over and over. If we know his schedule we can semi-predict where and when he is going to be someplace. To a drug dealer, drugs are expendable to a degree. The cost of doing business. They know some of the drugs will be seized or lost at some point. The markup is so high; they can make up for the loss in no time. But without cash, they can't pay for a new supply so they have to borrow either the drugs or the money."

I went on, excited as my idea grew. "Banks don't loan money to buy drugs, so you have to borrow from some nasty people with very strict lending policies. You miss one payment to these guys, they don't come for your car, they come for you. If we can take his bank or keep it from him, then we can mess him up on at least one transaction, then Joey will be the one hiding and we'll be the least of his problems."

I looked back at Dee and asked, "So, can you hack into the camera system and see if it's his?"

Dee looked me straight in the eye, and with a serious tone she said, "Somehow, I think you already know I can."

Mad said, "She can hack any system out there, but what if she gets caught?"

Dee laughed and said, "Mad, you are so sweet to worry about me. Honey, we are talking about hacking a drug dealer's camera system. If I get caught, a hacking charge will be the least of my worries."

Sam reached in her pocket and pulled out her phone. "Let me see what I can find." She was dialing as she walked up the steps and out onto the deck.

Dee said, "For my part, I need to know what kind of system he has. Then I can tell you how long it will take to get control of it."

I said, "I only saw one maybe two cameras. It wasn't anything fancy, and didn't look professionally installed, so I think it's just an off the shelf boxed system."

Mad said, "New plan! We will still have Hennery escort us towards St. Morgan. We stop at the little island where I can take a look at the graves. After he's gone, you and Sam cut between the islands and go to Demon's Moon. It will take you two or three days to get there and the same to get back and say one day to look around."

He began pacing. Finally, Mad went on obviously thinking on his feet. "In a week, Joey will be like Don Quixote fighting windmills and have forgotten all about the two of you. Sam can still call her friends and get the scoop we need. Rick, that will let you see your rock before the crap hits the fan."

"We'll tell Hennery so his men can hear. You are flying out of Puerto Rico and going back to the States. That rumor should help get Joey back to his normal state of paranoia."

"So what about you two?" I asked.

"Dee and I will do some island hopping. I have several friends to visit. If there is a rumor about Joey's money, they'll know. Arrr! Pirate treasure be it old or new, I love the search."

Dee said, "When we get closer to the island tomorrow, I can hack his uplink no matter what system he's got."

"Let me see," I said. "Mad you're going to check with your treasure hunters. Dee, you're going to hack his security system. Sam is going to check with her friends and find some of Joey's bad habits and hopefully some enemies. I get to stay out of sight and look at my rock." I smiled. "Sounds like a plan."

Sam came back down the steps and said. "I made some calls and they all told me the same thing. Joey went nuts when he saw me on St. Morgan. I told them I had left the area."

Dee and Sam went to Bob's for supplies. While Mad gave me the location of Demon's Moon, we shared our concerns about this harebrained scheme of mine.

We decided to go tell Officer Hennery Mad's carefully constructed version of what we planned to do tomorrow. We walked to his boat and there was no one on board. Our next stop was Bob's. We found Officer Hennery sitting at the table with his men.

Bob looked worse; the color of his bruises had turned blue and that sickening yellow color. He still gave us a big smile when we walked through the door.

"The lovely ladies are down the street shopping," he said.

"Thanks, Bob, but we're here to see Officer Hennery," I answered.

Officer Hennery said, "I see you've taken my suggestion and are getting some supplies."

I answered, "Yes, sir, we have decided."

Officer Hennery got up and said, "Let's go out on the dock where things aren't so crowded."

I started speaking again, "It's okay. We're heading out in the morning and not stopping 'til we see an American flag flying over some piece of land. Then I'll get on a plane and fly back to the States as soon as possible."

Officer Hennery said, "I understand how you feel. For your part, I think it was a case of mistaken identity. Sam, on the other hand, has made a bad choice of people to get upset at her. For her safety and yours, you are making the right choice. Mad, like I said, once you get away from them, you'll be fine. I don't think Joey has a beef with you. You can probably stay on Sabee if you want. We will be stationed here for a while."

Mad spoke, "I'm going to visit some friends further south, out of French waters."

Officer Hennery said, "I think you'll find Joey doesn't operate just in French waters anymore."

I asked, "What about the boats being taken? Where has that happened the most?"

He answered, "Not in the direction you are heading. It has occurred mainly to the north and northeast, one to the west. Nothing has happened to the south or east of where we are now."

I said, "We'll be out of your hair soon."

Officer Hennery said, "I have some good news for you. The weather is great, the water is fine, and there is no better fishing in the world."

We all laughed nodding our heads in agreement.

Then Officer Hennery asked, "Mad, I was told you have some mighty fine scotch on board your boat. Could you spare me a taste, or possibly two?"

Mad answered, "I sure do. It's very smooth and sweet. It just might be as old as your last girlfriend."

Officer Hennery let out a belly laugh and said. "Men, stay with Bob. I want to get a taste before the women get back."

We started toward the boat with Officer Hennery talking loud and laughing the whole way. He waved us down the steps and he stayed on top. Before we could go far, he said in a quiet voice, "Gentlemen, I don't care if that tale of where you are heading is a crock of shit or not. You need to get as far away from these islands as fast as you can. The two men that beat up Bob are Grier and Bulza. They are thugs that work for Joey. Hurry, hand me a drink, so they can see me drinking something."

Mad picked up a bottle of Scotch a poured him about two fingers and handed it to him. He slugged it down, and then staggered back coughing.

He said, "What the hell was that?"

Mad said, "Scotch. You said you wanted Scotch."

Officer Hennery said, "You white people drink that stuff. I just said Scotch because I knew the men wouldn't want any. Do you have any good dark rum? I need to get that taste out of my mouth."

Mad poured him two fingers of Jamaican dark rum and gave it to him.

"Gentlemen, at first light I will escort you in whatever direction you want to go. Once you are out of sight of this island, go and keep going until you are out of these waters."

He drank the rum in one gulp and smacked his lips. "Now that's a good drink! Gentlemen, see you in the morning."

After he left, Mad said, "May I ask a question about you and Sam?"

"Of course."

"Are the two of you having sex?"

That took me by surprise, but I answered "No!"

"Are you gay?"

I said, "No. Believe me; being with her has crossed my mind. But she is a one-man woman and is in love with this Arnold."

"Whoever he is, he's not being a man and stepping up to the plate."

"That doesn't matter, she still loves him."

"You've stepped up to the plate and he's out of the game, so batter up!"

CHAPTER 20

At first light, we prepared to leave. The plan was to slip out of the harbor and start toward St. Morgan. Officer Hennery would have no problem catching us after we cleared the channel and started racing the wind away from Sabee.

The *Alchemist* was fast and cut the water with ease. Mad's *Valhalla* seemed to be just as fast. Her stainless hull may not have that new sparkle, and the fiberglass and teak showed signs of wear, but she still carried herself with style and grace as she sliced through the waves. There was a big smile on Mad's face as they tacked away. *Valhalla* is truly Mad's little piece of heaven. The *Alchemist* was true to her name as well, changing wind and water into new adventures and destinations.

Just before noon, a boat came out of Sabee. To my surprise, it turned away from us and soon disappeared off the screen. Sam had spent the entire morning on the phone, reconnecting with old friends on St. Morgan and surrounding islands, trying to glean even the smallest amount of information about Joey.

Sam came up on deck and stood beside me. She closed her eyes and enjoyed the breeze for a long moment before speaking. "It takes a long time to get an answer to a question without asking the question. No one has seen Joey since that night we were on St. Morgan. The rumor is he's out of control and scary crazy. No one knows if Clarence has him in lockdown or if he's just gone into hiding. There are a few people that I trust checking things out."

She chuckled, "I'm going to make some calls to a few of Joey's arch enemies on a couple of the other islands and see what they have to say. Before I get lost in conversation with these charming individuals, would you like me to bring you a bowl of gruel?"

"Ah, yes, nothing like fresh gruel. Why people bother with steak and lobster, I'll never know!"

Sam came back up the steps with a ham sandwich and a cold bottle of water. "Sorry, this will have to do. I don't have time to burn the gruel."

I took the sandwich and said, "Thank you. There is nothing worse than non-burnt gruel."

She smiled, clearly trying to hide a worried look and said, "No one believes me when I try to tell them you're not Arnold. If I can't convince my friends you're not, then no one can change Joey's screwed up mind!"

"Don't worry about it. But Arnold is going to owe me big if I ever meet him," I said. Sam turned away and climbed down the stairs.

I looked at my idyllic surrounding and thought it was truly a beautiful day in paradise. Suddenly, I got a memory flash, a real memory of my grandmother. She was standing on a hill in North Georgia, looking down at her house in the valley. It was sunny and warm but off in the distance dark clouds were building. She pointed to the sky and said, "This is the calm before the storm." It was exciting because that was the first real memory I have had since waking up. It reminded me of the unseen storm clouds surrounding me from the hidden memories roiling in my subconscious.

We arrived at the island by late afternoon, giving Mad more than enough time to see the tombstones before dark. The *Alchemist* slid into the slip just like she had earlier. The island engulfed us as the palm trees camouflaged her mast and we all but disappeared.

After tying off and securing everything for the night, I looked up to see Mad wading ashore.

He said, "Dee is tracking a signal she found coming from the island. She really gets into this covert stuff. Especially after I told her some of the things Joey has done."

I asked, "What do you think happened to Hennery?"

Mad answered, "I don't know. He seemed ready to go last night. Maybe he got new orders."

As we walked by the slip, Mad stopped and looked at the stones lining its walls. He studied the surrounding area then pointed toward a clump of coconut palms. "There, see that?" Mad led us over to a small block structure built into the hillside hidden by the trees. "There is one of these on every island with a cistern."

We briefly inspected the single room, but found nothing unusual. Then Sam led the way up the jagged rocks to the water cistern. Mad leaned over and looked inside and said, "They're all the same. Someone spent a lot of time and energy building them on these little places and making sure they left no record."

We kept walking and climbed in silence until we got to the flat piece of ground where the tombstones lay in a neat row.

He looked at the stones and said, "Well, they are made of the same rock as the carving on Demon's Moon. Smooth as glass and very hard."

He stepped on the level area and crossed himself. Then he lightly rubbed a stone, like he was caressing it. He said, "These carvings are much larger than the one on your rock. They show a lot more details. These carvings are over three hundred years old, but look and feel like they were just made. The edges are sharp and clean. The swords are the same as the others. They have the Spanish cutlass grip and guard, but the blade is too narrow and the wrong shape for a typical cutlass of that era. The tip is angled like an Oriental sword. The Spanish cutlass came to a point. This tip is serrated, unlike any sword I have ever seen. It would tear the cut and make a nasty wound. This would have been a pirate's ultimate weapon. Lightweight for speed, short for close quarters, and making a cut that would disable your enemy in short order."

Sam asked, "Why would someone go to the trouble of placing the stone here, have these magnificent carvings made, but not put their names on the stones?"

Mad knelt beside the stone and continued to wipe all the dirt and dust off its surface for a long while.

He spoke in almost a whisper, "I don't want to commit sacrilege, but I'm pretty sure I know what they've done although I don't know or understand why." He started clearing the dirt from around the edge of the stone. He did it in a slow, respectful manner. Sam and I sat on one of the rocks that surrounded the graves on three sides feeling this was something Mad alone needed to do. When he finished, he crossed himself again.

I had not considered Mad a very religious man, but he was doing this in an almost ritualistic manner.

He said, "Rick, step down here." He pointed to a spot on the ground beside the stone. "Be careful not to touch it until I tell you. We're going to stand the stone up and lean it against the rock you're sitting on. Sam, we may need some water to clean the under side of the stone. Would you get some, please?"

He continued cleaning around the stone's edge while we waited for Sam to return. When she returned, I got into position. Mad said, "Let's hope Odin will turn his blind eye to what we are about to do."

We lifted the stone into an upright position and leaned it against the rock. He slowly started wiping off the dirt.

Sam handed him the water and he poured it over the surface, rubbing it gently. He studied it for a long moment then said, "I don't recognize the language." Pointing to a date on the stone, he went on. "This must be when the person died. In 1694, the Spanish were heavily involved in this area. He wiped off the cross at the top of the tombstone. "This is not Spanish. The cross is plain almost primitive. The Spanish were really into crosses. Some priests would have a unique design just for their parish. I have traced crosses back to a particular priest, church, and dates."

He pointed to the carved words. "This inscription is probably something like 'Loving Father,' mother, etc. followed by the name of the person and date of death, 1694. I have no clue what this could be," he added, pointing to the bottom of the stone at three circles in a triangle shape. In each circle was a different design.

Sam pulled out her cell phone. "I will send Dee a picture so she can try to find the language and get it interpreted for us."

While Sam called Dee, and Mad prepared the next two stones, I made myself useful and got some more water. I returned to find Mad staring at the carving of the swords. He said, "There's something rolling around in the back of my mind about these. Ah! It will bubble to the surface sooner or later."

We carefully stood up each stone. While Mad rinsed them off I looked toward Sam. She was still on the phone with Dee.

Mad said, "That's interesting. Each stone is in a different language. This one seems a little familiar, maybe Old German or even Norse."

He started mumbling to himself, trying to make sense of the writing. I looked at the other stone. Just then I heard Sam say, "It's Portuguese. Dee is working on the translation."

Mad mumbled, "Rest, Calm, Relative."

Suddenly, I was standing here, not in the present but when these stones were first placed here. I knew these men and felt the sadness of their death. I also felt anger and rage toward the one who killed them. My head felt like it was about to explode and I felt sick to my stomach.

Sam tapped me on the shoulder, "Rick, are you okay?"

Her touch startled me and I answered, "Ah, Yes!"

Looking back at the stone I said, "The first line reads: *'Vengeance Is Mine Sayeth The Lord.' Followed by 'Rest in peace thy loyal servant Brother Zachariel.'*"

"That's it! Vengeance yada, Rest in peace yada, loyal servant Brother Anael,'" Mad said, reading another stone.

Sam said, "Rick, you know that is not in English, right?"

We all stood there looking at the tombstones in silence until Sam asked, "What were those names?"

Mad repeated, "Brother Anael."

I repeated, "Brother Zachariel."

A strange puzzled expression came over her face. She dialed a number on her phone and walked off.

We just stared at the stones until Mad said, "Damn it! Like the swords there is something I just can't –"

Sam interrupted, "The Portuguese name is Oriphiel! Those are all names of Archangels."

Mad almost fell as he stepped back. "Of course, that's why the names seemed familiar! These are their old names!" He pointed to the bottom of the stones. "Those are their holy symbols of power."

Dee's voice came from the phone. "Mad are you all right?"

He just stood there staring at the stones. Dee asked again, "Mad, are you all right?"

He answered with a slight sound of disgust in his voice, "I am now. What kind of a sick freak would put the names of Archangels on tombstones?"

Sam said, "Mad, I don't think it's a divine statement. It could have been someone like my father, who changed his first name to Gabriel, named his only daughter Samantha, the female version of Samuel. To add insult to injury, he gave her a middle name of Lydia."

She looked at me and said, "Don't ever use my middle name or I shall smite thee."

Mad started laughing and said, "Your dad does have a twisted soul."

Dee's voice came over the phone, "Lydia is a nice name. My parents stuck me with Freya."

Mad chuckled and said, "Fitting. Freya, is the Nordic goddess of love."

Dee said, "Woo, I like that. So what's your middle name, Mad?"

Mad smiled and said, "My mother was Spanish and to honor my father's Nordic heritage, she blessed me with Thor."

Dee said, "The god of thunder. I like the feel of that."

Staring at the tombstones, Sam said, "Confess your sin, Rick, and tell us your middle name."

"Michael!"

119

There was silence for a long moment before Dee said, "Two Archangels, a Nordic god..." she cleared her throat, "and a goddess; quite a foursome! Okay children, keep playing among yourselves, I've got work to do."

I said, "The swords. I thought the tips pointing down meant surrender. After reading these tombstones, it sounded like they were more interested in revenge."

Mad said, "According to naval protocol between countries, when a captain surrendered his ship, he would stick his sword in the deck of his ship and step back, relinquishing control of his weapon and vessel. To a pirate, however, it means we lay claim to this, or we are taking whatever they stabbed with their sword. It was also a warning to surrender: if you make us fight, we will give no quarter and take no prisoners."

Sam asked, "So who were these guys?"

Mad answered, "At this point, I'm not sure. The Caribbean gives up her secrets slowly, but it's a safe bet they're not Archangels."

We carefully placed each stone back in its resting place then we stood in silence while Mad spoke in a low voice in a language I did not recognize. After several long seconds, he raised his head and gave us a sheepish grin. "Odin doesn't approve of a warrior's grave being defiled so I asked for his forgiveness. Whether they believed in one god or another wouldn't matter to Odin. He would be more interested if they lived and died honorably."

Sam's phone rang. We both watched as she had a brief conversation, then hung up and said, "That was Dee again. She found some interesting stuff and wants us to come to the boat."

After carefully walking away from the graveyard, being sure to leave everything the way it was found, I looked back while waiting my turn to jump down from one of the many rocks we had climbed to get up there. I knew the graves were no more than ten feet away and yet they were completely hidden once again. The island had kept them safe for over three hundred years and was still doing her part.

CHAPTER 21

We were back on Mad's boat in short order. His museum slash library was gone. Computers, monitors and cables lay everywhere. Dee bounced between keyboards and screens with choreographed yet chaotic moves, wearing a swimsuit even smaller than the one yesterday.

An elbow to my ribs reminded me there was another woman present. Sam also turned heads when she walked into a room. She was the type of woman you wanted to be with, and not just because of her looks.

Dee spoke, "There's a signal coming from the island and it's not even encrypted. I'm running a scan to find any traps, tags, cookies, et cetera, that would alert him if someone had tapped his uplink. I need more time checking it before I look any further. I want to make sure he's that stupid and not just acting.

"Now, about Joey. Thanks to the phone number Sam gave me, I have been tracking him by the GPS on his phone. He's on St. Morgan and has been staying in the same place since I've been watching." She pointed to one of the screens showing a map of the island. A little yellow happy face blinked over his position.

"I'll be able to listen in on his conversations in a couple of hours. Again, making sure there are no booby traps and he's really that stupid.

"OK. About the money. I ran a search in most of the usual places and found no accounts in Joey's name. I didn't expect to find anything, but stupid is as stupid does. I am now running a face recognition search on all picture IDs for accounts that have been opened in the last five years."

Mad was smiling like the Cheshire Cat. Sam was staring at Dee. I, who have trouble turning a computer on, was amazed by the effortless way she ran the numerous computers and searches.

She pushed a button and a picture ID came up on the screen. "But I did find something very interesting."

Sam said, "That's Clarence Le Nau, not John Pecard."

Dee hit enter again and said, "Then he's not Joe Roberts." She hit enter again. "Or Mat Kantz?"

Sam's mouth dropped open, as did mine. I asked, "Could that be Joey's money?"

Dee said, "Don't know. All I have to this point are pictures and names. These are old accounts and could have been opened before Clarence came to St. Morgan. Each was opened in a different bank and different country. I can tell you whoever set these up is good, very good. There are all kinds of spooky things watching these babies. I'll get in without being found soon enough." There was a "since of I've been challenged" tone in her voice.

She walked over to Mad, sat on his lap, gave him a big kiss, and said, "Have I told you I really get turned on when I do this stuff?"

Sam cleared her throat and said, "Okay, then I guess we should be going."

Dee slid her hand under Mad's partially unbuttoned classic Hawaian shirt, pinched one of his nipples and said, "Don't worry, we have all night. There's more I need to show you." Dee got up from Mad's lap and returned to her computer. "I was going to give you a satellite view of Demon's Moon, but all the satellites for that area are mysteriously dark. I don't know why and won't try to find out. It smells like one of those big ugly government things that goes bump in the night and scares little hacker girls.

"In the morning before you leave the area, I want you to turn off your phones and take the batteries out. That way no one, including Joey, can keep track of you."

She pointed to the blinking happy face on the screen, then handed Sam a laptop and a phone.

"If you have to get in touch with us, use these. They'll be harder to trace. Remember, keep the batteries out of them. I don't know who's out there."

I asked, "Why do you think the satellites aren't functioning?"

Dee answered, "They're not off, they're blocked. It's probably nothing. The military may just be playing with a new flying saucer or the satellites were having a bad day. Little hacker girls don't play with the government toys anymore."

She looked at Mad and said, "That's where little girls get into trouble and they don't even get spanked."

There was that naughty schoolgirl look again and it was all directed at Mad. Some of it must have splashed on me because I got another elbow to the ribs.

Mad looked at us and said, "She's such a tease and does it without even trying."

Just then, one of Dee's computers spoke in a sexy female voice, "It's OK! No one is watching."

Dee said, "Let's see what the cameras are keeping an eye on." She tapped a few keys. "Okay, it's an eight-camera system. Number one shows a nice plane. Number two a different view of the plane. Number three woods and a path? Number four a path? Number five a path? This guy is weird! Six and Seven are different parts of the path. Number eight. What do we have here? A big metal door and a very fancy lock."

Sam asked, "Can you give me a full screen of that?"

Dee clicked the mouse, the large screen behind Mad's desk lit up. "Big enough?"

"Now show me the woods and path."

Click. It appeared on the big screen.

"Okay, now the door again."

Another click and the door appeared on the big screen.

"I know that place. We would go there each time we came to the island because it was cool inside. It was a bomb shelter for the base. We called it the dungeon because of its thick concrete wall and heavy metal door. A bunch of us came here once on a dare with Joey."

Dee said, "Whoever this belongs to, they intend on keeping people out. That is one high-end lock system."

Out of the corner of my eye I saw Mad give a little yawn, so I said, "We'll go back to our boat and let you children play. If we don't see you in the morning, we'll see you in about a week on Bent Key, unless something changes."

Dee walked over and straddled Mad again. He said, "Remember what I said, 'Batter, Batter, swing Batter!'"

I smiled and answered, "See you in about a week."

After we got on deck, Sam asked, "And just what was that about?"

I laughed and answered, "Just Mad being Mad. "

"Then it was something to do with sex no doubt."

With a chuckle I said, "Lets get off the boat before the rocking starts and we get seasick."

After we got back to the *Alchemist*, Sam was quiet for a long time, then she asked, "What do you think Clarence is into? Everyone knows he's a crooked cop, but those accounts seemed to be far more than, 'I'll just turn my head while you overcharge the tourist.'"

"I don't know. It may be connected with Joey."

Sam continued to pace in the fantail.

"Sam," I asked, "why does Mad dislike Joey so much?"

Sam let out a deep breath. "That happened several years ago when he lived on St Morgan. His traveling partner at that time was Laura. Joey had become the go-to man on Morgan for anything drug-related. Mad knew Laura had a drug problem and was working with her to keep her straight. Somehow, she got some drugs from Joey. They were bad or she overdosed, either way she died."

Sam stopped pacing and stared at the deck. "Mad went crazy, tracked Joey down and shot him. He didn't die, but it used up one of his nine lives. Clarence arrested Mad for attempted murder.

I said, "Joey must have nine lives."

Sam shook her head in agreement. "Clarence wanted to avoid an investigation and protect his brother. He presented Mad with an offer he couldn't refuse. Joey would not press charges if Mad would leave St. Morgan permanently. Mad took the deal. Knowing there was nothing he could do, he moved to Sabee and became a recluse. Later, he got into treasure hunting, and I've only seen him a couple of times a year since all that happened."

I said, "He seems to be back on track with his traveling companions." Sam gave a little smile. "How long were you and Joey friends?"

Sam said, "Just one summer. The first summer he moved here. Everyone treated him like an outsider. Being one myself, we clicked. Joey changed after Clarence moved up in police department. His Napoleon complex exploded. He became angry, violent, and obsessed with being a bigger man than his brother. That's when he started dealing drugs and our friendship ended."

"How was Arnold connected to Joey? Did he work for him?" I asked.

"No! Arnold came to town months after Joey killed my friend. He met and started hanging out with some of Joey's inner circle. It took a while, but he got closer and closer to Joey. We contacted the DEA. They were very interested, and Arnold started supplying them with intel about Joey's operation.

"Arnold discovered that Joey wanted to expand and supply drugs to the U.S. He had found a dealer and was going to meet with him in person. Arnold and several others were invited along as bodyguards. Joey wanted to make a big impression. We told the DEA about the meeting. They told Arnold to go through with the trip and they would handle everything. When they got to the meeting something went horribly wrong. There was a shoot out. One of Joey's cars caught on fire and exploded. Several people were killed. After the dust settled, everyone was accounted for... except Joey and Arnold. They found the remains of two burnt bodies in what was left of the car. The bodies were too badly burned to ID on site so the DEA took them. After several weeks, they told us one body had been ID'd as Joey, and the other one was Arnold."

Sam started pacing again. "You can imagine my surprise seeing that dead man on St. Morgan. I don't understand how they could have made that big of a mistake."

I said, "That's easy, Clarence was the next of kin and falsified the report to cover up for his little brother."

Sam said, "It's not fair that son of a bitch is still alive!"

I said, "The DEA made one mistake, they may have made two. Arnold may still be alive. We'll look into it as soon as we finish what the two of you started."

She looked at me, drying her tears. There was a questioning look in her eyes that I didn't understand. She said, "This is not right. You're involved in something you're not ready for and don't fully understand. Joey is evil! He is responsible for Laura's death and lots of others. He murdered my friend and her mother, as well as everyone who could testify against him."

"Don't worry. I'm a big boy and can take care of myself. Besides, I'm not alone. We have a Mad Viking and a Killer Computer Geek, an Archangel Vampire Slayer, and a Smart Pig. Evil doesn't stand a chance."

She smiled and said, "I'm going below and try to get some sleep. See you in the morning."

I now knew more about Arnold and even understood why she held out hope that he was still alive. In a way, I hoped he was either dead or really sick because if he was still alive and hiding, leaving Sam to face Joey alone, he needed to have his ass kicked. He should act like a man, and as Mad had put it, step up to the plate. In more ways than one.

The last time we were here, there was silence as we listened for the boat following us. This time there was Dee, and she was quite vocal in her approval of Mad. He had evidently stepped up to the plate and hit several home runs.

CHAPTER 21

The next morning Mad and Dee were nowhere to be found. They had left sometime during the night without a sound. Sam and I soon got under way. Slipping behind Baneterra, we soon left all signs of land in our wake.

We fell into the comfortable routine of life on a sailboat. There were many long conversations about nothing in particular. Sam talked without really saying anything. She remained guarded about her past. That may have been because she knew I couldn't remember mine. Overall, it was a pleasant trip and I enjoyed Sam's company.

We sailed toward our destination and on the afternoon of our second day, we picked up a blip in the radar; just where Mad's coordinates said should be.

We had seen only two larger ships on our voyage. Both were at the edge of the horizon. No sign of pirates wanting to take our boat or Joey's people wanting to collect the reward.

As we got close enough to see the island, it was just a shadow at first, much like any other island, but as we got closer, the place seemed dark and foreboding. There were no shades of green or brown from trees and sand. The waves splashing against the dark rock even refused to make light-colored foam.

We finally saw the opening in the jagged rock that lined the crater's floor. We furled our sails and motored closer, looking for a good spot to anchor. Sam stood on the bow watching for rocks, coral, or anything that might damage the boat. This would not be a good place to have an accident. Help was a long way off.

Sam turned and said, "Take it easy, there's stuff all around. This looks like something from Lord of the Rings." She pointed to the jagged rocks along the crater's rim.

I asked, "Sam, are you sure we're still clear? We are getting close."

"I don't see a problem. It's clear all the way into the bay. There seems to be a wide and clear path all the way through."

We kept going and soon passed through the crater's ring and into the bay. The water was clear and calm. I had expected the sun to be beating down on the dark rocks to make this place unbearable, but there was a cool breeze caused from the hot air rising and pulling in the cooler air from the ocean.

Sam motioned me to stop and said, "Unless you want to beach us, we're close enough."

I looked at the bay and realized large dark rocks surrounded us. Some were just below the surface while others lurked much deeper. Something seemed odd about the rocks. It took me a few moments to realize, there were no barnacles, coral, or sea fans attached to the rocks. I looked down in the water and saw no fish, just the dark sand bottom. The bay seemed to be barren.

We put anchors out at both the bow and stern, not wanting the changing tide to move us into the large rocks on either side. The light was quickly fading. Sam stood on the bow, looking toward the beach and cliff face then asked, "Where did Mad say the rooms were?"

I answered, "The big room should be in the middle, straight ahead of us with several rooms on each side."

Sam said, "Well, they must be hidden because I can't see anything."

The crater floor was an almost a perfect circle, divided equally between water and land. Ahead of us was the peak of the craters rim. It stood around two hundred feet high. The rim seemed to be made entirely of the black glass-like obsidian. The sheer cliff face appeared smooth all the way to the water, where the height on each side had dropped to less than fifty feet.

The water had taken its toll on the smooth surface of the rim. There were cracks and fissures all along the water line. You could see where large slabs of the once smooth wall had broken off and fallen away. The top of the entire rim was jagged and torn. In moonlight, it would probably resemble teeth or even fangs. Sunlight did not reflect from any surface on the crater's wall. It seemed to take in the sun's energy and give nothing in return.

I now know what Mad meant when he told me there was no reason for this place to exist. This is a depressing place and seemed somehow unnatural, even alien.

This place gave me an unusual feeling. Not a feeling of impending doom or that we were in danger. This was not a happy place. It was a place you wanted to leave. A shiver ran down my back. One glance at Sam and I knew she felt it too.

I got the map out Mad had drawn of the island. After getting my bearings, I pointed to where the crater's rim met the water line, and said. "Up there is my rock. We'll have to see it in the morning."

Sam said, "You don't sound excited."

"Well I'm not. I may even be a little sad. I've been looking for this place a long time. I hadn't thought of what I would do once I found it. For now, I'm going to prepare you a great meal. All you have to do is sit up here and enjoy the breeze."

Sam smiled and said, "First mate, fetch me a glass of wine first."

I ducked down the hatch and returned with a glass. "Yes, my lady, this is a very nice Cabernet Sauvignon. It is the perfect wine for the dish I am preparing."

She reached for the glass and took a sip. "Yes, very nice, now snap to it. I'm getting hungry." She chuckled.

After a couple of minutes, I heard Sam come down the stairs, cabinet doors opening and closing. She stuck her head in the galley and after grabbing the bottle of wine, she said, "Are those gourmet beanie weenies or is this one of those recipes handed down from generation to generation in Georgia?"

"My own creation," I stated.

"Hmmm, food poisoning this far from civilization could be dangerous!" She ran back up the stairs.

I picked up our plates and flatware, and went on deck to find a place for us to eat. To my surprise, there was a small table set up on the fantail complete with a tablecloth and candle. I picked up the wine, topped off her glass, then poured myself a glass. Lifting my glass, I said, "To good friends, new adventures, and whatever happens next."

I went below and returned with some garlic bread and penne pasta covered in a vodka crab sauce. I placed the dish in front of her.

She took a bite and said, "You my friend have hidden talents, but what, may I ask, makes this the perfect wine for the meal? Is it the slight earthy oak taste with the hint of floral bouquet and its smooth finish?"

"No, it's the only wine we have!"

"Well then, I agree it is truly the perfect wine."

As we finished our meal, the boat rocked and we heard a scraping sound. I got up and said, "The tide is changing. We must be dragging an anchor."

I went to the bow. The line was still tight and the anchor seemed to be holding. I heard another scrape along the hull. "The stern anchor must have broken free." I ran to the back and pulled on the stern line. It, too, was tight and the anchor holding.

Sam asked, "Is anything wrong?"

"One of the anchors must have come loose for a minute, but they have hooked up again. There are no waves and the tide seems to have slowed. I think she's okay until morning."

I came back and sat beside Sam as she spoke, "It's just the walking rocks," she laughed.

"Walking rocks?"

"It's an old wives tale about some people who made a deal with the Devil. The Devil tricked them and turned them into stone. Now, they are doomed to walk the floor of the ocean, trying to earn their freedom. Some local sailors to this day will toss coins in the water before leaving port and ask the rocks for safe passage."

"Whooo, really?"

She continued, "Yes, really. It is a known fact that most of the maritime disasters are cause by these rocks. Think of all the times some ship hit an unseen object in safe waters and sank. The rocks even change the currents, causing ships to run aground and break up."

"Just why do they play these tricks on ships?" I asked.

"There is something on board that ship they need to buy their freedom from the curse. It could be gold or even a soul the Devil wants to claim."

"Just how do you know all this?"

"Nama was a voodoo priestess on the island where I grew up. Well, she was my fifth grade teacher, but we all knew who she really was." Sam laughed.

"Your teacher was a Voodoo Priestess?" She gave me a look like 'of course didn't you have one.' "Would you like to share any more bedtime stories?"

"No, it's late. Just don't make any deals with the Devil and you should be fine. Good night." She started laughing as she went below and got each of us a pillow.

It was nice sleeping close to Sam again under the stars. Even if it was on a Demon's Island surrounded by cursed people walking the ocean floor.

I woke up to the smell of bacon frying and fresh coffee brewing. There's no better smell in the morning. Sam came on deck with a plate of bacon, eggs, and toast. "It's not the yummy meal you made last night, but it will get you through the morning."

After eating, we decided it was time to go and find my long sought after rock. We waded to shore and walked onto the beach, where we saw a tall, light brown, granite obelisk.

Walking toward it Sam asked, "That thing is huge, where did that come from? I didn't see it last night."

The granite was in direct contrast to its surrounding. Not only was its light color strewn with flakes of gold, but the way it glistened and sparkled reflected every ray of the morning sun.

We walked toward the obelisk. Something had been etched in its surface. Whatever it was appeared to be in several different languages.

We looked at each grouping and Sam asked, "Can you read any of these?"

"No! Can you?"

"No!"

"It would be nice if I had remembered a useful arcane language."

Sam said, "I'll take pictures and send them back to Dee when we get a chance."

We walked toward the cliff face and started our climb. Several hours later, we reached the top and I saw my rock in person for the first time. The object of my quest was smaller than I had imagined and somehow anticlimactic. I had found the boat with red sails, Mad, and the rock, but felt no closer to finding who these people were or proving their existence.

"The swords are the same, as on the tombstones. I guess putting a skull with swords through its eyes, on the grave of an archangel might be a little risky," Sam said.

"The tombstones were made from this black rock and must have come from here. The swords have the same strange tip."

I got closer to take a better look and felt something under my foot. It was a smooth rectangular shaped stone approximately a foot wide by a foot and a half long. I bent over and wiped off the sand. There was an inscription carved on the stone in a language I was beginning to know only too well.

Sam asks, "Well, can you read it?"

I wiped more of the sand away and saw the last line and read the date and quote that answered several of my questions. "1694, An Eye for an Eye."

My knees got weak and I almost fell as I leaned back against a rock. Sam asked "Are you all right?"

I answered, "The village idiot has left the building. I think this skull with the daggers through the eyes is Captain Ivan McBride. The three graves we found were the Demons, McBride claimed to have killed. This island must have been their hideout."

Something at the boat caught my attention. "Sam, where's the channel?"

Sam looked and stammered, "Ah, it was there last night."

There were large rocks scattered all over the mouth of the bay, showing no opening, much less one large enough for the *Alchemist* to pass through.

I said, "The channel must be deeper than it looks or this could be low tide. We got in, so you know there's a way out."

Looking back at the carving Sam said, "Will this give you a few more pieces to your puzzle?"

I said, "Maybe, but I still don't know who they were, where they went, and what they were doing."

Sam laughed and said, "Well, we've seen your rock so let's climb down and see the rest of this tourist attraction. Maybe we'll run into one of your demon people in one of the rooms and we can get your answers."

CHAPTER 22

Climbing up to see my rock had been a time consuming task. The crater's rim defended her secret by issuing numerous cuts and scrapes on the way up. Climbing down, on the other hand, was quick and easy.

Once back on the dark sand we walked along the sheer wall toward the crater's center and the big room Mad had told us about.

We found an opening leading into one of the smaller rooms. The doorway was barely five feet high, and narrow. Windows on each side of the door were just slits cut through the thick exterior wall.

The room was the same size as a cheap motel room and its only feature was a small ledge cut out of the back wall. It may have been for a bed or just some place to sit.

"This must have been someone's living quarters," I said.

There were several things unusual about the room. The ceiling was at least ten feet high. The ceiling height seemed excessive because at the time a five-eight man would have been considered a giant. Despite only one door and two small windows, the place was well lit. The next thing I noticed was the floor, walls, ceiling, and even the ledge were clean. There was no dust, cobwebs, or anything. The place was shiny, like it had just been wiped down with furniture polish.

Sam looked at me and said, "After three hundred years, give or take a decade or two, the place still looks good. If they do windows, I want them to start cleaning my place."

We looked at each opening as we worked our way to the large center room. Each was the same, and all were clean and shiny. Before going into the center room, I looked at Sam and said, "I hope this isn't like the Hotel California."

Sam interrupted me and said, "Hold it. Stop right there!"

I looked around to see if I was about to step on a snake, or maybe something was crawling on me.

Sam continued, "I love the Eagles and that is one of my all time favorite songs. I have some great memories attached to that song, and this place is not going to be one of them."

I tried to speak; there came an "Attt!" from Sam.

I tried to speak again. "Attt! Do you want to sleep with the walking rocks?"

I started to open my mouth. "Attt!"

Not wanting to sleep with the rocks, I started humming, "*It's a Small World*" and got a thump from Sam's hand on the back of my head as I went into the big room.

This room was maybe four or five times the size of the other rooms. One long counter went along the back of the room. Behind the counter was a doorway leading to a room the same size as the other living quarters, but on the back wall of this room was a doorway that led to another larger room. I looked inside and said, "This looks oddly familiar."

Sam asks, "Do you see something?" She stuck her head in the room and said. "Your déjà vu is working overtime I see. Except for being bigger and darker, you are right, it is exactly like all the others, empty."

"Very funny. This must have been for storage." I found it interesting even this far from the opening and deep under the crater rim, there was still enough light to see a lot of detail.

We went through the rest of the rooms on the other side. They were all the same clean, shiny and empty. Coming out of the last room, we decided to take a break by going back to the boat and get something to eat.

After eating, Sam started trying to find a language on the obelisk she could translate.

I stayed on deck looking at the island and up toward my rock. The centerpiece of my quest had not provided me with answers or even a new clue. It was made from, and part of, this island. The rooms were all empty without so much as one piece of graffiti scratched on a wall. My search had lead me to a black barren island in the middle of No Damn Place. I hoped there would be something on the obelisk to rekindle my quest.

It was hot, very hot. The breeze had stopped and the sun was beating down. I went down into the cabin; got a small cooler, put some ice in it, and some adult beverages.

I looked at Sam and said, "Let's go to the bar. I think it will be cooler."

She wiped some sweat from her forehead and said, "I'm with you."

In the hour or so since we had left the beach, everything had changed. The water was uncomfortably warm and the sand was blistering hot. Walking back into the big room in the cliff wall it seemed cooler than before, almost like walking into a cave. The air seemed fresh and clean, although I could not feel a breeze.

Sam set up one of the beach chairs and said, "Rick, do you think Dee is sexy?"

I laughed, shook my head and said, "Dee is sex twenty-four/seven. She is every schoolboy's fantasy and every old man's dream. She would cause a mother-in-law to have nightmares and husbands to go crazy. Her girlfriends all hate her, and her only friend is possibly a flaming gay male. Sexy? Hell yes! Not in a good way, but in an animalistic lusting way. Not in 'I want to take you home to meet mom.' Or 'I want to introduce you to my friends' way."

I paused then added, "I think most men would prefer their women to be ninety-percent class and ten-percent trash. That trash percentage in the privacy of their shared bedroom. Mad's trash percentage may be higher and he likes it to be on display a lot more than most. Why do you ask?"

"I just saw the way you stared at her and wondered."

"Hold on, I saw you staring, too."

Sam answered, "She has a fantastic body. I wondered how she keeps those suits in place. I wondered what she would look like when she gets a little older and gravity starts doing its thing. We both know gravity will do its thing!"

"Dee may not be everyone's cup of tea, but she is a very intelligent woman. When her abundant attributes start heading south, she will still find a way to make things work for her benefit," I said.

Sam smiled, picked up the camera and started looking at the pictures of the obelisk and said, "This language has some similarities to Spanish, or maybe Portuguese. I think this part says, "Brothers of Mark are welcome." or something like that, maybe not. Now that we have found your rock, do we have to find Mark's brothers?"

We both laughed and just sat for a while looking through the open doorway and windows at the boat, water, and jagged rocks that now seemed to be blocking our exit.

I got up and started walking around the room, looking at the walls. They were as smooth as glass, showing no cracks or blemishes of any kind. I turned toward Sam and said in a loud voice. "Hello!"

Sam jumped, then screamed. "What are you doing?"

I said, "There should be an echo in an empty room this size, but there's not."

She shook her head in agreement and said, "No dust, no cobwebs, no furniture, no people, and no echo. This place is full of a lot of nothing, and I will be glad to get out of here as soon as the tide changes."

I had felt that way since we got here, not spooked or anything; just the urge to be someplace other than here. This place seemed to give off a strange energy and moving around seemed to lessen its effect. I walked behind the bar. Sam was now walking around the room looking at the walls and rubbing her hands over the smooth surface.

I went into the room that we thought was the living quarters of whoever ran this place. Like Sam, I was walking around the perimeter of the room letting my fingers rub on the smooth surface.

I felt a sharp stinging pain on one of my fingers. "Ouch."

"Are you okay?"

"Yes, there's something sharp on the wall and I cut myself." I bent down and saw a thin wavy line running down the wall. I traced the line with my finger very carefully till it formed the shape of a square.

"What is it?"

"I'm not sure." I knocked on the wall with my knuckles and then on the square, I looked at Sam "It's hollow." I kept rubbing my hand on the wall around the square. There was no handle. I sat down on the floor in front of the square and thought for a long minute on how to get it open.

"Open sesame!" I said.

Sam bent over laughing, "You really thought that was going to work, didn't you?"

"Hey, it was worth a shot." Sam was working her way down the wall looking for a handle. I lay back on the floor to let her pass and asked, "Have you got any ideas?"

She kept running her hands over the wall and said, "Maybe there's a hidden handle someplace."

I looked at the tip of my finger and said, "Be careful it could be sharp."

I picked up my foot and put it on the wall to stretch. Sam stepped over me looking for the handle. Something moved under my foot. "You found it!" I said. Sitting up to see that the square had pivoted in the center and the wall was open.

Sam asked, "I found what?"

I looked in the hidden compartment and unlike the rest of the room, it was pitch black.

"What do you see?"

"Nothing just a big black spooky hole!" I answered.

"Oh! Man up! Reach in there and pull out some gold pieces of eight or maybe a silver bar or two. You know, a pirate treasure. Arr," Sam growled playfully.

I looked at her and said, "You're the one who didn't like treasure hunters and even made fun of me when you thought that was what I was doing."

"Okay. Okay, I'm sorry. I shouldn't have made fun of you or your rock. Now stick your hand in there and show me what you've got!"

I raised an eyebrow and said, "Okay, Dee." I felt a slap on the back of my head.

Gingerly, I reached in the compartment and felt something. I took hold of it and pulled. It was a stack of paper. I reach in and pulled out three more stacks all about the same size and all blank.

"Is there anything else?" she asked.

"I don't think so." I stuck my hand in until I could feel the back of the compartment. I placed my hand against the back wall and there was a different texture. I kept feeling around until I found an edge then pulled. Something heavy fell over. It startled me and I jerked my hand out, making Sam jump.

"Oh, woman up! It feels like a book of some kind," I said.

I carefully pulled the large heavy leather-bound book out and placed it on the floor. Embossed in the leather cover was the skull with daggers through the eyes.

Sam said, "Rick, this could be the clue you hoped to find."

I slowly opened the book to the first page. It seemed to be in the same language as on the cover. All I could read was the dates, 1688. I turned through the pages and read them. The last entry was in a much-improved handwriting and read 1716. I said, "It's going to take a long time to translate all this."

We skimmed through the book and found several pages blank. Well back in the pages we found two drawings, one of some black squiggly thing drawn on a forearm. The other drawing was of someone wearing a tattered, dark-hooded habit. A plain cross hung from the rope tied around his waist. The odd thing was his left arm hung to his side. Coming out of its sleeve and angled across the lower part of the habit was a sword, the same sword as on the tombstones.

Sam said, "Looking at the dates there seems to be an almost daily entry of some kind."

With the light fading and the cool breeze returning, we decide to head back to the boat, taking our stuff and our newfound treasures. The day had been long and hot, and we were both very tired. Before going to sleep, I went below, dug in my pocket and got some change. Returning to the deck, I walked around the boat throwing the change in all directions.

Sam laughed and said, "Nama would be proud."

CHAPTER 24

I slept straight through the night without interruptions from walking rocks scraping against the hull. Sam was still asleep, not a fake sleep either, a deep sleep, the one where there's just a little drool in the corner of her mouth. God, if she knew I had seen that she would be so embarrassed. She is truly a beautiful woman and the more I'm around her, the more I want to kick Arnold's ass for what he's putting her through, even if he is dead.

*****

I had just finished making breakfast the next morning when I heard Sam say, "Rick, have you seen what your bribe has done?"

"No." I handed her a plate of waffles as I looked in the direction she was pointing. The channel was clear all the way out of the bay to open water.

"It is simply amazing what a buck forty-seven and a high tide can do."

Sam stood looking at the channel and said, "I think there are fewer rocks today than yesterday."

"Let's pull anchor and get through the opening before they come back," I said.

I finished pulling the stern anchor and walked by Sam to the bow. I asked. "Aren't you going to help?"

"I am. I'm staying out of your way and watching for rocks."

Once the anchors were on board, I heard the motor start and felt the boat turn toward the opening. I kept lookout this time while Sam slowly steered us over the rocks into clear and deeper water.

Sam called to me, "Now come back here and be a good boy and eat all your breakfast. That way you'll have the energy to hoist the sails, swab the decks, and do the dishes."

I really liked her sarcasm and wit; it kept me on my toes. That and her looks made her a great traveling companion. Probably not as much fun as Dee, but then I'm not Mad.

We had a good wind and after everything was set, we soon settled into the routine of traveling under wind power.

We were going to sail all day and late into the night. Sailing at night, I realized the courage it took for those early captains to hurl their ships into the inky blackness not knowing if they would sail off the edge of the world or strike land before daylight. Even with all this technology, I find the darkness just beyond my bow unnerving. Radar might keep us from running into another ship or an island; it would not keep us from hitting Sam's walking rocks. But, since I had paid them off at Demon's Moon and the charts showed deep water all the way to Bent Key, I felt somewhat safe.

There had not been any reports of boats being taken in this area. Still we wanted to spend as little time in open water as possible. Two people alone out here would be easy prey for a group of armed thugs.

We took turns at the helm, but Sam spent most of her time trying to translate the journal. At sunset, she came on deck with a cold drink.

"What's up?" I asked.

"Dee told me Joey has sent his boys to everyone he thinks I know. Telling them not to talk to me or else. That explains why I haven't been getting calls or emails. They are terrified."

"Well, so much for plan B."

"Dee has found out a lot of stuff about Joey. She can't wait to go over it with us at Bent Key. I think there's some kind of a connection with the journal and the people you're looking for."

"And what is that?"

"The person keeping the journal was named Jeremy. In the first part of the journal, he used some English words and phrases. He was on a boat until something happened in 1687."

"So how does this connect to my people?" I asked.

She said, "That captain's name was... drum roll, please." She pointed at the skull on the journal cover. "Wait for it, wait!"

"Captain Ivan McBride?" I said in surprise.

"Give the lad a cookie," she said.

"Interesting, very interesting indeed."

"He wrote something in the margins in many different languages. It must be important because it's almost hidden and printed very small."

She went back to translating and I kept us on course until early morning. With nothing on radar, I set the alarm to sound if we got within 25 miles of anything and threw out the sea anchor. I lay down on the deck and caught a few winks.

The sun came up on a clear day and we were back under way. Sam brought me a cup of coffee and wanted to know how much further it was to Bent Key. "By my precise calculations, I figure to be there around noon, give or take a day or two."

She smiled and said, "At least they're precise."

I thought about the new pieces to my puzzle and the time passed quickly.

"Land Ho!" I shouted down the hatch a few hours later. "Shiver me timbers! Land Ho!"

Sam came on deck, went to the GPS, and after a minute or so said, "Your course be plotted, sir. They be on the southern tip of ye island. At a place called Le Marin there be plenty of safe anchorage."

"You know Rick, that phrase I keep finding in all those different languages; there is one I think you can read." She placed the book in front of me and pointed to something very small on the page.

I said, "I can barely see it, much less read it."

141

She handed me a magnifying glass. "Here, old man, I'll take the helm. I marked a couple other pages where he wrote something in a similar language."

I said, "They all have a common theme. Each one mentions something under or beneath. I think someone was hiding in the basement, keeping tabs on these people for some reason."

Sam said. "I didn't see a door any place, did you?"

"No, we stopped looking after we found the hidden compartment. If I had a secret passage, I'd put it in the storage room. That way only the person running the place would know."

It wasn't long until we saw the harbor and Mad's boat. It would have been impossible to miss. Dee was jumping up and down on the fantail topless. That was the first time I had paid attention to the name of Mad's boat. Somehow, with Dee jumping and waving, Valhalla seemed more than appropriate.

Sam said, "That girl is going to have back problems when she grows up."

"I just hope she doesn't get a black eye. They may try to arrest Mad for assault." I was getting used to the smacks on the back of my head.

We slid in beside them and started tying up. Dee had put on a swimsuit cover up which just made things worse. The sense of mystery was back. I continued tying off the boat and trying not to look at her, knowing Sam was watching me. Finally, with everything done, I turned to face Dee and looked her straight in the eyes. They were blue. I hadn't expected that with her brown hair and olive skin.

Sam asked, "So, Dee, have you found any new stuff on our favorite drug dealer?"

"Lots, and Mad has found the swords. Come on, he's waiting."

She vanished down the hatch. We crossed over to their boat and followed her. Mad was sitting at his desk. Behind him on the big monitor was a large drawing of a sword. The same sword we saw on the tombstone and now the journal.

Mad said, "I give you the ultimate weapon of its day." The picture on the monitor was a drawing of the sword showing a lot of detail. "A man by the name of Bishop Marko allegedly commissioned these swords. No one thought they existed because of the weirdness of the story, and a myth was born."

"Who was Bishop Marko?"

Mad said, "He started out as a priest in this area. He had political contacts close to Queen Ann of Spain and through some questionable moves, he increased donations to the Church and money going to Queen Ann. He soon became a Bishop over most of the Caribbean.

"He wanted to be the high Muckedy-muck of the new world. He told Queen Ann that if she gave him the power over the new world, he would convert lots of souls to Christianity, thus expanding her empire." Mad spun on his chair with a smile.

"The Queen said, 'That's nice but, I need gold, silver and sparkly things to pay my bills. These wars are expensive. I'll give you a couple of years; show me what you've got.'"

Somehow, I couldn't see Queen Ann speaking that way.

Mad continued his storytelling. "Now, Bishop Marko went to the new world and found it was harder than he thought. The savages were stubborn and didn't want to give up the gold and sparkly things. Upon his return, the Queen was impressed, but not enough to put him in charge of that part of the New World, but she did give him a very fancy ring and cross. The Spanish love their crosses.

"Bishop Marko did a lot of begging and made some big promises. She gave him two more years and said go forth and get me big piles of shiny things. This is where the swords come in. Bishop Marko had brought another gift for the Queen, but since he didn't get the job full time, he decided to keep it for himself.

"Bishop Marko had enslaved or captured two small men from a far off land. These men had given Bishop Marko a dagger with strange powers, in hopes of winning their freedom. Marko took the dagger and said it wasn't enough. He wanted more. The men said they only had enough material to make twenty-five swords and daggers. Marko agreed to set them free once the task was complete."

Mad glanced at the screen again then turned back to continue, "The swords were said to be as light as a feather. They would never rust, break, or need to be sharpened. The terrifying part was cuts from these swords would never heal. Also, just a touch of the blade would make people scream in agony.

"Time goes by, the two men and twenty-five swords were sent to Bishop Marko, who was waiting in the new world. The men and swords never arrived, thus a myth was born."

Mad pointed at the papers scattered. "I read up on Bishop Marko and he was quite a piece of work. He tortured a lot of people by burning them; several of his enemy's mysteriously bled to death, from very small cuts.

He wore a white cloak with the cross from the Queen around his neck and her ring on the middle finger over the white glove on his left hand. He claimed to be the Queens' left hand over the new world.

"Even without the swords, Marko did get a lot of shiny stuff for the Queen. It and Saint Marko were lost, when the Spanish Treasure Fleet sank in 1715 off the coast of Florida."

Mad pulled up another picture of a man's forearm showing a dark squiggly mark. He said "I don't know what this is but the mark matches the tip of the sword."

Sam said, "That picture is in the journal!"

I stepped to the edge of Mad's desk and laid the journal in front of him. Mad had been so into telling us about what he had found. He had not noticed the journal.

"What is this?" Mad asked.

"We think it's an almost daily record of life on Demon's Moon!" Sam said.

Sam explained about Jeremy and Captain Ivan McBride. "But we didn't recognize a lot of the language it is written in."

Mad was spellbound by the book. I don't think he heard a word Sam was saying. He slowly opened the book, stared at the first page for a minute, before carefully turning each page after. "This is magnificent. Truly magnificent! A record of a man's, no a people's, life over three hundred years ago." He pointed to one of the sections of small print in the margin and said, "This is Norwegian. It says, 'They hear from under the earth.' Did you find a cellar, dungeon, secret passage?" Mad was out of control.

I said, "No we stopped looking after finding the journal."

"You need to make another trip."

"We came to the same conclusion, after Sam translated some of the languages in the margins."

Mad looked through the journal and said, "This is in Old Latin. He was learning the language so this is really bad Old Latin. It's going to take a long time to translate."

Sam asked, "On Demon's Moon, could you read any of the stuff on that big rocky thing?"

I said, "By big rocky thing she is referring to the obelisk."

"What obelisk?" Mad asked.

Sam showed him the pictures she had taken. Mad said, "I have been there twice and never saw that. The picture is too small. I can't see the writing."

Dee spoke up, "Enough with all the old stuff, I'm hungry. Let's go get something to eat and drink. I have lots of news about our beloved Joey."

Getting something to eat sounded like a great idea and we agreed to meet on the dock after freshening up a little.

CHAPTER 25

Sam showered, changed, and put on makeup, all in the time it took me to find a clean t-shirt. Man, I thought, did she ever look good. We met Mad and Dee on the dock. Mad, like myself, had dressed in shorts and a t-shirt. He did have a very tall walking stick made from some kind of dark wood. Dee was wearing a skimpy nothing. Showing more of her boobs than most women had, excluding Sam of course.

We walked off the dock and started down a street made of sand and crushed shells. There were some scattered sections of asphalt or concrete where the road had been paved at one time. We passed several buildings that had taken the brunt of a hurricane or two.

There are a few things that are common throughout the Caribbean. Each locale runs on island time, which means whatever you have planned will be at least two hours late. Also, if it ain't broke, don't fix it, and if it works at all, it ain't broke. If it is broke they will fix it tomorrow. That gets a little confusing because tomorrow is always tomorrow. Next, pot, weed, marijuana, whatever you want to call it, is an herb, not a drug. Rum is a staple, like milk, sugar, or bread, so get over it!

We followed the street, passed several more of the leaning wood-framed buildings. Turning a corner, we saw a ship on the ground next to the road surrounded by mismatched umbrellas.

Mad said, "Welcome to Randy's Shipwreck Bar. A hurricane blew his fishing boat up here. He couldn't afford to fix it, so he turned it into a bar." The sound of laughter, steel drums, and the smell of spicy food said a good time was about to be had by all.

For the next couple of hours, we laughed and talked. Shared fish head soup, conch fritters, fresh conch salad, and jerk chicken. We all had several drinks before we would let Dee get down to business.

She finally interrupted the fun. "Believe me, I hate to be a party pooper but there's some really important stuff I want to tell you. Remember, I wasn't sure if Joey was stupid or just acting stupid?" We all nodded in agreement. "Well, it has been confirmed. Not only is he stupid, he is the king of all things stupid. I don't remember how much I have told you, so I will start with our trip to St. Morgan."

"You went to St. Morgan? Are you crazy?" Sam said

"Oh please, he doesn't want us. He's looking for you and this sexy little smart Pig." She blew me a kiss. "The first night we went to several bars before finding where Joey's boys hung out. We went there the next night and struck gold."

She sipped her drink before continuing. "Joey's office is called the freezer because of the snowflake on the door. That, my friends, is a Snow Locking System. The best money can buy and totally impossible for mere mortals to open. The door on Baneterra has the same lock."

I started to ask one of the twenty questions racing through my head.

Dee raised her hand and said, "Let me finish. Joey keeps his drugs in five safe houses scattered around the islands. That way one raid can't put him out of business."

Mad spoke up, "Last week a boat bringing in his shipment had a problem. It caught fire and sank, losing the entire shipment. Joey got a lead the men who sank his boat were on Sabee acting like they were sport fishermen. He sent his muscle to find them."

Sam and I looked at each other.

"The reason Officer Hennery didn't join us was he had to pick up two bodies floating in the water east of Sabee."

Sam asked, "Was it one of those guys from Sabee?"

Mad said, "It's hard to ID a body with no head, hands, or feet."

Sam exclaimed, "Joey has turned into a sick freak!"

Mad said, "It's those new boys he has, they're the freaks. A lot of his old people are upset and scared."

Dee said, "Joey has another problem. His supplier got busted and he's trying to find a new source."

Sam asked, "How did you get Joey's man to tell you all this? He has everyone scared to death."

Dee said, "A little cleavage goes a long way. A lot of cleavage goes even further. The poor things only have enough blood to operate one head at a time. Men get so distracted by boobs and shiny objects."

Sam smiled and nodded her head in agreement, so I kicked her under the table. She just kept smiling, and I noticed two men watching us from the shadow of one of the buildings.

Mad cleared his throat. Dee looked at him with a grin. "But my charming Mad got most of the information."

Mad explained, "While Dee was keeping the young man occupied, with, I'd guess, a shiny object or two, I noticed the bartender was getting upset. It seems the young man was her boyfriend.

The more her boyfriend looked at Dee's shinny things. The more she talked. Joey collects money every week under armed guard. He is taken to Baneterra, where he flies to some unknown bank. He tells everyone his money is in Fort Knox and protected by the U.S. Military."

Dee smiled and continued, "No one goes to the island because it is heavily booby-trapped. He returns the next day and it starts all over."

Mad continued, "Before he leaves with the money, it has to be sprinkled with baby powder. Then it's wrapped in clear plastic and covered in red duct tape. Each bundle is either thirty-five or forty thousand dollars."

I said, "The claymore mine I saw on Baneterra may be the U.S. military protection he is referring, too."

Dee said, "You are correct, my sexy memory-challenged friend. While you were on your little trip, he made a money dump. I watched him open the bunker, a.k.a. Fort Knox, deposit the money, and fly off with empty bags."

"You watched him?"

Dee smiled and said, "I own his security system and can watch his money and all five of his drug houses."

We sat there for a few minutes thinking. Sam got up and said, "I'm going to the little girl's room."

Dee said, "Me too!" They walked into the bar leaving Mad and me sitting on the patio.

Mad put his hand over his mouth, faking a yawn and asked, "How many did you count?"

I looked at him in surprise. "There are two by that crooked building," I whispered.

He answered, "That makes at least four. The good news is they're not pros. The bad news is they're not pros. So we have no clue what they'll try."

"So how do you want to handle it?"

"Dee can take care of herself and I know Sam can. What about you?"

"I can handle myself. My guys don't have guns. How about yours?"

He said, "No, they're just local boys wanting to make a name for themselves and get some quick cash."

Sam and Dee came back and sat down. Mad started to speak. Dee cut him off, "We know, the bartender told us. Four of his regulars were talking about seeing Sam's picture and reward. They are going to jump us between here and the boats."

Sam said, "I just got a call. Remember Sharon the waitress on St. Morgan?" I nodded my head. "Joey went to her house, kicked the door down, and accused her of being a snitch. He beat her up and shot her in front of her kids. She's in the hospital, they don't know if she's going to live. That son of a bitch has to be stopped!"

I said, "I've been thinking of what we can do, but first we've got to get back to the boat."

We all glanced at each other. Mad said, "If everyone is ready, Rick, you lead the way. I'll bring up the rear."

CHAPTER 26

We paid our check and started our single file walk back to the boat. Staying close to the buildings checking each door we walked by making sure it was locked. Each time we came to a space between the houses, I stopped and looked for any kind of movement.

Mad whispered, "You act like you've done this before."

I glanced back smiled and said, "Couldn't tell you. It's an amnesia thing."

Mad chuckled, "So, it's the old amnesia excuse, is it?"

We turned the corner and saw the street was dark. I stopped, looked back, and said, "Here we go. This is where I would plan an attack." We turned the corner and walked in to the darkness. The temperature dropped and I got a sudden chill.

From across the street, we heard footsteps then loud screams. I turned and saw four men running toward us waving machetes over their heads. They fanned out, each picking his target and ran toward us.

I braced myself and waited for my attacker to get closer. He was a heavyset dark-skinned man with short-cropped hair. We made eye contact; there was a terrified look in his eyes. Mad had been right; this man was not a trained killer. My attacker let out another scream as he got in striking range and swung the machete down toward me. With my left hand, I hit his forearm blocking the machete's path. I jammed my right fist into his throat, not hard enough to crush his wind pipe, but hard enough to hamper his breathing. He stopped; a look of surprise followed by fear filled his eyes. I grabbed him by the front of his dirty food-stained t-shirt and pulled him face first into the wall behind me. Blood splattered leaving a dark streak as he slid down the wall. Both his hands gripped his throat as he gasped for air.

I looked to see Sam's attacker slam into the wall. She grabbed him by his dreadlocks and slammed his face into the wall again. After kneeing him in his kidneys, he fell to his side clearly unconscious. She tossed the machete out into the street, smiled, and said, "It's not nice to play with knives."

Dee's man lay on his back, Dee sitting on his chest with her knees pinning his arms. She was holding his machete to his throat. Even in the dark, I could see confusion and fear in his eyes.

Mad's man, however, was still ready to strike, standing with his machete raised high.

Sam screamed, "Oh no, Mad!"

Holding his walking stick in one hand, he raised the other hand toward us and we froze. He placed his hand back on his walking stick, which was resting on his attacker's shoulder. Mad was keeping the man from falling, by making several back and forth movements with the walking stick. He lifted the stick from the man's shoulder, placed its tip on his forehead, and gave his attacker a slight push.

The man fell backwards like a tree, a thud echoed when he hit the ground and dust curled up around him as he lay motionless.

Mad shrugged as Sam ran over to him. "I just wanted to see how long I could keep him standing."

We all went to where Dee still held down her attacker. I bent over and looked at the man on the ground. He was an older, dark-skinned man, scraggy beard, nappy hair, dirty clothes, and he reeked of pot and cheap wine.

Dee looked up to us with that naughty schoolgirl giggle and said, "I like being on top."

I ducked and put my hand on the back of my head expecting a thump at any second. Dee looked at me and with concern in her voice asked, "Is something wrong? Are you okay?"

"I'm all right. Just a nervous tick I've developed," I answered.

Mad winked at Sam and said, "I think she's more than a nervous tick!"

Blood trickled down the blade of the machete Dee continued to hold to the man's neck. She touched the blood with her finger and showed it to him. Then she made a cross on his forehead and started mumbling

151

something in a language I had never heard. Her body started to shimmy and shake. She leaned backward holding the blade high in the air. The man under her did not move, but his eyes opened even wider. She continued the mumbling and shaking for several minutes.

Jumping to her feet still holding the machete high in the air, she walked over to the man Mad had pushed over. She wiped her finger on the side of the machete and rubbed a cross in blood on his forehead, then spit in his face. She did the same thing to the two men that had attacked Sam and myself.

She went back and sat on the chest of her attacker and spit in his face. Then she leaned back and gave us all a little wink. She rolled her eyes back, showing only white. Bent forward until their noses were almost touching, she spoke in a low unearthly voice.

"These people are under my protection. If any harm comes to them, it will come back to the person causing the harm tenfold. If you know of harm coming to them and do not stop it, you will receive the harm tenfold yourself. Do you understand?"

The man blinked his eyes.

She pointed for us to start walking toward the boat. As we walked away, she started chanting in that strange language again, her tone could only be described as sinister. Abruptly, she stopped and let out a bloodcurdling scream. Leaning forward until she was again face to face with the man she said, "You will be able to move once I lift the curse. Then gather your friends and leave this place. You need to make sure nothing happens to my friends. Do you understand?"

He blinked.

She again spit in his face. "Pray I never set eyes on you again, because I have your blood." She let out an evil laugh that made my skin crawl, jumped to her feet, and started dancing toward the boat waving the man's machete over her head.

CHAPTER 27

After getting back to the boat, we had several good laughs about Dee's performance as the Voodoo Queen of the Caribbean.

The reality of the attack by the men with machetes slowly took hold. Dee without any sexual overtones sat on Mad's lap, sinking her head onto his shoulder. Sam's phone rang and she went out on deck. I thought of the men running at us waving their machetes.

Sam returned, sat down on the steps, and said, "Sharon didn't make it."

Mad growled, "We have to stop that bastard."

Sam said, "But how? Believe me, it's been tried before."

I looked at Mad and asked, "Do you think we can blow the door?"

Dee answered, "It's very heavy. It took all Joey's strength to pull it open. Why do you want to blow it up?"

I answered, "You said it couldn't be opened."

"I said a mere mortal, which I am not, couldn't open the door. I know someone who designed the system and she put in a back door. So with a certain card and a certain code, you too can be better than a mere mortal and open the door in under three seconds."

By morning we had come up with what everyone agreed was a good, simple plan. We would go to a spooky island owned by a crazy murderer, get around all his booby traps, and pick an unpickable lock, then replace his real money with shredded paper. And, take the drugs out of his five houses so he couldn't give it back. Finally, we would blow up Fort Knox so he couldn't replace the bogus money.

All I had to do was convince people I was Rick Blane, tell them I was leaving the area because I was afraid of Joey. Let them know Sam had already left with some people during the night.

We divided up the list of supplies. Mad was getting us a powerboat to help get us on and off the island faster. For what we were planning, speed could save our lives. He also had a few other items on his list that we needed but would be harder to come by.

Since we had come up with our plan, Sam had been on the phone nonstop. I wasn't sure how she was going to pull off her part. Like Mad's part, I really didn't want to know. Mad said one of us may need to have deniability.

The next morning Sam and I stopped at Fort De Feeney, a cruise ship stop on the island, where I would carry out my part of the plan. With all the tourists and cops, there would be less chance for another attack.

We know from Sam and Dee's conversation with the bartender last night, Joey's people had Sam's picture. She stayed on the boat and kept out of sight while making phone calls and working on her part of the plan.

I went shopping. There was no way to know how long we would be out or when it would be safe for us to go into port. I mixed in the stuff from last night's list. At a glance, other than quantities, nothing on the list was unusual. Once the stuff got back to the dock, it was apparent to everyone I planned to be at sea for along time. When asked where I was going, I said I was going straight to Key West and would not be coming back to these islands.

After putting all the supplies on board, I asked for the police station. I told the people on the dock about the attack last night. That I had been mistaken for someone named Arnold, and a man named Joey was trying to have me killed. I showed them my passport. "See, I'm not Arnold."

Some of them had heard about the trouble. I told them the woman I was with left with the other people and I was going to leave as soon as I filed a police report.

The small group on the dock gave me directions to the police station. I filed the report giving a generic description of the men. I put in the report that I did not know the other people. I had met a woman on the trip to St. Morgan. She said her name was Sam something. I spent a week or so sailing with her. Last night, I find some nut-job, name of Joey, was trying to kill me, because of her and some guy by the name of Arnold.

"He thinks I'm Arnold." I explained my name is Rick Blane and showed them my passport. "I'm not! I don't know Arnold or where to find him. I don't know where that woman and the other people have gone and don't care. You just need to tell Joey who I am and that I'm going home."

The officer started asking me questions. I kept saying I don't know or I don't care. He stopped questioning me after an hour, handed me back my passport and said he was sorry about the problems, but he hoped I would return someday to his lovely island.

By the time I got back to the boat it was mid-afternoon. I went below to tell Sam about the report and to ask about my performance on the dock. She was missing; I stuck my head up through the hatch and looked around. There was no one standing close and she was not topside.

"Sam," I repeatedly called in a whisper as I went from room to room. I was standing in her bedroom when I heard a door creak behind me and saw her peep out of the closet.

Sam said, "Just a few minutes before you got here I heard someone whispering from the dock. A voice asked if anyone was onboard. The boat moved as someone stepped onboard. I found a place to hide. Whoever it was only did a quick check of each room, probably just to see if anyone was onboard."

"Boy, Joey's guys are fast. He was checking out my story. Let's get out of here. What did you think of my performance on the dock?" I asked.

"You sounded like a scared little boy. They laughed their asses off after you left."

I went topside and started preparing to leave. Several of the people I had told my story to were waving. Each had a big smile. I smiled and waved back.

After getting past the big cruise ship anchored in the harbor, I got the sails up and Bent Key became a distant memory in short order.

Sam stuck her head up through the hatch and said. "I just talked to Dee, Joey got several calls saying you were sailing alone and you were not Arnold. Your passport said you were Rick Blane of Atlanta, Georgia. You had met some woman called Sam on the plane flying into St Morgan. The person making the call read the entire report to Joey. He told Joey you didn't know where that woman and the others had gone. He said you were so scared that you started crying like a little girl and just wanted to go home."

I looked around and said, "It's clear, you can come out of hiding."

Sam came up on deck and continued, "Joey told his man not to worry about you, but he had better find the other people. He wants that bitch dead before Friday." Sam put her hands on her hips, "You called me That Woman!"

I grinned but sounded wimpy. "Please be careful. I'm a very sensitive person and I've had a rough day."

By early the next morning, we were tucked away in our hiding place on what we now called Grave Island. Mad was going to stay several miles away, anchored by a small reef island. Now, all we had to do was complete our little project and wait.

Every so often, we took a break and looked through the journal for English words and dates. Some of the names were funny like Big Nose John, who may have later been referred to as No Nose John. Most of the others, like Smoking Ear Ed, were only mentioned once or twice.

The handwriting greatly improved over the years. I noticed several blank pages toward the end of the Journal and after that the entries got farther apart and some sections seemed to be in code. The handwriting rapidly declined into a large awkward script. The comments seemed to become less friendly and the island was referred to as this dark cursed place. There seemed to be several different groups on the island that would leave, stay gone for a while, then return for a short stay and leave again.

The computer moaned in a female voice. Sam shook her head and said, "That's Dee, she just sent us an email." With a click of keys, she opened the message. "They're in place and she wants me to turn on my phone. She has some news."

Sam turned the phone on and it started ringing immediately. She answered, putting it on speaker.

Dee's voice came out of the speaker. "Rick... No, let's use Arnold. I heard Rick was crying like a little girl. Joey has been having fun telling everyone how he scared the pants off some tourist. So, Arnold, Mad thinks we have time to do it today, He wants to know if you want to get it over with."

I answered, "We can be ready in a few minutes. Let go!"

Dee said, "Hold on a minute."

The goal was to prove to everyone I was not Arnold and convince them I was afraid of Joey and running away from him. We knew that part would be easy because Joey needed to believe other people were cowards. I hadn't expected it to bother me, having those people believing I was afraid, but it did.

Dee's voice came through the speaker again. "Mad has the headsets, so we can all stay in touch. When you get there, I'll guide you through the booby traps. Oh, before I forget, I think the door is rigged somehow. After unlocking the door, he opened it just enough to slip his hand in and did something. The angle was bad so I couldn't see. There may be a switch to turn off, or a trip wire to unhook."

Sam and I exchanged nervous glances.

Dee continued, "Okay, folks, I'll be watching you in real time. Sam, tell me when you get to the island. I'll switch the video feed to a recording I made yesterday. Mad says we need to do this now. What do you think? Last chance to put it off?"

I nodded my head yes. Sam said, "Okay! We agree. Come on over, we'll finish up and be waiting."

CHAPTER 28

We heard a boat coming and Sam went up the steps with one duffel bag to put on the boat. I heard her screech, "Mad!"

I threw two bags up the stairs then looked out through the hatch. My mouth dropped open. "Mad!" I said, "We need something light and quick not a –"

Mad cut me off. "She is only twenty-four feet and there is nothing lighter than a Zodiac. We all know two Yamahas are faster than one." He made that Tim Allen sound and said, "More power, and more power," then trailed off making monkey sounds.

Sam tossed the bags to Mad, looked at me shaking her head. "Men!"

I smiled at Mad and mouthed "More power." Then I handed him the rest of our stuff, got on board, and we were off.

Sam took the helm when we got close to the island. She passed the place where we had anchored, saying it was the safest place, but the next one is on the other side of the island and would give us a hiding place. That is if this yacht would fit.

Soon we saw what she meant. It was a crack between two large rocks, with a small spit of sand, way too small to be called a beach. A narrow path led up the steep bank and headed toward the center of the island.

I saw her glance at each side of the boat then at the crack. Without hesitation, she turned toward the opening and didn't cut power, until the nose of the boat was well between the two rocks. She cut power, threw the engines in full reverse and the bow slid gently onto the sand just as she shut off the engines.

Mad crowed, "She's so good!"

I nodded in agreement, a death grip still in place on the top support.

"I didn't want the waves to push us in to the rocks and maybe puncture one of these inner tubes." Sam pointed to the floats surrounding the boat.

Mad patted my shoulder. "Let's try to do this thing without blowing off major body parts."

Sam pointed toward the path. "This will take us through some of the old houses and comes out near the hangar. Fort Knox is down a path to the left. If you want, I'll lead till we get to that point."

"That works for me," I said.

We inserted our audio buds and checked in with Dee. We waited until she started the video. Sam led the way. When we got to the houses, I remembered what had happened and got a creepy feeling. I wouldn't want to be here on a moonlit night. Hell, I didn't want to be here now. Sam led us past the old houses and along a stone fence. It wasn't a path; more like a place where there was less brush, but true to her word, we came out near the hangar.

She pointed. "Okay, it's down there, about two hundred feet on your left dug into a mound of dirt."

A ridge of earth surrounded this end of the island. Probably something the government had done when they built the airstrip.

I dropped my bags, gave Sam a wink, and said, "Mad, there are at least two trip wires by the hangar." He nodded. "Okay, Dee, it's just you and me, Babe. Take charge and tell me what you want me to do."

Dee answered. "Oh, I love a man who can follow directions. I don't see you yet, so walk down the path slowly and keep your eyes open! Have I told you I like to watch?"

Sam smacked me on the back of the head, handed me the door decoder, and said, "Be careful."

Mad said, "Once you find the booby traps, I'll take a look and see what kind of toys we have."

I pulled a roll of bright orange surveyor's tape out of my pocket and showed it to Mad, then I started down the path looking at every stick, leaf, rock, and spider web I came across. I heard Dee's voice low and sweet in my ear.

"Baby, I see you. There is something about three feet ahead of you."

I moved to the right and slowed, looking so hard it made my eyes water. "I don't see anything."

Dee answered, "It's there, baby, just past that dark spot on the ground."

"Okay, I've got it. Mad, it's a black trip wire, about eight inches off the ground. Leading back into the brush. Can't see what it's hooked to. I'll put some tape over the wire. Day glow orange is such a romantic color don't you think, Dee?"

Dee said, "If you say so, baby. This is a cheap system. You're in black and white."

"How far to the next?" I asked.

"You just keep doing what you're doing, and I'll let you know when you get close to the next spot."

I stepped over the wire and slowly walked down the path.

Dee's voice came in low and gentle again. "Be careful with this next one. He stepped around something, not over like the other one."

I looked close and saw something in the center of the path. "Got it," I said. "Mad, it's a land mine. On top of it is something that looks like a black spiny sea urchin. I'll mark it with the tape."

Mad came back, "Geez! Don't put the tape on those prongs, that thing was unstable when it was new, thirty years ago. Put the tape near it, not on it, please."

I ripping off a piece of tape, thinking, *Mad is rattled. This thing must really be bad news!*

Dee said, "Okay! Baby, we know what we're looking for now. There're three more trip wires to go."

With Dee's help, they were easy to find and mark. Soon, I was looking at a huge steel door in a steel frame mounted to a concrete wall buried in a mound of dirt.

"Lucy, I'm home," I said lightly.

Dee answered without banter, "This part I can't help you with. Once the door opened, he stuck his hand in and did something. I couldn't see what he was doing, so please be careful."

"I will, so what's the secret Batgirl combination?" I asked.

Dee said, "Okay, baby." I could hear the nervousness in her voice. "Slide the card through the slot, Push 6..9.. pound, then 6..9.. pound, and then 6..9.. pound. Slide your card through the slot again, and you will get a green light."

The green light blinked and I gave the door a push. It didn't move at first, then creaked open just a touch. I peeked in and saw a piece of wire. Carefully feeling around, I found it was looped over a nail. I gently removed the wire and opened the door a little more. There were no loud noises so I opened it some more and saw the wire swing free. It was attached to a claymore mine mounted directly over the door.

I said, "It's okay children, you can come out and play now." I opened the door wide and looked at the contents of the room, then I sat down by the door and waited for the others.

Dee asked, "So is there anything in the room?"

160

"Oh, yes, let's wait for the others."

I heard Dee as she guided them to where I was sitting. I stood when I saw Sam cross the last trip wire. She smiled, walked up to me, put her hand on each side of my face, and kissed me on the lips.

"Don't get any ideas. I'm just glad you're all right." Then she lightly smacked me on the back of my head.

I mumbled, "Okay."

Mad and Sam looked around and burst out, "Holy Shit! Joey has been a busy boy!"

"Would someone please tell me what they see?" Dee pleaded.

Mad said, "The back wall is stacked floor to ceiling with red duct-taped bundles!"

Dee said, "Now that we are through the traps and looking in Fort Knox, I need to tell you Joey is on the move. He's at the marina and will be heading out soon. I didn't want to put more pressure on you while you were finding the traps."

Sam said, "He could be here in two hours, maybe less. Do you think he knows something?"

"I don't think so. He's coming alone, probably to get money for the big deal."

I said, "We can still do this before he gets here."

We carefully took down bundles to cut open and replaced most of the money with the copy paper we had been cutting and taping. Then we re-taped each bundle and put it back exactly where it came from. We managed to substitute our fake money in fourteen bundles, before Dee told us he was almost there. That was when we noticed the baby powder had spilled out onto the floor and the place now smelled like a nursery.

I said. "That son-of-a-bitch is not as stupid as we thought. Take our stuff and get out of here, I'll clean this up and meet you by the hangar." I took my shirt off and rubbed the powder into the dirt.

Dee's voice came into my ear, "Baby, he's on the island. Get the hell out of there."

I stepped out, closed the door, and started down the path, pulling the tape off the trip wires and trying not to blow myself up in the process. I got to where Sam was waiting. We turned off the path and almost got to one of the houses when we heard a voice. Everyone froze. We couldn't see him for the brush, but he was close. He stopped and said to the person on his cell phone, "This place still gives me the creeps."

My heart was beating so hard I was certain he could hear it. He continued talking standing right in front of us.

Finally, he said, "I'll be back soon. Hunt that bitch down. I want her dead before I do this next deal." He started clearing the brush off the runway and we ducked into the remains of the closest house.

The roof had fallen. Pieces of timber and roof tiles lay scattered on the floor. There was just one room, maybe five-hundred square feet. The building looked to be of Spanish design complete with arched windows and very thick coquina walls.

The creepy feeling was even stronger inside. It felt like ants were crawling on my skin. I glanced at Sam. She was rubbing her legs and arms. Mad was looking at his exposed skin to see if something was on him.

We heard a phone ring about halfway down the runway and could hear his voice, but could not understand what he was saying. The conversation was short and he started whistling while walking back toward the hangar and us.

Mad asked, "Dee, did you hear his call?"

"Yes, and it's sad. She was so young, full of life and pretty, too. We will all miss her so. One of Joey's men reported to him, Sam had been killed."

"Yuck!" I said, "I've been kissed by a dead woman."

Sam shook her head. "Believe me, I know the feeling, and that was not a kiss, it was a peck. If I had really kissed you... Well, anyway, it will be a long time before you get another one."

Joey started the plane. Mad peeked out a window and said, "We need to stay put until he is long gone in case that paranoid bastard circles back over us."

I looked at the window where Mad was keeping an eye on Joey's departure and noticed something. The keystone in the arch of the window was black. Part of the roof was covering the window next to me. With a little effort, I saw the keystone in that window was black also.

The engines throttled up to full power and the plane started down the runway. We each looked out our window and saw the plane lift off. It barely cleared the treetops before dropping out of sight. The plane banked toward Sabee but did not gain altitude.

I said, "He is going to scud run low and fast, far away from here before popping up on someone's radar."

Mad said, "We might as well get off this creepy rock. We can't do anything until he comes back and takes the bait. Then it'll take me two, three hours tops, to set up the fireworks."

I stood up and walked over to the window by Mad. The black keystone seemed to be made of the same rock as the graves and Demon's Moon itself. Mad saw what I was looking at, rubbed his hand over the stone, and said, "Another connection to Demon's Moon."

Sam asked, "What do you think, another isolated coincidence?"

I said, "I hope it's like a Seurat painting and with a couple more dots, we'll be able to see the whole picture."

We gathered up our stuff and started our trek back through the brush to the boat. Every house we passed had the same black stone in each window.

Finally, we got to the Zodiac. Sam backed us out while Mad and I kept the inner tubes, as she called them, from getting snagged on the rocks. We passed the end of the runway and saw Joey's boat anchored in the small bay.

We soon pulled alongside the *Alchemist*. I told Mad to wait; there was something I wanted to give him. Sam smiled and went below returning with the journal.

I said, "We are going to be looking for secret passages and a hidden room on a black rock. Translating this will give you something to do, and hopefully keep you out of trouble while we're having fun."

Sam handed him the journal. Mad cradled it in his arms and asked, "Are you sure?"

I answered, "It couldn't be in safer hands."

CHAPTER 29

We left for Demon's Moon the next morning. There had been no recent reports of missing ships. Joey was busy trying to find a new supplier. Sam was dead and Rick Blane was running home to hide under his bed.

Sam came up on deck. I thought for a dead woman she sure looked good. Hell, for a live woman she looked good.

With a big smile on her face, she said, "Now you get to be a tourist and chase down these mysterious people. Mad is really excited about the whole thing. He thinks his people and yours are the same. He and Dee are going to hang out with some friends until Joey picks up our fake money, then we can blow the hell out of everything he owns on Baneterra."

I nodded; things sounded good so far.

Sam continued, "Dee is working on the translation and will let us know if she finds anything interesting. I don't care what Mad says, he thinks there is treasure hidden someplace in the pages of that journal."

I said. "I don't think so, when they turned pirate and didn't hoard the money they spent it like every other pirate."

Sam answered, "Oh, come on, you know it's more exciting to chase treasure than bales of cotton or barrels of molasses."

"Hold on, girl, you told me island people don't like treasure hunters. Now you, Mad, and probably Dee are looking for treasure. I have been looking for these people for a long time and never thought there was treasure."

"Come on, you've already convinced us something was going on. Let your hair down. Have fun, be a treasure hunter."

The trip to Demon's Moon was uneventful and soon the dark mass loomed on the horizon. This time the dark forbidding wall of the crater's rim looked comforting.

Sam stood on the bow as before and guided us through the jagged tear in the crater's rim. I slowly passed through the opening and into the bay. She turned with a big smile and said, "It's clear all the way to where we anchored last time."

After securing the boat, I reach in my pocket pulled out some change and started throwing it in the water around the boat.

Sam gave me a wry grin. "So, is that to avoid shallow water? I know it can't be a bribe for the rocks."

With a grin I answered, "Just hedging my bets. If we need to get out of here in a hurry, I don't want to worry about your walking rocks."

Sam answered, "Let's go while we still have light. Dee translated the last page of the journal and emailed it to me before we lost contact. I'll get it and some flashlights. We can read it over there. It may give us a clue."

Sam handed me the backpack loaded with supplies and soon we were ashore. This time the room did not seem as large or as strange. We walked across to the counter, where we opened the pack and got out the email. I walked into the room we thought to be the living quarters. Even knowing where the journal had been hidden, it was almost impossible to find the spot. I rechecked the compartment and it was empty.

Sam was still standing at the counter. "Okay, this is what Dee has translated."

She read: "'They have not returned on the date they gave me. So, this means we are free, free to leave. We will remove everything from this cursed place.' Dee thinks the last page seemed to have been written in a hurry. 'I must go down to the place where I was told to never go. I wish to take nothing of theirs with me. I pray they are no longer there. I saw no sign of them in their hidden world. I leave all their orders, even though their words vanished after being read. I leave this journal, for I want no connection or remembrance of this cursed place.'"

I considered the information in the message. "It sounds like he left something in the basement."

Sam said, "He really wanted to get off this island. Now the trick is to find a door that has been hidden for three hundred years."

We picked up our flashlights and walked into the back room gently rubbing our hand on the smooth surface trying to feel for any imperfections that might give a clue to the hidden passage.

After checking the room and finding nothing I said, "It's time for my secret weapon."

Leaving the room, I returned with a lit cigar. Sam said, "So now you're going to start smoking?"

I answered, "No! But, the cigar is. The cracks are too small for us to find, but maybe smoke can."

We walked around the room, letting the smoke float up the wall, watching for any sign of movement. When we got to the back wall, the smoke vanished into the corner.

I said, "And we have a winner." The smoke was sucked in around the entire back wall. "One hell of a door."

Sam said, "Now if we only knew where they put the door knob."

We spent the next hour looking every place we could think of for a handle, button, or lever to open the passage. I walked back into the room and stared at the wall. Could it be that simple? If no one knew of the passage, then why would you have to hide a handle?

I went over to the wall and gave it a push. Nothing happened at first. Then a crack appeared in the corner of the wall. "Sam come here!" I yelled. When I stopped pushing, the crack closed.

I said, "It's an Occam's Razor. The simplest answer is usually the right one." I placed my shoulder to the wall and pushed. The wall opened slowly revealing a landing, leading down into the darkness. Something clicked and the door stopped opening. It stayed in place, a latch of some kind holding the door open.

"Shall we enter the Netherworld and search for ye treasure, My Lady?" I invited with a sinister grin.

"A dark mysterious spooky island, protected by cursed souls turned into walking rocks and a secret passage leading to underground caverns. What will you come up with next? UFOs? Maybe Atlantis?"

"Just trying to show you a good time."

Sam said, "I know you've forgotten a lot of stuff, so let me explain. This is not a good time. To start with, there is no spa, no strawberries dipped in chocolate or champagne. Oh, yeah, there should be a masseuse named Pierre and –"

I stopped her. "Okay, this is not Fantasy Island." Looking down into the darkness, I stepped onto the platform. "Let's see what's down here."

The walls of the cavern were not like the ones in the rooms. They were rough and absorbed the beams from our flashlights. I walked down several steps to the floor of a small room.

There were three tunnels leading out of the room. I pointed to the tunnels running in opposite directions and said, "It looks like these run under the living quarters on each side of the bar."

Sam was standing beside me, looked down each tunnel and said, "That could be where they listened from."

We started down one of the passages, moving slowly and looking at everything before taking the next step. The walls were dusty, but there was no sign of life. I think of caves being damp, musty smelling, and cold; not this place. It was dry and maybe a little cooler than the outside.

Sam called me over. "Look at this." She directed her beam to a smooth square-cut rock with a piece of leather attached, forming a handle. She pulled the leather strip and the rock moved just a little. We could hear sounds coming from the room above.

Sam said, "I'm going to go up there. See if you can hear me."

A few minutes later I heard her walk in the room. I heard her say, "Can you hear me now?"

I answered, "Yes! Loud and clear."

"Hello, can you hear me?" she asked again.

"Yes, I'm right here!" I shouted.

She mumbled, "Must be the next room over."

"No, this is the one!" I yelled. She walked out of the room and I barely heard her ask the same question next door. I heard her walk by the doorway and into the bar.

She got to the doorway and asked, "Could you hear me?"

"I could hear you perfectly and even a little when you went next door. I was yelling. Couldn't you hear me?"

"Not a peep."

"This is an interesting place. Sound up there is amplified and seems to only travel one way. Who were these people and how did they know about acoustics?"

We checked the other passage running under the living quarters and found one opening in each room. There were several openings at different places around the bar.

I said, "That leaves us one tunnel and it must lead to your treasure." We started down the passage, checking each step before taking the next. I heard something and stopped.

I glanced at Sam. "Do you hear that?"

"Yes, and it has gotten a lot cooler."

We came around a corner and the tunnel opened up into a room about the size of the bar. It was still cave-like, with ragged walls and ceiling. There was sunlight coming through a crack in the far wall.

"This looks like a good place for stacks of gold or maybe a treasure chest or two."

Sam shined her light on the walls and in every corner. Treasure fever obviously makes even smart people act crazy.

The only things we saw were two small tables with benches carved from the rock sitting in the middle of the room. Something had been placed on top of one of the tables. As I got closer, it appeared to be black material of some kind laying long ways on the table. A rope was drawn tight against something wrapped in the cloth.

Sam stood at the end of the table and said, "It's a hooded robe." She lifted the hood that had been hanging off the end of the table.

I loosened the rope and opened the robe. Lying inside were four sheathed swords. "This could be what he left for them," I said.

Sam said, "So they never came back. That must have been some trip."

"Maybe they found Pierre and the spa," I answered.

The guard on each sword was a little different, not the elaborate swirls and loops of the Spanish, nor was it the plain yet efficient guards of the British. The hilt was like the blade more on the Oriental design. The leather grip was red and wrapped in braided silver wire.

We each picked up a sword and pulled them from their sheaths. They were bright and shiny as if just cleaned.

"These are the swords Mad showed us in the picture."

"The picture did not show the tips were black," Sam answered. There seemed to be a translucent coating that covered an inch or so of the sword's tip.

"The other drawing was of a forearm with the tip on the swords on it?" Sam said.

"I think they are suppose to burn human flesh if touched," I answered.

Sam instantly touched her finger to the blade. Paused for a moment then started jumping around shaking her hand. "Ouch, boy, that burns! Ouch!"

I said, "Don't give up your day job. After three hundred years they may have lost something."

"Let me see your sword. Give me your arm and let's see if it works on you."

"You aren't going to cut me," I said.

"Oh, come on, man up. I'm not going to cut you. I'm just going to see if you are chosen."

I stuck out my left arm and showed her where to place the tip to match the drawing. She placed the sword to my forearm.

"How long is it supposed to take?" I shrugged my shoulders.

After a long moment, I grabbed my forearm and started dancing around the room, "Shit that burns! Damn!"

"You have the nerve to tell me to keep my day job?"

I glanced at my arm. "Nothing. Your turn." I took her sword, placed it to her forearm, and after a while removed it.

"We aren't the chosen ones."

"We both already knew that."

Sam picked up one of the other swords, dropped it immediately, and said, "It shocked me!"

I said, "Static electricity," and picked up the same sword and got the same jolt. I touched the remaining sword, getting the same shock. Then I picked up the sword Sam had touched to my arm and it felt like shaking hands with an old friend. When I touched the sword I had placed to Sam's arm, I got an uncomfortable feeling that was not there before. Sam got the same results, only feeling comfortable holding the sword, which had been touched to her arm.

I said, "Mad is going to go crazy over these swords. The workmanship is incredible. The ripples in the metal look like water, I have never seen anything like this.

We both heard a noise coming from further down the tunnel. Still holding our swords, we carefully found the sound to its source. It was water dripping into a cistern carved into the rock. That was large enough to hold two thousand gallons or more of fresh water.

Sam said, "This must have been built for the people on the island."

I saw a door like the one at the bar. It opened into a small cave that led out to the other side of the island.

Sam tapped me on the shoulder, pointed to some steps that led up and out of sight into the mountain. I closed the door and we climbed the steps. They turned, forming a spiral. Light increased as we went higher. The steps opened onto a small platform surrounded by jagged rocks. It was a place where the people on the island could be watched.

I could see the *Alchemist* and the beach without any problem. Sam was looking out over the other side.

Sam said, "They wanted to keep an eye on these people for some reason."

I leaned against the wall and stared into the blade it was almost hypnotic. Maybe they are, because before I knew it the sun was setting. I looked at Sam who was staring into the blade of her sword and said, "Sam, we need to go."

She jumped as if I had woken her from a sleep. "What? Oh. Okay."

We went back to the table and tied the robe into a bundle around the swords. I picked up the bundle and it was heavier than I expected.

We got to the stairs. I stopped and asked, "I wonder how many other secrets this place holds?"

CHAPTER 30

Once we left the caverns, the urge to leave kept growing and with everything loaded on the *Alchemist,* we decided it was time to go. Sam took her position on the bow looking for rocks. It was a futile effort. There was barely enough light to see the water's surface, much less a dark-colored rock several feet down. Staying in the center of the channel, we idled through the jagged opening. The bribe had apparently worked because we soon found ourselves in deep water, ready for our trip back to a more populated area.

We decided to go back to our hiding place on Grave Island, because it had been the only safe place we had found. With Sam supposedly dead and Rick running from the big bad Joey, we had to stay in hiding until our plans for Joey hopefully turned the tables and had him looking for somewhere to hide.

Standing alone at the helm staring out into the darkness, I thought of the early sailors and how much courage it took to sail in those days. I have a GPS and know within a few feet where I am. I have well-defined charts, showing me the water depth and landmasses. All they had was a hand-drawn map showing land out there somewhere. The maps gave them a general direction within a hundred and eighty degrees more or less and sometimes distance within a few hundred miles.

I have sonar telling me how deep the water is under the boat. They had a string with a rock tied to its end, with knots tied in it, which told them the water depth and their speed.

Radar tells me where other boats are and shows me land. They had some poor guy in the crow's nest or standing on the bow looking for the shadow of land on the horizon or white caps revealing a reef.

Even with all these toys, as Sam calls them, sailing at night made me tense to say the least, but those guys put their life on the line every day using nothing more than a map scratched on a piece of paper and a rumor.

Sam stuck her head up through the hatch. "Has anything changed?"

"No, we're still alone in the middle of nowhere. When the sun comes up, we'll hang all the sails. I'd like to get where we could at least call for help if needed."

She nodded in agreement and said, "Rick, I found something in the robe with the swords. There are four daggers and leather-bound books. I don't know if they are journals, ship logs, or personal diaries. Each is in a different language, so until we get help they're just really great looking books. I think we have another clue to help us find out what they were doing on Demon's Moon."

She handed me one of the books. The cover was embossed with the skull and swords. The writing inside, if you could call it that was strange and unlike anything I had ever seen.

Sam took the book and put it back with the swords then asked, "Rick, could you describe the handle and guard of the swords?"

I gave her a quick glance and got that "just do it" look. "Okay, they were all the same. The grips were red leather, wrapped with a silver braided wire. The guard was about a half-inch wide and seemed to be made of silver; a simple grip and guard, but very effective. The blades were dark; you could see some rippling where the metal had been folded over itself for strength. The tips were serrated and blackened. Good memory, don't you think?"

"You're such a good boy. Now, I am going to hand you the swords one at a time. I don't want you to look or pull them from their sheaths. I want to see if you can pick out the sword you were carrying in the tunnel. Don't look. Here's the first one."

I tapped it with my finger, remembering the shock from earlier. Slowly, I took hold of the grip and felt the braided wire and the leather. "No, not that one."

"Now from behind door number two."

"Funny, you don't look a thing like Monty Hall." I gingerly touched the next one. "No, that's not it."

"Door number three."

"Yuck! That's not it either."

"Last but not least, door number four," Sam said.

I took hold of the grip and said, "Now, this is a sword! It feels like I'm shaking hands with an old friend." Pulling it from the sheath, it became an extension of my arm.

Sam said, "Okay, look at the grip and blade."

Even in the dim light from the hatch, I could see a blue tint to the blade, guard, and grip. Sam showed me the blade of the sword she was holding. There was a crimson tint on the blade and guard.

Sam said, "These colors appeared after we brought them on board."

I answered, "Or, after they touched our flesh and started possessing our souls."

Sam said, "Woo, they're cursed. Seriously, when I touched the blue sword it felt like ants were crawling on my hand. Then, when I pulled it from its sheath, the feeling got even more uncomfortable."

I caught myself staring at the blade, almost in a trance. Glancing at Sam, she too was staring and had a blank look on her face. I said, "Sam." She jerked her head in surprise. "We need to put these things away."

She stammered, "Yes, we do."

I sheathed the now blue sword and handed it to Sam. She disappeared down the hatch, returned, and said, "That was interesting; it had the same effect on me back at the island."

We took turns at the helm for the rest of the night, while the other tried to nap on the deck. Daylight broke on another beautiful Caribbean day. We hung the sails and made best speed in the direction of Grave Island, our safe hideout. Sam kept checking her phone for a signal every

173

couple of minutes. Suddenly, there was a loud noise and we both jumped. It was the phone ringing.

Sam smiled as she picked it up and said. "I had almost forgotten what it sounded like."

We had been out of touch for less then forty-eight hours so that was not likely. It was Dee. Sam walked off as they did the girl talk. Sam had to explain what we had done. Dee had to tell us where they were and what they had done.

After a few minutes, Sam handed me the phone and said, "I think you need to tell Mad about what we've found."

I took the phone and heard Mad ask, "Rick, how did it go?"

"We found the passage. Remember the picture of the sword you showed us? I think we found four of them."

"No way! How do they look, are they rusty? No, they can't be. How long are they? Oh my God, be careful, don't cut yourself!"

"Mad. Mad, they're ok, we're ok. It gets even better. Each sword has a dagger and a book each in a different language."

"You got to be kidding me, that's…," and the phone went dead.

I looked at the phone and said, "Lost the signal."

Sam answered, "We're still way out, I'm surprised it worked at all."

"What news did Dee have?"

"Joey has gone totally berserk. The men who lost his shipment were found hacked into pieces. Several people he talked to about us are missing. He sent those thugs of his on a murderess rampage.

"I told Dee we were going to stop at Grave Island till things calmed down a little. Mad and Dee are a day or so east of there; they're safe."

I said, "Well, let's go where they are, if it's safe."

Sam quickly answered, "No! There's uh…, we can't go there yet"

CHAPTER 31

The day was clear and sunny with just a few puffy white clouds scattered about the sky for highlights. Even in this idyllic setting, life sometimes throws you a little green dot. In this case, there were two green dots at the edge of the radar screen to the north. It was hard to tell their direction of travel. They would show up on one sweep of the radar, but not the next.

The dots were not on our direct course, but I got an uneasy feeling. To be safe, I turned more easterly and tried to avoid contact, we were still in bad guy country.

This course is shorter and hopefully we could be anchored up before dark. Our old course took us away from Sabee and was longer and safer. Now, we had to avoid reefs and shallow water; not fun in a sailboat at night, but with Joey's boats on the prowl, we needed to get into our hiding place as soon as possible.

I mumbled, "Frying pan or fire?"

Sam said, "It depends on whether you like the taste of cooking oil or charcoal."

I answered, "The shortest distance between two points may be the quickest, but I'm not sure it's going to be the safest."

The blips dropped off the screen for more than an hour before reappearing. Our new course to Grave Island now had us sailing between Sabee and Baneterra. Joey's imminent trip to his Fort Knox could make this interesting. The dots reappeared and this time they were heading our way.

I gave a concerned chuckle and said, "Ahh Sam, honey, we're going to have visitors."

She smiled went down the hatch and said, "It's probably those Jehovah's Witnesses. Quick, turn out the lights; we can hide in the bedroom." She came up through the hatch and placed the two swords in a slot beside the instruments.

I said, "Those may scare a Baptist, but it won't faze a Jehovah's Witness."

She picked up the binoculars and started scanning the horizon. "Two boats coming this way in a big hurry. They must have heard about your cooking."

"I hope they don't want to stay for dinner."

Sam kept watching then said, "It doesn't look good for the home team. There are two boats; four men in each and one guy is huge!"

I took the binoculars and after looking through them said, "That's the big guy I had the run in with on the dock in St. Morgan."

Sam smiled and said, "What did Hennery say their names were? Bulza and the other one was Grier?"

I answered, "Something like that."

"Do you think he's looking for another swimming lesson?"

I said, "Give them the Queen's royal wave as they pass. These assholes are cowards and bullies. Seeing fear in someone just emboldens them."

Sam said, "If they board us, the Red Lady and I will show them fear."

They passed on each side of us and looked us over. Then they crossed behind us and came up on each side of us.

Bulza said, "Grier, that's the asshole I had the problem with at Nick's place."

Grier was a short stocky man with dark greasy hair, he smiled and said, "Then you must be Arnold and the lovely lady is Samantha. Joey is going to be so happy to see you."

I said, "Sorry, never heard of them."

He pointed to a picture of Sam and everyone pulled out guns. The good news is they all had Tech Nines, which are not known for their accuracy. The bad news is they throw out so much lead it usually doesn't matter.

Their bravery blossomed once they felt we were unarmed and pulled their boats alongside. I glanced at Sam and got one of my déjà vu moments. There was something in that steely look I recognized.

Grier shouted, "Drop your sails!"

I put my hand to my ear, but shrugged my shoulder as if I couldn't hear him.

He shouted again and I pointed at the sails. I shrugged my shoulders. He pointed the Tech Nine toward the main sail and fired. A raged line of holes appeared across the sail about a foot apart. Like I said, not very accurate, but there were about ten holes.

Sam took the wheel while I loosened the lines and dropped the sails. I walked back to Sam and she asked, "Do you have a plan?"

I answered, "Other than staying alive? I'm playing it by ear."

As the *Alchemist* slowed, the other boats closed in, one on each side. I said, "Stay next to the hatch, I've got a plan." She stepped in front of the hatch. Two of the men from each boat grabbed the rails of the Alchemist and pulled the boats together.

"Boys are you sure you want to do this? We're very close to Sabee. Officer Hennery and his men may come by at any moment."

Everyone in the boats laughed

Then Grier and Bulza motioned for one man from each boat to board us. As they climbed over the rail, I saw my chance. They were blocking us from the other shooters.

"Sam, you know, I've never done this kind of thing before!"

That cold feeling came over me and time seemed to slow down. Every image became sharp and clear. I turned to Sam and pushed her down the hatch. The look of shock and outrage was priceless. If I lived through this, she was going to kill me, I thought.

I placed my hand on the grip of the sword; it seemed to almost jump out of the scabbard with eager anticipation. Pivoting on my right foot, I took one step to my left toward one of the men. In a fluid, almost effortless, motion, I brought the sword down, catching the man from Bulza's boat between the neck and shoulder. There was no resistance to the blade as it cut through his body to the center of his chest. I pulled the blade out with surprising ease as the man fell backward off the *Alchemist* and on top of Bulza.

Turning toward the other man, I saw his eyes grow larger and fill with anger. His cockiness had vanished. They had convinced themselves that killing two unarmed people would be easy. He started raising his weapon, as I took two steps toward him, lunged and pushed the sword tip through the center of his chest. The anger in his eyes was replaced by shock, as I pushed him backward, off the *Alchemist*, and into Grier's boat.

I turned and dove toward the hatch as the sound of gunfire exploded around me. I felt an old and much too familiar burning sensation in my left arm, followed by the same feeling in my right side. Something I remembered about myself. I don't like being shot; I mean, I really don't like it. Just before hitting the floor of the cabin, I saw a flash of red. The sword Sam was holding nicked me on my already wounded arm.

Grabbing my arm, I screeched, "Sam, duck!"

They fired non-stop for several minutes, out of fear and anger more than trying to hit anything in particular. We could hear the bullets tearing into the hull, shards of fiberglass and the smell of cordite filled the cabin. Finally, their motors started and the boats pulled away to new positions.

I stuck my head up through the hatch to see where they were and what they were doing. One of the men on Bulza's boat was dumping a body overboard. Then they started hosing the boats down like nothing had happened. One of the men in the other boat was placing a bandage on his arm. He must have been hit in the crossfire.

I sat down on the steps and said, "Well, they're cleaning the boats and deciding how they want to kill us this time." Pain shot through my arm. "Were you trying to cut my arm off?"

She answered, "If I was trying to do that, it would be lying on the floor. I should cut it off; you shoved me down the steps and, look, you made me break a nail!" She displayed the center finger of her right hand in my face. "See! Now what did you do to make them so angry, anyway?"

"I equaled up the odds a little. It's now six to two!"

"You've been shot!"

I answered, "Only twice and don't forget hacked on by a sword! But I'm sure it doesn't compare to your broken nail."

Sam looked at my injuries. "They're just flesh wounds. I'll put a little bandage on them and you'll be fine. This!" she said, holding her finger in front of my face again, "is broke off into the quick. Now that's real pain!"

I said, "There's something about the cut from the sword. It hurts more than both gunshots combined."

Sam looked at it closer. "It barely broke the skin but it does seem to be bleeding a lot. If the blade was treated with something; we need to clean the wound."

She tore open an alcohol wipe and said, "This is really gonna hurt." She started rubbing the cut vigorously. She was right it hurt like hell. After about a week of rubbing, she stopped and placed a bandage to the cut and held it there for a moment. When she removed it, the bleeding had stopped.

I heard the boats start up again and listened as they moved to a new position. I glanced out through the hatch. They were sitting on each side of the bow out about a hundred feet. Well, they had learned their lesson about shooting each other, but were too far away to do much with those peashooters.

We heard Grier's voice. "American Pig, I am going to take you to Joey dead or alive, it makes no difference to me. If you come out now, maybe Joey will let you live. If you make him wait, it will be a slow and painful death."

I stuck my head out of the hatch and said, "Grier, I have a better idea. Why don't you go back to killing babies and raping goats? We'll get back to our vacation." I saw him raise the Tech Nine and start firing, rounds hit all around the deck, not even coming close to the hatch.

I heard Grier scream something at Bulza in a language I didn't understand. "Don't be a coward. Stand up and be a man."

I sat down on the steps, stared up at the ceiling of the cabin. I saw a bright light followed by a stabbing pain in the side of my head, I gritted my teeth. "That son of a bitch is really pissing me off!" Overcome by a sense of déjà vu, I punched the ceiling of the cabin just behind the opening of the hatch with my fist. The carpet buckled and tore. I put my hand through the tear and pulled on the lever. A hidden panel swung down.

179

I unfastened an AK-47 attached to the panel, pulled off a banana clip, snapped it into place, put a round in the chamber, and passed it to Sam.

I pulled off an M-16 with a grenade launcher, loaded in a grenade, and snapped on a full clip. After dropping another grenade in my pocket, I closed the panel and saw Sam was staring at me with one eyebrow raised and an odd expression on her face.

I said, "Before you ask, I don't know. It's where I would've put one."

Sam alternated her gaze between me and the rifle in her hands. "This is the plan. They are a little in front of us and can't see the hatch. We both get on deck staying low and behind the cabin. We both stand up and start firing. When they hit the deck, and they will hit the deck, I put one of these grenades in Bulza's engine compartment. He goes boom. We both fire on Grier till he waves the white flag. If he gives us any shit at all, I blow his ass into the water, too."

Sam reached up and pulled the panel open. She took another clip and stuck it in the back of her shorts. She flashed me a grin, then said, "A girl can never have too many accessories." She looked at me for a long moment, then gave me a big kiss and said, "Rick, there's something I need to tell you."

A breeze came through the hatch and I gave a shiver. "Sam, I'm getting ready to blow something up. This might not be the best time."

"OK."

"One more thing. They're close and I'm not sure how large the explosion is going to be, so stay low just in case."

"You don't know how large the explosion is going to be?"

I answered as I started up the steps, "It is going to be big. I'm just not sure how big." I gave her a wink.

I heard her mumble, "Men!"

While we were getting into position, Grier said, "So are you going to keep hiding like cowards?"

I looked at Sam and said in a low voice, "On three. One, two, three."

Sam jumped up and took a Rambo stance, firing from her hip. Her muscles were tense, but still rippled from the recoil. The sound of an AK-

180

47 is distinct and commands respect. Hearing it makes you want to duck whether you're the one being shot at or not.

Everything went back into slow motion. Bulza and his men were ducking even though they were not being fired on. I had a clear shot and launched the grenade. It hit the engine compartment and broke through the fiberglass cover. For a microsecond I thought it hadn't worked, then the cover lifted off the boat and everything exploded into a huge fireball. Two bodies flew out of the boat and Bulza was blown through the windshield, over the bow, and into the water.

Sam stopped firing; she had ducked behind the cabin. Shaking her head, she said again, "Men!" In no time, she was back in her Rambo stance and ready to fire on anything that moved in Grier's boat.

I said, "Grier, toss all your guns overboard. I'll let you pick up your friends and we'll call it even."

He answered, "You don't know who you're messing with!"

I said, "Well dirtbag, it seems you don't know who you are messing with." I opened the grenade launcher, ejected the casing, and reloaded. "I'm going to count to three. If you don't throw your guns overboard, I'll blow your ass into the water."

Grier didn't answer.

"One. Two."

A man in the back of the boat jumped up. Sam was firing before he could aim his weapons. I launched the grenade and it made that pop-whooshing sound, just before the fireball filled the sky. One man blew up and out of the boat with the explosion. Grier was nowhere to be seen.

Sam kept them covered while I got us out of there. I started the pod and backed away from the smoke and flames. Both boats were still afloat but burning. The hull and sails were riddled with holes, but had little effect on our speed. I put us on a course to our hiding place.

Sam called Dee so she could send someone to pick up survivors. Just as we got to our hideout, we saw our radar screen light up with boats coming from all directions to help the sinking vessels.

CHAPTER 32

Safely tucked into our favorite hiding place on Grave Island, we felt a little more secure, but still kept our swords close by just in case. We could hear helicopters flying in from some of the bigger islands looking for Grier's and Bulza's boats. Soon all the commotion stopped and we sat in silence for a long while

Sam looked at me with a sad or maybe concerned look and said, "I'll fix something to eat, then we need to talk."

I nodded my head in agreement. There had been something on her mind for the last couple of days. With things happening so fast, our conversations had been short and dealing only with urgent matters.

Sam handed me a zippered plastic bag of her jerk chicken. It came with instructions to be slow cooked, not burned. I placed the pieces on the grill attached to the stern of the boat and watched the sunlight fade.

The smell of the chicken cooking was incredible. I've always heard the only difference between a good meal and a great one is about four hours. The last food for either of us had been about eight or ten hours ago.

I must say the red beans and rice, fried plantains, jerk chicken and some beer did make for a great meal. The only sounds made through dinner were the almost sexual moaning sounds I made as I ate. I'm sure Sam even made one or two.

While cleaning our dishes, I could tell she was struggling, trying to find the best way to start a conversation. We heard a helicopter flying past us on the other side of the island. We stopped and listened until the sound died away.

The phone rang and we both jumped. It was Dee, calling to check on us like a mother hen. There were six survivors, suffering injuries from burns and lacerations. Two men had been shot multiple times, none of the wounds were life threatening. One of the men had received injuries only in his ass. The medic said he must have been hiding under a seat with his butt in the air, when the boat exploded.

Sam laughed. "That must have been Grier. He was on his knees hiding, that coward."

Dee said she would call back when there was more juicy gossip.

The sun had set when Sam seemed to notice my bandages again. "Sit still, I'm going to get some stuff and clean those little boo-boo's. Don't want you to get infected."

I said, "But you're the one injured. How is your finger?"

She flashed her middle finger with vigor. I laughed. She said, "It will grow back, but you shouldn't remind the doctor of her injury. Things could get quite painful."

I started removing the bandages and noticed the cut Sam had given me. It was dark and didn't look like a cut, but more like a tattooed line where the cut had been. "Hey, look at my arm." The place where Sam had touched the blade to my forearm was also dark and showed every detail of the blade's tip.

Sam looked at her arm and said, "It must take time, you can't even see the outline of mine."

We both heard the sound of a boat heading towards us, from the other side of the island. We quickly turned out all of the lights. The boat was going slow, as if looking for something. When it got just behind the *Alchemist* it stopped, then without warning we were hit with a blinding spotlight.

We dove for the deck as a voice came from a bullhorn. "Ah! Yes, it is Mr. Arnold and Miss Sam. A friend of yours has sent us to bring you to him."

Still lying on the deck, I asked, "And who might this friend be?"

The voice came back with a chuckle. "Well it be Mr. Joey Le Nau, of course. It seems he is tired of the rumors of your death and wants to see to it personally. So, we going to take you to him one way or other. But I will get paid lots more if I gets you there alive."

Sam said, "Big John, is that you?"

He replied, "Yes, Miss. Sam."

Sam asked, "Why are you doing this?"

He answered, "Well Miss Sam, that little son-of-a-bitch has much on me, and he wants to pay lots of money, nothing personal Miss Sam. I've always liked you."

Looking around I saw the spotlight was shining directly on the hatch. There was no chance of us getting to the guns.

Sam started laughing and said, "Never a dull moment with you, Mr. Blane."

I glanced back and said, "Well, at least we have our new friends."

Big John said, "Stand up or we'll start shooting."

I answered, "I think we'll just stay down here."

"Please stand up. You're worth lots more alive. My boy's gettin nervous."

I looked at Sam and said, "Let's get up. I can fight better standing, can't you?"

She gave me a nervous grin and answered, "I don't know, I've been told, I'm pretty good lying down." I raised an eyebrow and flashed a grin.

We each placed our sword on a chair under the table in easy reach and out of sight of the boarding party.

I said, "OK, we're standing up."

We stood up and Big John said, "Hold your arms up and turn around. I want to make sure you're unarmed." After we did what we were told, he continued, "I'm going to send my men on board. Don't try anything or they will kill you dead and that'd make me unhappy." As the boarding party walked in front of the light, I saw two men staying on the boat with rifles and got a glimpse of Big John holding the bullhorn.

Two men carrying pistols and plastic strip ties came over the stern of our boat. When they got between us and the men on their boat, I yelled, "Now!"

We each grabbed our cutlass and spun around to gain momentum. I caught my man across his chest, then turned the blade over, and cut back across his stomach. I kicked him in the chest, he fell overboard making three separate splashes.

I looked to see Sam stand half-crouched, sword at her side. Her attacker stood over her with his gun raised. He slowly tilted forward then fell over the side of the boat. His head separated from his shoulders making two splashes when the body hit the water.

The spotlight rocked back and forth and we ducked behind the table. I heard odd sounds come from Big John's boat, followed by a strange gurgling noise and suddenly everything got deathly quiet.

Sam asked, "What just happened?"

I asked in a loud voice, "You still want to take us alive?"

We waited. There was no answer. I picked up a pistol dropped by one of our assailants, aimed it at the light, and pulled the trigger. The light popped, hissed, and went out. Nothing happened, no shooting or shouting. We both slowly peered over the rail and saw one body lying in the boat that did not appear to be moving.

I dropped back to the deck and asked, "What the hell just happened?"

Sam answered, "I don't know, but whatever it is, we need to get the hell out of here!"

Keeping low, we untied the *Alchemist* and started backing out. Their boat was blocking us, but it soon moved aside. Sliding by Big John's boat, we got a good look at Big John. He appeared to be wet and his throat was cut.

We glanced at each other, mystified by what had happened and sailed silently away from Grave Island into the darkness.

CHAPTER 33

Sam took a deep breath and said, "OK, I know a place we can go and be safe."

"That is if we can make it through these shallow waters at night!"

"Give me the helm and turn off all the lights, even the running lights."

I looked at her and saw a determined, serious look.

"Do you trust me?"

I smiled and said, "With my life!" I stepped aside and started turning off the lights.

"We'll run with the pod for now, but we'll need to hang every sheet we have and pray for wind soon."

I wanted to turn the radar on, but I knew the light from the screen would bother her. She was doing this old school, sailing by the seat of her pants, using her memory and the moonlight to get us through the coral heads and jagged rocks. She took the *Alchemist* through the shallows like a sports car on a winding mountain road, never once cutting power.

After several very tense hours, Sam spoke. "We're out. We'll have deep water to our destination."

"It's a light wind, but I'll hang every sail that matters. By the way where are we heading?"

She pulled out a chart, unfolded it, and pointed to a little speck south and east of our current location. "That's where we can meet up with Mad and Dee."

Just then the phone rang. It was Dee with more news. Dee talked loud and at a furious pace. I looked at Sam who was holding the phone away from her ear saying, "Yes, I understand, we will." This went on for thirty-minutes at least.

Finally, Sam said, "I'll tell him right now."

Hanging up the phone, she just stood there shaking her head. "Well, Mr. Blane, I have some good news, some bad news, and some really bad news. Which would you like first?"

I opened my mouth to speak, but she continued without stopping.

"As we just found out, Joey knows I'm not dead and you didn't leave town. He thinks you're responsible for taking his shipment and that I am your accomplice."

"A smart boy that Joey."

Sam smiled and continued, "He has ordered every one of his men with a boat to hunt us down. There will be a big reward if we are brought to him alive. If dead, he will only pay if he can ID the bodies."

I asked, "So, that's the really bad news?"

She continued, "No, that's just the bad news. As you heard, there were six survivors from our encounter with Grier earlier today. One of those men will have to go through reconstructive surgery. It seems Grier had a good portion of his ass blown off. The doctors are baffled how that was the only part of him that was injured."

I said, "I know, I know. That's the good news!"

She winked at me and said, "Now for the new, interesting, and bizarre twist of the day. Officer Clarence Le Nau has issued arrest warrants for Rick Blane aka Arnold and Samantha Van Helsing aka Sam. The warrant is for the murder of two men on Grier's boat and we are wanted for questioning about two bodies found near Sabee."

"Sabee! Hennery was there and knows we had nothing to do with that."

Sam said, "There is a laundry list of warrants, everything from assault to piracy. Grier told Clarence we were trying to steal his boats. He also said we were the ones who had been taking all the missing boats in the area. We are considered armed and dangerous. You can bet every police officer in the region is looking for us, along with Joey's thugs."

Sam pointed to the chart. "We've got to get there and fast!"

"What's there?" I asked.

"Death Island, but I call it home!" she said and gave me a sinister grin.

I glared at her. She chuckled, "Its real name is St. Giles. People started calling it Death Island because it was once a leper colony, a dumping ground for anyone with an unknown illness."

For the rest of the night there was little conversation. We both watched the sails and willed wind into them. We also watched the radar screen hoping to see the landmass appear; even though we knew it was hours away. We also didn't want to see those little green dots indicating boats, especially one heading in our direction.

Just before daybreak, a dot appeared to the northwest on a heading directly toward us. Then another dot came into view from the east-northeast also coming in our direction. It was on a course that would join up with the first boat before reaching us.

Sam, without saying a word, went into the cabin. She opened the panel, loaded the M-16 and AK-47, and slid them out on deck. Picking up the two swords, she came back on deck. "There might be a chance if it is the police, but we'll need to fight for our lives if it's Joey's men."

The dots merged on the screen becoming one. We both turned and looked out into the darkness. Suddenly, we saw dim flashes of light and heard the faint sound of rapid gunfire. This went on for several minutes, then stopped as suddenly as it had started.

Watching the screen, we saw one dot speed away, leaving the one sitting dead in the water where they had met. To our surprise and relief, the boat moving was not coming in out direction. I stared back into the darkness wondering what had happened. Suddenly, a huge fireball filled the night. The boat that was left had exploded and was burning.

I started up the pod and put it to full throttle. We needed to get every mile behind us as fast as possible. I already have to pay for the repair of several hundred bullet holes. So what if I destroy a twenty thousand dollar pod pushing the engine past its limits? It's just money. The owner is going to be pissed at me anyway.

CHAPTER 34

Sam took the helm just after first light. She is a great sailor and turned every breath of the wind into speed. After several hours, she pointed to the horizon. "There's our destination." I could see a dark land mass in the distance.

"Doesn't look very big."

"It's just big enough. Any larger, country and tourist corporations would want it. Any smaller and we couldn't live there."

We kept sailing toward the island. "This is similar to Sabee in that there is only one way to get on the island; no beach or bay. Father built a pier that can hold several boats."

The phone rang; it was Dee. I took the wheel while Sam talked. This had nothing to do with women talking while driving. It seemed to be the prudent thing since Dee was talking even faster and louder than before. Sam walked around on the stern answering only "yes" or "OK" as Dee babbled.

Finally, Sam screeched, "OK! OK! I understand! I'll let you know!"

She picked up the binoculars and looked toward the island. "That son-of-a-bitch!"

"What is it?" I asked.

"Clarence has some of his men sitting just off the pier waiting to arrest us."

She handed me the binoculars and took back the wheel. We were close enough to see the boat. I could also see the white ring around the island caused by the waves crashing against its sheer cliffs. At the end of the island closest to us was a jagged spear of rocks pointing toward the heavens. Staring at the solitary rock, I had a déjà vu moment. No, this was more, much more; I knew this place deep in my core.

Sam said, pointing a green dot moving to the radar screen. "That must be Clarence. We could beat him to the pier for all the good that would do."

I gave the screen a quick glance and returned to looking at the tall, thin, solitary sentinel. "Sam does that place have a name?" I asked pointing in the direction of the rock.

She answered, "I have heard it called several things, Lighthouse Rock, Devil's Finger, most of the locals call it The Monk's Tongue."

My head snapped toward Sam and I said, "Did you say Monk's Tongue!"

"Yes."

I stared back at the rock, my mind racing, like it had when I woke up in the Miami hospital. Images, so many images, or were they memories? Were they real or fabrications of my subconscious trying to heal itself? I struggled to make sense of what was happening and abruptly suffered the feeling of an ice pick being jammed into my temple.

This must've been what my shrink was talking about when she said I would have memory attacks and would need to take a deep breath, relax, and trust my gut. That was very hard to do when your head felt about ready to explode.

I opened my eyes to Sam kneeling beside me with a concerned look on her face, placing a cool damp cloth to my forehead. "Are you OK?"

"Yes! And, I have a plan."

Sam gave me one of those "you stupid shit" looks and said, "Does it involve fainting and lying on the deck?"

"I didn't faint. Real men don't faint, we just take short naps." Sam helped me up and had to steady me until the dizziness passed.

"So what's the plan, or do you need to take another nap first?"

I returned her earlier glare. "I don't know, but it has something to do with the Monk's Tongue." I took the wheel and turned us away from the pier. Our course was toward the end of the island and that somehow familiar rock. I was heading straight toward a crack between the island and the solitary rock.

Sam spoke up in a calm voice. "You know crashing into the island and sinking the boat is not a workable plan."

I smiled. She always used that calm voice when she was concerned. "Yes, I know, but if we get close enough to the cliff, Clarence's men won't

190

see where we are going. We have to slip around this point and get to the backside of the island without being seen."

"That's your whole plan?"

"Of course not, I'll work out the rest, when we get around this point. Hold on, we're going to cut it close." I cut the point closer than I had planned. We scraped a couple of rocks, but nothing to cause major damage.

Sam spoke as we scraped the last rock and cleared the point. "Rick, I have been trying to tell you something for a while. I need to do it now before you kill me in some kind of a fiery boat crash!" She let out a deep breath. "Arnold is alive."

For a second, my emotions wavered between anger and disappointment, but right now, I needed to find something and I wasn't sure what it was. "Sam, I'm very happy for you. Arnold is truly a lucky man to have someone like you."

She smiled and said, "Yes, he is!"

"Sam, I need to ask you a very important question."

"Of course, anything!"

"Do you trust me?"

She gave me a big smile and said. "As someone recently told me, with my life!"

"I hope it won't come to that!" I kept us a safe distance from the sheer cliff face and glared at each imperfection as we passed.

Sam watched me for a short period then asked, "What are you looking for?"

"I don't know, but something is here. I just hope to remember it when I see it!"

Sam asked with growing concern in her voice. "Remember?"

Keeping us parallel to the island, I finally spotted a gash in the cliff face. It seemed to be twenty to thirty feet wide.

I said, "Voir que cela marque nous sommes ici."

Sam replied, "Rick, speak English, you're doing that French thing again."

I said, "Really? OK, we're here."

I turned the *Alchemist* toward the opening and said, "Whatever it is I'm looking for is in there. As my grandmother would say, better hold on to your drawers, things could get interesting!"

Sam braced herself on the rail and said, "I would if I wore any."

OK, why does it sound sexy when a woman says she is not wearing underwear, but really gross when a man says he's going commando?

"Sam, I want you to know I've never done this kind of thing before. Hell, I haven't even seen it done on TV." I chuckled.

"That might bother me, if I knew what we were doing. So I'm just going to close my eyes, take one or your little naps, and wait for a loud crunching noise."

There wasn't time to drop the sails as we slipped into the opening. My eyes adjusted to the light and I saw it was a dead end. We were on course to hit a solid rock wall looming directly ahead. My first instinct was to start the pod, throw it in full reverse to slow us down, but we were still going to hit, and hit hard. I closed my eyes and braced for impact.

The front of the *Alchemist* started rising out of the water as we aggressively slowed and came to a full stop. I had expected to hear the sound of fiberglass crashing into rock. Instead, I heard a whooshing, sliding sound like fiberglass sliding against mud or sand. The stop was abrupt enough that it threw me against the wheel and Sam almost lost her balance as her feet slid on the deck.

"That wasn't what I expected," Sam said as she regained her footing.

Just then, we felt the stern of the *Alchemist* being pulled to port. Appearing behind us was an opening in the cliff. The current gradually pulled us into a channel toward sunlight at the end of the channel. The stern bumped against something. That made the bow turn slowly to port and we drifted into a lagoon under a cliff overhang. Multiple rays of sunlight flooded in through cracks in the walls and ceiling. The lagoon was large enough to fit several boats the size of the *Alchemist*.

"*Asile!*" I said

"English," Sam replied.

"Sorry, sanctuary!"

CHAPTER 35

Sam gave me a strange look, but said nothing. After securing the *Alchemist*, I took her by the hand, stepped off the boat, and led her up the stairs along a narrow path to a huge set of oak doors. I slapped them with my open hand, smiled at Sam, and said, "We'll open this later."

I led her around the lagoon to another staircase. We climbed up to a small room. In front of us was the back of Monk's Tongue. A crack in the rock faced toward the pier and Clarence's men. Another crack to the left looked down the side of the island toward the secret entrance to the lagoon.

I said, "Clarence isn't there. He must think he is chasing a Flying Dutchman."

"Rick, are you OK?"

"Why do you ask?"

"Oh, no reason, you passed out cold a few minutes ago, brought us through a secret passage into a hidden lagoon, and have been babbling in French. Are you sure you're OK?"

"Better than I have been in a long time" I took her by the hand and started down the steps. Soon we were standing in front of the big doors. I slid the metal bar back. The sound echoed through the lagoon, as did the creaking of the oak timbers when the doors opened. I could see more steps leading up into the island.

The steps were wide, made of the same black rock we found on Demon's Moon. I looked at Sam. "Me thinks we have a connection." After several steps, we found ourselves in a huge room. Small passages led off from each side. Straight ahead, I saw more of the wide steps.

We crossed the room and continued our climb. Soon we came into another huge room. Again, passages led off from each side. Straight ahead were still more wide steps.

This time at the top of the steps was a carved stone door, very much like the ones on Demon's Moon.

I smiled at Sam who had an unreadable look on her face. "Well, Alice, will this lead us out of the rabbit hole?" I slid the hasp back and pulled hard. Light flooded in as the door opened.

I stepped into the room and came face to face with a suit of armor. Across the room behind the desk hung a painting of Sam's necklace, the wooden stake crossed with a hammer. Sam stood beside me and took my hand, as the heavy door closed behind us.

Two men walked in through the door next to the suit of armor. I recognized them from Atlanta, the plane, and from seeing them on St. Morgan: Hanz and Franz.

One of them asked, "Sam, how did you and Arnold get in here?"

I said with some irritation in my voice, "I'm Rick!"

The other man said, "Shit, he's still messed up! You weren't going to bring him here until he was fixed."

There was a slight pause as everyone looked around the room at each other.

Sam growled, "No, he is not fixed, and now, I think he's worse. He's channeling some dead relative, but I had no choice. Clarence and Joey are after us!"

"We know! We've been trying to keep them off your ass."

Sam said, "Well you've not done a very good job!"

Something was happening to me. My vision got blurry, and someone was dimming the lights. My brain felt like it was going to burst out of my skull.

Sam stepped in front of me, placed her hands on each side of my face and said, "Rick, I need to tell you a few things. These two oafs are my brothers, Hanz and Franz." She took a deep breath. "Rick, look at me."

194

I looked into her eyes, my mind racing, trying to make sense of it all. There was something about the way she stared at me that wasn't registering, and I felt dizzy.

Sam said, "Rick!"

"Yes!" I answered while putting my fingers to my temples.

Sam said in that low calm voice, "Rick, you are Arnold!"

CHAPTER 36

I could hear voices, but they were too far away to make out. I slowly opened my eyes and tried to focus. I was in a hospital room. A nurse dressed in white, wearing one of those little white nurse hats like they wore in the fifties stood at the foot of my bed reading something on a clipboard that hid her face.

I asked, "Where am I?"

I heard Dee's voice screech, "Rick, you're alive!" Turning my head in the direction of her voice, I saw those ample attributes of hers coming bouncing toward my face.

"Am I in heaven or is that you, Dee?"

She crammed my face between her breasts, and a sweet strawberry smell filled my nostrils.

A voice I didn't recognize said, "Young lady, he has brain damage, are you trying to kill him with those things?"

Two thoughts collided in my brain. First, as I took another breath filled with the smell of strawberries, I thought there could be worse ways to go. The other was the voice must belong to a Nurse Ratchet, to stop this kind and caring woman from showing her concern over my well-being. I voiced neither; instead, I tried to focus on the wart I knew would be on the

195

tip of the nurse's nose. To my surprise, she was young, very attractive, and without a single visible blemish.

"Rick, are you all right?" I heard Sam's voice and saw her push by Dee.

"What did you say?"

She looked at the nurse and asked, "Has he lost his hearing?"

The nurse answered, "His vitals and hearing are fine, I think he just fainted, but I need to clean and dress those wounds."

"Sam, you said something about Arnold!" I turned to Nurse Ratchet, "I didn't faint!"

"Not now, Rick, we need to …"

"Why not now? I'm not going anyplace!"

The nurse told me to sit up and take off my shirt, so she could get a better look at my side. As I pulled the t-shirt off, I heard Dee say, "Oh my." That self-conscious feeling flooded over me and I looked down at my chest.

I handed my shirt to the nurse who was staring at the angry scars across my chest in shock. "Just a little something from a previous life." I lay back on the bed.

I heard a male voice and recognized it as one of the men Sam had introduced as her brother. "Sam, what does he remember?"

"Nothing."

One of the brothers said, "Well, we know where his reset button is."

The nurse touched my side and I flinched from the pain. "That's from a small caliber bullet." She didn't sound surprised.

I answered, "So is the one on my arm."

I heard a male voice chuckle then ask, "Sam, did you shoot him again?"

Sam snapped, "No! How about you, Hanz, did you shoot him again or you, Franz, did you shoot him again?"

Both men said, "No" and put their hands up as if to say, "We surrender." One of the brothers pointed to himself. "I'm Hanz."

Sam shook her head and, with quite a bit of disgust in her voice, she said, "Men!"

I reacted to that statement with some concern and asked, "So each of you have shot me?"

"It's not as bad as it sounds."

I glanced at the nurse who had a surprised look on her face as well and asked, "When has finding out that you have been shot by three different people ever sounded good?"

The nurse shrugged her shoulders. Dee said, "Boys, we should go and let them talk."

Dee walked over to the men and led them to the door, one of the men turned toward us and said, "Sam, tell him about your necklace."

Sam snapped, "Franz!"

The man laughed and said, "I'm Hanz," and closed the door.

The nurse stood up and said, "I can finish up later; you need to talk." She quickly left the room.

"Sam, what's going on?"

"Rick, I don't even know where to start."

"At the beginning is usually a good place."

"Yeah, but which beginning? We've been over this before."

"Let's pretend I have amnesia."

"You mean amnesia again."

Sam, you're really giving me a headache."

She smiled then said, "A long time ago in a galaxy far, far away..."

It was my turn to give her that look.

She started over. "OK, let's go back to Miami, where you got mugged."

"You were involved in my mugging."

"No, but we were there." I started to speak; Sam raised her hand and continued, "I have gone over this with you before. So trust me, it will be best if I tell you the whole story. Then I'll answer your questions, or this will take weeks."

I narrowed my eyes and said, "OK."

She continued, "I'm going to cover just the highlights first and fill in the details as needed."

I nodded in agreement.

"Hanz, Franz, and I were in the restaurant waiting for a client. You came in and sat two tables down from us. Shortly after you ordered, a gangbanger came in with his posse. Sometime later, another group came in. Hanz recognized their leader from a previous job and went outside before he was recognized."

She paused, obviously trying to decide what was most important next. "You finished your meal, paid your check, had the owner call for a cab, and went outside. You walked to the end of the building where a man pulled a gun on you. There was a struggle, the man hit you on the head with his gun and it went off. He took your backpack and billfold, and ran off.

"We heard gunshots inside. Each group thought it was an ambush and started shooting. The same thing happened outside, and it soon turned into a running shootout.

"Hanz said you got up and staggered back toward the front of the building. A gangbanger ran out and used you as a shield, while shooting at everything in sight. You were hit several times by return fire.

"Hanz knew you were going to be collateral damage, so when he had a shot, he took it. Just as he pulled the trigger, the man turned you slightly. The shot took out the bad guy, but also grazed your skull. That pretty much ended the shootout and everyone ran for cover."

I exhaled.

Sam continued, "We rushed you to the hospital. After patching you up, they found you had amnesia. You had no ID or memory, and since Franz had shot you." She glared toward the brothers. "We decided to bring you here to the island so our specialist could work with you, until we could find out who you were. Are you with me so far?"

198

This matched up with what the detectives in Miami had told me. I eyed her with cautious skepticism. After all, she and her two brothers had each confessed to shooting me. I nodded my head in agreement. "I'm with you so far, I think, but why can't I remember being here?"

"I'm doing this in a time line to help you relate to all that has happened. After bringing you here, we kept looking for a missing person's report, which was not filed until three years later. Per your instructions before leaving on the trip, a detail you will have to get from someone else, because I never understood it.

"To help in your recovery, the doctors had you work out with my brothers. They started calling you girly man; you called them Hanz and Franz because they kept saying 'we are going to pump you up'. No matter how hard the workout or how sore you were, each day you said 'I'll be back' like Arnold Schwarzenegger in the *Terminator*. We needed to call you something, so you became Arnold. The names Hanz and Franz stuck to my bonehead brothers. The catch is neither one wanted to be Franz so if one does something good Hanz did it. Franz does all bad things. They did the same thing with their real names, Jim and Tim, neither wanted to be Tim."

"So this is my brother Darrell and this is my other brother Darrell?"

Sam laughed and said, "Something like that. Any questions so far?"

I said, "Yes, I know how Franz shot me in Miami starting my journey! But, please tell me how you and, ah, Franz each carried on the tradition?"

"I'm getting to that. First, you need to know they were accidents and both were your fault."

"I'm somehow responsible for two different people shooting me?"

Sam stammered, "Yes, but we're getting ahead of ourselves. Your workouts with the boys became more and more intense. You seemed to be driven and practiced every day, learning different forms of martial arts, hand-to-hand combat, and became more than proficient with multiple firearms, but your real expertise was with that damn bamboo stick thing. I think you called it Kendo. From the first time you picked it up, you were on! No one could touch you. The boys even brought in an expert from Japan; a man who had practiced his entire life and you cleaned his clock."

I detected the sound of pride in her voice, but that vanished in the next breath. She pushed her little finger in my face and said, "See that? It's crooked! You broke my finger during one of our practice sessions. That made it very hard to grip a pistol and aim. We were on an assignment got onto some trouble and your big butt got in the way of my bullet. I nicked your rib." She took hold of the necklace, the emblem of their company, a silver hammer and stake of the Vampire slayer. "This stake is that sliver of rib."

"Assignment." Pain shot through the side of my head, closing my eyes I said. "Tell me later."

I placed my hand to the side where the doctors had told me part of my rib was missing, raised an eyebrow and with a little sarcasm said, "Interesting. A little morbid, but interesting. Is it a trophy, like a deer head on the wall or a keepsake of some kind?"

She snapped back an answer, "Don't over-think it, OK?"

I said, "All right. Could you get the nurse? I need an aspirin. My headache is coming back."

With concern in her voice Sam said, "Do you think you're going to faint?"

I growled back an answer, "I didn't faint. I just have a headache."

Sam said, "Let's take a break. This is a lot for you to take in all at once." She called for the nurse.

"Sounds good. First, let me see if I have a grip on what you've told me so far. Franz shot me, giving me amnesia, and then brought me here to nurse me back to health where I turned into some martial arts, gun-shooting, bamboo stick wielding geek."

Sam smiled as the nurse came back into the room and said. "Good so far, especially the geek part."

I took the aspirin and lay on the bed while Nurse Nancy-Paul (formerly Nurse Ratchet) dressed my wounds. She truly had the southern accent that I tried to fake; hers sounded better and was quite charming.

Then I realized all the stuff Sam told me, bizarre as it was, hadn't freaked me out except for finding out the three of them shot me. (Have I told you, I don't like being shot?)

Nurse Nancy-Paul finished and I asked, "Could I get up and walk around?"

"Of course, if you start to feel like you're going to faint, just sit down."

Popping up out of bed, I barked through gritted teeth, "I didn't faint!" The room started to spin.

"Are you OK?"

"Fine. I just need some fresh air."

Sam and Nancy-Paul rolled their eyes at each other, but they got under each arm and led me through the door and outside. I promptly sat down on a stone bench. Nurse Paul brought me a glass of water. After a few minutes, I noticed Sam staring at me. "What?"

"At times you can be quite an ass!"

"Me! I just broke your finger. Hell, you shot me!"

"That was an accident and you know it."

"Hello! Amnesia." I pointed to my head. This amnesia gig may have some advantages after all.

We sat there not speaking, until I noticed a building built into the cliff face beside us. It reminded me of that temple from Indiana Jones and The Last Crusade. "What is that?"

"That is the monastery. We got on the island through there and our new back door. This building is our hospital, where we take care of the sick and injured. It's also were we do research."

"Research?"

She took me by the hand and led me across a large patio to a stone wall about three feet high. She explained, "This is what my father calls the Garden of Eden."

Below us about thirty feet or so were lush green patches of plants and trees divided by walls much like the one next to us.

"There are plants growing here from every continent. Several we've been unable to find any place else. Father lets a select group of doctor's work here, hoping there is a cure for some disease hidden in those plants."

Sam pointed across the garden to a big wall and said, "The Spanish built that around the entire island, to make this island a fortress. Instead, they turned it into a prison and left people here to die, hence the name Death Island. No one left here alive because neither the Spanish nor any one came back to help them."

I looked around at the walls and the gardens. Something wasn't adding up. There was a foreboding feeling about this place that didn't match with the idyllic setting. I turned to Sam and asked, "What do you do here, other than research?"

Sam gave me a serious look and asked, "What do you mean?"

"Let's see, martial arts, weapon training, scars, and bullet holes I didn't have before. What did I do here?"

Sam let out a self-conscious laugh and said, "I would tell you, but then I would probably have to kill you. So it may be better if you remember on your own."

At first it wasn't funny, because there has to be a little bit of truth in a joke to make it work and I didn't know the truth. I gave her a stern look and said, "Give me my bamboo sticky thing."

"We try to help people that can't help themselves," she gave me a strange little grin, "by dealing with the things that go bump in their night."

I stared at her, trying to understand what she was saying. The doors opened and Nurse Paul came out. "You're needed in the Monastery, now!"

CHAPTER 37

We were met at the front door of the monastery by Hanz and Franz. Well, in my case, Franz and Franz since they have both evidently shot me.

Sam asked, "What's up?"

Franz said. "Clarence is at the pier with a warrant, wanting to search the island, for the two of you!"

Sam said. "He can't do that! Where's father!"

Franz glanced at me and said, "He's off the island dealing with another bigger problem."

Sam said, "Shit!"

Franz asked, "Arnold, getting any of your memory back?"

"Not yet, but some things are beginning to make a little more sense."

"Well, get better. We're going to need you. For now, let's deal with Clarence. Sinking Joey's boat really pissed him off. Good Job!"

I noticed Mad coming to stand beside Hanz and Franz. "I was wondering about you."

Mad smiled. "Looks like the two of you haven't learned to play well with others."

Hanz asked, "Did you sink one of little Joey's boats?"

Sam raised two fingers. "We blew up and sank two of his boats."

Hanz said, "Holy shit, sis, you're a bad ass! Look Franz, she even has a tattoo."

I looked and her sword mark was now as dark as mine was. Mad stepped toward us, his eyes the size of saucers. He grabbed each of our arms, turned them over, and stared at the marks. His mouth dropped open, but he seemed unable to speak.

One of the brothers said, "Look, matching tats. How sweet."

The other one said, "Dad's going to be pissed, you know how he feels about tattoos."

Sam snapped back, "They're not tattoos." Both brothers raised their eyebrows.

Mad said, "They're not tattoos. They're more like brands." With a smile growing on his face he continued, "You've definitely found them."

I answered, "Four of them anyway."

I heard the sound of a buzzer and Sam said, "We need to deal with Clarence."

One of the brothers said, "I'll get rid of the son-of-a-bitch."

Sam said, "No, let Tim handle him, he's more diplomatic."

The brother said, "I'm Jim, but thank you."

We all followed Tim-Jim to a room where we saw Clarence on a security monitor pacing back and forth, Tim pressed the button on the intercom and asked, "What do you need Clarence?"

"You know damn well why I'm here."

"I just got up from a nap. So bring me up to speed."

"Let down the damn drawbridge. I have a warrant to search the island for your sister Sam and a Rick Blane aka Arnold."

I looked at Sam and mouthed "Drawbridge?" She whispered, "Later."

"Clarence, Clarence you know we're not under your jurisdiction, so take that warrant and stick it up your ass. If you think your boys guarding the end of our pier let someone sneak pass them, get some new boys. Now, go away before I send some of dads flying monkeys after your ass."

I looked at Sam and said, "And he's the diplomatic one?"

We watched as Clarence went into a rage shaking his fist and shouting obscenities. After about ten minutes, he stomped down the pier, got in his boat, and left heading back toward St, Morgan.

CHAPTER 38

Just then, alarms sounded and bells started ringing. Hanz said, "Damn, the desalinization plant is down again."

I asked, *"Has the fresh water in the caverns dried up?"*

The brothers looked puzzled, turned to Sam, "What did he say?"

I was puzzled and started to repeat myself. Sam looked concerned and placed her hand on my mouth. "He's channeling some dead relative. Rick, please speak English."

I stared into Sam's eyes. "Has the fresh water in the caverns dried up?"

One of the brothers asked, "Caverns, what caverns?"

Sam said, "Behind the wall in father's office, where Rick fainted."

Sam led us through the dining hall and into the room where the passage was hidden. I pushed on the wall and the heavy door opened. I turned to Hanz and Franz. "We'll need some flashlights. And, I *didn't* faint."

Sam left with the boys, quarreling with them about their not being able to find their heads if they weren't attached.

After they were gone I asked, "Mad, did you know I was Arnold?"

"No, I had some suspicions after you had left for Demon's Moon the last time. Rick, she couldn't tell you, the doctors were worried."

"About what?"

"Rick, you're in uncharted waters. You have something akin to double amnesia. Some doctors think it was the physical injury that wiped your memories. Other doctors think your brain has shut down because, it doesn't want to remember."

That seemed absurd. My expression must've told Mad I thought he was crazy. Mad explained, "Sam came up with a plan to get close to you and nudge your memory. She stayed in touch with the doctors and her brothers were usually close by, for protection."

"Well, they haven't done a very good job. Joey tried to kill me several times."

"Joey's not what they've been protecting you from."

"What then?"

"I don't know, but it has something to do with those scars on your chest. Sam is going to tell you everything. The doctors think it would be worse not to at this point. She has nothing to hide and wants you to remember."

I looked around, "What is this island?"

Mad let out a snort, "That is a story in itself and one you became a big part of, for now all you need to know is Gabriel, Sam, and the boys, are the good guys, and they work with other good guys. Sometimes the police and others are kept from doing the right thing because of rules and regulations; let's say on occasion Gabriel's guidelines are far less stringent.

"I don't understand."

Mad smiled, "You will in due time."

Sam and the boys returned with the lights and I led them down the steps into the first big room, pointed and said, *"Go through the doorway and –"*

Sam calmly said, "English."

"Sorry. Go through the doorway, down the steps, turn left." I got a sharp pain in my head and flinched. No one noticed because they were busy exploring.

One of the brothers said, "Cool, we've got a bat cave."

"After you look around, follow these steps down to the big wooden door."

Sam was keeping an eye on me without being too obvious. Mad asked, "So what do we call you, Rick or Arnold?"

206

Sam's head snapped toward Mad like he had said something wrong. I chuckled. "It doesn't matter. I'm from the south and can have two names like Nurse Nancy-Paul." I paused and looked at Sam. "I'll be like your brothers. Rick gets the credit and Arnold gets the blame. Arnold can be my evil twin."

We got to the door and sunlight trickled in as it opened. Mad stepped into the light and said, "Amazing, simply amazing."

We walked toward the *Alchemist* and Mad said, "Holy shit, looks like she has been through a war."

While Mad checked out the bullet holes, Sam went on board to get what Mad was really interested in seeing. She came back with the swords covered with the robe and said. "There is a ritual we have done and I want to see how it works on you. I want you to hold the grip of each sword and tell me how it feels."

Mad gave me a glance like what the hell is going on. I said, "It's not a trick, just an experiment."

She handed Mad one of the swords. "Hold onto the sheath, then take hold of the grip."

Mad took the sword, actually shaking with excitement. He placed his hand on the grip, narrowed his eyes, then closed them. "It's like there is a low voltage electrical charge tingling my hand. What is it?"

Sam said, "Here, try this one."

Mad took hold of the grip and closed his eyes. "The same, but different somehow. Let me feel the other one again." He placed his hand on the first sword's grip and instantly said, "No!" jerking his hand back. Then he placed his hand back on the grip of the second sword. "This one feels warm, soothing. That one is cold and prickly."

"Hand that one to Rick and hold this one."

"Oh, a blue one. I wasn't expecting them to be in different colors." He took hold of the grip but abruptly let out a screech. "It burnt me!" He looked down at his hand.

"Now this one."

Mad looked at it, and sounding more like a question, he said, "Red?" He touched the grip with one finger and jerked it away. He shook his hand, looking puzzled.

Sam pointed to the mark on her arm, pulled the red sword from the scabbard. "I think they somehow choose their owners."

I handed Mad his sword. He took hold of the grip and pulled the sword from the scabbard, then stared into the blade. The big door opened and I heard one of the brother's say, "Hidden lagoons and secret passages. It doesn't get any better."

I pointed across the lagoon to the other doorway "Through there is a secret staircase leading to a lookout where you can see around parts of the island."

Without saying a word, they practically ran to the doorway and disappeared. Sam shook her head. "They're just big kids."

After a long moment Mad asked, "How do I get the mark?"

Sam said, "Someone places the tip to your arm."

He took hold of the blade, "Do it!" shoving the grip first to Sam then to me.

Sam smiled and gave me a nod. I took hold of the grip, feeling an uncomfortable but bearable tingle in my hand. I placed the tip to his arm and after a moment or so, removed it and handed him back his sword. "It took a few days for it to show up on us."

Mad stared back into the blade in silence. The boys reappeared from the doorway. As they walked toward us one said, "Clarence and his men are gone."

I looked at Sam who was still standing on the boat. "We need to finish our conversation, especially the part about Clarence and Joey trying to kill me."

When the boys got closer they saw the bullet holes and splintered fiberglass and one said, "Damn, Arnold, she looks worse than when you – "

Sam snapped, "Franz, shut up!" Her voice echoed through the cavern causing Mad to jump and Franz to stop in mid-sentence.

After a few moments, she said, "I need to talk to Rick, alone, so go play in the tunnels or something." They turned on their heels and started for the big door.

Holding the sword and following in the boys wake, Mad stammered, "I'm going to show Dee."

CHAPTER 39

I stepped on board the *Alchemist*, picked up my sword and sat down. Holding it somehow calmed me. I saw waves of cobalt blue rippled like water through the blade. "The sword seems to have beguiled Mad, too."

After a moment or two, Sam glanced at me. "How are you doing?"

"I've adjusted to the confusion about my life in the last several months. These killer headaches and urges to take micro-naps are new. I don't like them at all. You said Joey tried to kill me?"

"It's a little out of the timeline, but probably more pressing."

We wrapped up our swords and Sam took them below deck; she came back with some drinks, sat down, and let out a sigh of relief.

"You don't know how many times, I have wanted to tell you. The doctors keep giving me these dire predictions of how you might react. I analyzed and over-analyzed your every word, wondering whether you had remembered something, or was it just an offhand comment? Should I nudge a little harder? Or, did I say too much? The whole time you were walking around happy and clueless. It was quite frustrating."

She took a sip of her drink, then looked down at the deck and drifted off in thought. After a long moment I said, "Sam."

She gave me a blank stare.

I prodded. "Clarence? Joey? Kill me?"

She glared at me, narrowing her eyes. Unlike her brothers, I remembered nothing of Sam's wrath and stared back showing no fear. The joys of amnesia. She finally mumbled something, probably, "Men," then more loudly she explained, "Other than hearing about Clarence or seeing him in town, he was not a factor. You were on this island recovering during the time Joey killed my friend, her mother, and the witness. After Clarence let Joey out, you went undercover and started the long slow process of getting into Joey's inner circle. After quite awhile, Joey invited you to go with him to Miami. You were to be a bodyguard; we followed staying as close as we could. It turned out to be a trap, planned to take us all out.

"During the shootout, you and Joey were busy shooting each other. I saw your head jerk, and you hit the ground like a ton of bricks. Joey stood over you, and took aim with a big smile on his face.

"Several shots tore into him at the same time; he crumpled to the ground beside you. Big John drug him into a car and left in a hail of bullets.

"Hanz came running over explaining while trying to shoot Joey; he got kicked in the ribs. Ribs you had broken in one of your stupid stick fights. The gun went off missing Joey, hitting you in the head.

I said. "So that's how you think it was my fault, for him shooting me in the head."

Sam said, "Exactly. The kick punctured a lung with his broken rib. He was coughing up blood, but refused care until we got you to a hospital. We came up with the homeless person being mugged story in case some of Joey's people were still around."

"They ran your fingerprints and found you on a missing person report. Your family was contacted and came to be by your side. Our bogus homeless story took on a life of its own. People claimed to have seen you, bought you food, and even gave you money.

"When we found out you couldn't remember the time on the island, our doctors got concerned. Evidently double amnesia is very rare and spooky bad. No one could agree on how much to tell you. Finally, the doctors decided, since your family was already there, to let them take you home. The doctors worked very closely with your family; in some cases, even staging things to get your reaction. The good news is you didn't go crazy; the bad news is you didn't remember."

I raised my hand to stop Sam and asked, "Hanz and Franz, how many more times did they try to kill me while I was living here?"

Sam gave me that look and said. "Let's try to stay focused. We stayed close and out of sight in case some of Joey's people came to pay an unwelcome visit. Your family and most of the doctors don't know about your time on the island. The doctors that did agreed it was time for you to take a trip. So after some planning and manipulation you were put on a plane to St. Morgan. That is a very short version of what happened between you and Joey. I will fill in other details as needed."

I rubbed my hand over the scars on my chest and asked, "What about these?"

Sam took a deep breath. "That needs to wait until you have recovered a lot more, because you told me, when you could remember, you wanted to forget."

The door opened. Mad stuck his head out. "Why don't you take a break? Dee says Joey is on the move and she thinks he is going for the money."

I followed Sam and Mad up the steps through the caverns, and realized how strange my life had become since arriving at St. Morgan. I have a crazed drug dealer trying to kill me, been on a creepy black island and found a secret passages and some strange swords. Let's not forget my bizarre bouts with blood memory, but somehow it all feels normal.

CHAPTER 40

Mad led us to a room where Dee had set up an impressive number of computers. She looked at me and asked, "Are you feeling all better?"

"Except for a strange strawberry craving, I'm fine."

"See, I knew you didn't have brain damage."

Sam gave me a concerned look. "Strawberry? I didn't know your sense of smell had been affected. I thought you just had a headache." She saw Mad and Dee laughing and started to smack me on the back of the head.

I covered my head. "Brain damage, brain damage, and my rib really hurts!"

"Good."

Dee said, "Joey is almost at Baneterra."

I said, "After he gets the money and gets out of our way, we'll go make him a poor boy."

Mad said, "The Zodiac is loaded with everything we need."

Dee said, "Here comes Joey," and pointed to the screen.

Joey came into view on the monitors, a bag slung over his shoulder. He stepped over the trip wires and around the land mine. Finally, he reached the door of his Fort Knox. He opened the door, sticking his hand in feeling for the wire. After a while, he removed his hand, looked around, and stuck his hand back in the door crack. A few moments later he opened the door slowly and stood there looking at the wire.

I realized what I had done. "Shit! I didn't hook the wire back."

He went inside then came out looking at the ground and at the surroundings. Went back in and came out with one of the bundles of money and started giving it a close inspection.

His phone rang. Dee checked another screen and reported, "It's his new supplier."

Joey answered. A voice asked, "Do you have enough money?"

Joey said, "Of course."

The voice said, "One o'clock. There'd better be no bullshit." The caller ended the call.

Joey went into a rage, throwing the bundle of money through the open door and stood there several minutes shouting. He went inside coming out sometime later with three heavy duffel bags. He hooked up the trip wire, checking it twice and closed the door.

Dee said, "Would it be too much to wish for him to trip one of the wires and blow himself up?"

Sam said, "Only the good die young."

Mad said, "Let's go take all Joey's money and blow the place to hell."

The hair on the back of my neck lifted as I realized we were going to a spooky booby-trapped island, with plans to take a paranoid drug dealer's money. There were at least two bounties on my head and every police officer in this part of the world probably had a shoot to kill wanted poster of me in his pocket. I gave a big smile and mumbled, "A piece of cake."

Mad gave Dee a kiss. "We'll tell you when we're ready, babe."

Dee said, "Babe, you're always ready."

Sam said, "By the time you get back, Dee and I will have some surprises lined up for Joey."

I said, "We'll be using the back door so you don't have to wait up." We walked out of the monastery, down the steps through the Garden of Eden, and through a small door that opened behind the drawbridge. We turned left, then walked behind a wall that led into covered slips, where I saw the Zodiac.

"I'll get under the tarp in case Clarence still has someone watching the island."

Mad pulled out of the slip and in short order I felt him open up the two Yamahas and we screamed across the water. The wind and engine noise was not as peaceful as sailing, but for now we needed speed. Mad said, "OK, you can come out of hiding." There was too much noise to talk, so I watched for trouble.

We got to Baneterra and Mad stopped at the place where Joey had anchored, not the hidden place Sam had taken us. He stuck the bow on the sandy beach between two big rocks. "We'll just be a few minutes, and I don't think Joey will mind."

Dee's voice came through our earpieces. "Joey is back on St. Morgan. You boys have fun. Remember, I like to watch!" I said, "Dee, that's just wrong."

Mad pulled back the tarp I had been under. There were four bags. "You take two, and I'll take two."

"You had me lying on explosives."

"It's just C4."

We got off the boat, climbed the bank and started down the runway. Mad asked, "So how are you adjusting to this new reality."

I answered, "I'm walking down a runway on an island owned by a crazed drug dealer who has tried to kill me several times! I'm carrying two bags of C4, with plans of blowing this place to hell, and it seems like just another day at the office."

"So, you're OK with it then?"

"Seems that way."

CHAPTER 41

Dee told us to stop at the hangar while she switched the cameras. We set the bags down. Mad unhooked the trip wires by the hanger, then started unpacking. Two bags were filled with equipment to make the stuff go boom and a couple of cameras. One had several bricks of C4 and thirty or so different colored golf ball sized objects with a wire sticking out of each. Mad started sorting them by colors. The last one was filled with empty bags so we could carry the bundles of Joey's money.

214

He reminded me of a mad scientist. "Did you use to blow up things in a previous life?"

Mad snorted, "Hell, I used to blow up things in this life. It's like riding a bicycle. Once you put your foot on the pedal it all comes back. In a previous life I was a Viking, who fought with courage, treated my enemies with dignity and respect. Well, that's what I hope Odin believed."

Dee whispered in my ear, "Rick, remember *Strawberry Fields* forever?"

"I love the Stones music."

"Stones? That was the Beatles."

"I knew it was one of those Australian groups." and started down the path, trying to hum some of the song.

"You're getting close."

"I got it." I tore off a piece of tape Mad had handed me and draped it over the wire. After marking all the wires and the land mines, I opened the door with Dee's sixty-nine code, released the trip wire and pushed the door open. A thunderous bang exploded from inside the room, followed by an even louder explosion pushing the heavy metal door against me and knocking me to the ground.

I lay on my back looking up at the sky through palm fronds. Everything felt surreal, until I had one of those rare moments of clarity. Being blown backward several feet by a bomb made me truly understand and believe. *This son of a bitch is dangerous!*

There was a voice way off in the distance saying something. I sat up and tried to shake the cobwebs out of my head. Then I heard Dee's panicked voice screaming, "Rick, are you all right? Rick, talk to me."

"I'm OK God. I always thought you were male, but you sound a lot like Dee."

I could hear Dee talking to Mad telling him to hurry; she didn't know if I was all right. I was trying to get up when he arrived and gave me a once over.

Mad said, "You're one lucky asshole. Not a scratch." Smoke and dust was still billowing out of the door. "I'll let it clear in case he set more traps."

Sitting there was not a problem. It felt good and as soon as someone answered the phone ringing in my ears, it might even be enjoyable. After a few minutes, Mad looked inside Fort Knox. "He wired a shotgun to the door. The blast set off the claymore; this U.S. Government issue door saved your life."

The ringing in my ears was clearing, so I got up and looked inside. The shotgun blast had put a huge dent in the door about chest high. The claymore mounted over the door had blown a crater in the floor just inside the doorway. Stacked on the back wall were Joey's bundles of money. He had taken all our doctored bundles and several more.

Mad asked, "What do you think?"

"Four maybe five trips and I'll have the place emptied."

"No, why do you think he set the shotgun?"

"You mean besides him being a paranoid freak? I got sloppy and forgot the wire on the door. It spooked him, that's all."

"The path is clear except for the land mine. I'll blow it up with everything else."

"Let's rock and roll. Dee, can you sing any of those oldies for us?"

Dee said, "Singing is not even close to what I'm good at, baby."

Money is heavy and the walk to the boat seemed to get longer with each trip, but knowing how it was going to affect Joey made each step a pleasure. On my last trip, Mad was working on Fort Knox.

He said, "I'm blowing up the planes and some other stuff just for fun, but this place is going to become a crater. Well, after I turn it into a fireball we can see from the island."

The door was bent from the blast. With some effort, we closed it and walked toward the boat. At the end of the runway, Mad turned and looked back. "This place still gives me the creeps."

This was not a place where you would want to sit with a drink and watch the sunset. From my first step on the island, an uneasy, restless feeling had crept over me. I had just wanted to get the job done and leave.

Mad got into the boat, looked around at all the bundles, "You've been a busy boy."

"Joey has been a busy boy. There's a lot of weight here, so I spread it around to keep us balanced."

"I'm glad you did, the extra weight is going to slow us down. Let's hope we don't run into trouble."

CHAPTER 42

I try not to be superstitious, and I know saying something doesn't make it happen, but I wish he hadn't said that.

Mad had to use the power of the motors, while I pushed to get us off the beach. Once we were clear, he turned us away from Baneterra and the twin Yamahas roared; the Zodiac plowed through the water.

Mad looked around at the bundles. "With all this weight she handles like a barge."

"Arrr, Captain. Should we throw ye cannons and cook overboard to lighten our load?"

Mad gave me a quirky smile, clicked on his headset. "Dee, we're on our way.

"Good, the man of the house is not around. I left the back door unlocked so just come in, and I'll be waiting."

Mad clicked his headset off. "That woman is going to be the death of me, but I'll go smiling."

Gunshots rang out; I could see the rounds hitting the water in front and beside us. The gunfire was coming from a police boat. The lights were flashing, while an amplified voice blared across the water, "Stop! You are under arrest!"

Mad looked and calmly said, "Got any suggestions because we can't outrun them?"

I looked around "Head for the shallows."

"That won't work. With this load we draw more water than he does."

I patted my pockets. "Got any change?"

"What? I'm in swim trunks. What would I be doing with change! You want to buy a coke or something?"

I looked in the cup holder and found a nickel and four pennies, tossed it over the side and mumbled to myself. *It's all I have; I'll pay a lot more next time.* OK, so I may be a little superstitious, but why take the chance of pissing off Nama's rocks? Shots rang out again.

I stood beside Mad. "Let me take her. Sam showed me a shortcut."

Another blast from some kind of automatic weapon caused a water spray that drenched us.

Mad smiled, stepped aside, and let out a belly laugh. "I hope you can get us away from them. Explaining this boat load of money would take some time and there is that whole guilt by association thing; traveling with an accused pirate wanted for too many crimes to mention. My reputation would be permanently tarnished."

I turned the boat to port and tried to push the throttles through the console.

"Where are you going?" Mad pointed. "That's a reef."

"Not all of it. Sam said to avoid the dark places and the really white places."

Mad screamed as I cut the boat sharply, then jerked it back the other way. "Rick, you can't do that. Holy shit, I know you're not going to..., when we get back, if we get back, I think a mental evaluation is in order."

"I've had several and the jury is still out."

I zigged and zagged through the reef, avoiding dark and light patches. A glance back showed me the police boat was closing. I said to myself, *Nama, if you're going to help this may be a good time.*

"Who in hell are you talking to?"

I looked at Mad; he had closed his eyes tightly and was holding on for dear life. "Hopefully, friends."

Suddenly white foam appeared just in front of the bow. I jerked the boat to the left and saw another white spot. I turned back to the right, only to see another rock jutting out of the water directly ahead of us. Back to the left I saw deep blue water. The sound of splintering fiberglass and screams filled the air. I looked back to see the police boat airborne with her bottom ripped open and bodies flying through the air. The boat broke apart as it landed between two large rocks.

Mad asked, "How the hell did you get through there?"

I heard Dee's panicked voice in my ear shouting, "Mad, are you all right, Mad? Babies talk to me. Oh my god, Mad, please talk to me!"

I glanced at Mad who was still staring at the police boat. "Mad." I pointed to my ear.

He turned on his earpiece, hearing Dee's desperate pleas. In a calm voice he said, "What's up, baby? Want to play dress up later?"

Dee sobbed, "Oh, baby, I didn't see them. They must have been hiding there all night waiting. I'm so sorry. Are you OK? Please, please are you OK?"

Mad said, "I love you, baby. We're on our way, no one's hurt."

Mad was looking over his shoulder toward the remains of our pursuers. With a strange expression on his face, he asked again, "How did you get through there?"

I laughed "I did what Sam said, and I avoided the parts that weren't water."

"That's what I mean. I don't see parts that are water."

I glanced over my shoulder and saw the boat wedged on what seemed to be a solid wall of large jagged rock. I pointed. "Ahh, it's right over there behind the boat. They couldn't make the turn. Sam brought the *Alchemist* through there, so I knew we could make it."

Mad narrowed his eyes. "I'm going to keep my eyes open next time."

I heard air hissing and saw several holes in the support tubes. "Take the wheel; I'll move some of the weight off our leaking tube."

"After seeing how you handled this boat, you're the captain, and I'm the first mate."

He dug down under a seat and found a repair kit. After patching the holes he could see and turned on the compressor. The tube filed with air which increased our speed. There were holes we couldn't find because, even with the compressor running, we struggled to keep the tube inflated. There was no danger of the boat sinking, but the flat tube was drastically cutting down our speed.

Dee said, "Under no other circumstances would I ever tell two men such as you to do this, but boys, you need to hurry. There are boats coming from all directions toward you."

Mad said, "Don't worry, we'll be there soon baby."

We ran the motors wide open and after shifting some of the weight, our speed picked up to just a few knots below what we had run on our way to Baneterra. The motors had to work a lot harder to maintain that speed but it couldn't be helped.

Dee said, "All the boats but one are on a rescue mission. So you're safe for now. The one boat that is coming after you came out of St. Morgan, but it's not a factor."

With time on our side, we swung wide around the island to keep out of sight. I saw the crack in the cliff face and kept the power on until well inside. "I don't know if it will work with the Zodiac. We may have to get out and push."

I added power and ran it up on the little piece of sand, where the *Alchemist* had stopped. "Now, we should start moving backwards."

Nothing happened.

"Guess we will have to do this the modern way." I put the motors in reverse and backed down the passage. When we got to the end, I switched forward and idled into the lagoon. Not as classy as on the *Alchemist*, but still impressive.

CHAPTER 44

Mad stepped out of the Zodiac, took a line and tied off the bow, while I shut down the motors and tied off the stern. In the quiet of the lagoon, we both heard the hissing sound of air escaping from the hastily patched tube.

Mad glanced at the *Alchemist* and the numerous bullet holes in her hull, then back toward the Zodiac now listing to port, caused by the rapidly deflating support tube. He let out a laugh, "Boy, you're rough on the equipment. Two boats shot up in as many days. I don't know if Gabriel's navy can handle you."

"At least I bring them back."

"That you do. Let's go tell Dee we're home."

Mad all but ran up the steps. He stopped outside Dee's room. "Is the lady of the house in?"

She squealed like a schoolgirl and ran to Mad. "Oh, baby, I was so worried. I don't know where they came from. They were just there. Are you hurt? Here sit down and let me look. Oh, baby, I was so scared."

Mad gave me a sheepish grin and a wink. I backed out of the door and walked into the dining hall.

Hanz was coming through the door on the far end of the room and said, "Well, you are acquiring quite a record."

"What do you mean?"

Hanz said, "It seems one Arnold aka Rick Blane and an unidentified male accomplice ambushed a police boat while on patrol. Arnold and this unknown male shot at and wounded several police officers. Later, Arnold and the unknown male blew up the police boat and made their escape. Arnold, for a girly-man, you're getting quite the reputation."

"I do what I can, but Mad is going to be pissed, finding out he was just a sidekick."

Hanz grinned. "Everyone knows the sidekick is where the action is. The other guy is just fluff."

I nodded my head in agreement. "Where's Sam?"

"She took Franz to work on a killer surprise for Joey. When word gets out about your new and improved reputation, she will have no problem sealing the deal." I waited for him to tell me what she was doing.

Mad came in, "Boys, Dee just got a message from Sam."

We walked into Dee's computer heaven and she read us the message. "Sam says everything is falling into place. Reports of Arnold injuring six police officers and destroying two more boats have convinced Joey's people to work with us."

"Would someone please tell me what is going on? Hold it. Six cops and two boats?"

Dee said, "You're a bad ass."

Mad said "It's island talk! Now you know how the pirate stories got so twisted."

Dee laughed. "The plan is simple. We use Joey's management style against him. He keeps his people under control through fear and intimidation. His crazy behavior and those new men have made some of his people very nervous. Sam is talking to a select group of his people, making them an offer they can't refuse."

I chuckled. "Does it involve a horse head being put in someone's bed?"

Dee answered, "No, they would just use that to make soup or something. Arnold will pay them a visit if they don't agree."

Hanz asked, "Where did the swords come from?" He reached for one. Sparks jumped from the grip toward his hand, making a popping sound.

He jumped, jerked his hand back, and said, "Did you see that?" He reached for the grip again, and received another jolt.

Mad picked up the sword, nothing happened. I walked over and separated the four swords on the table, touching each grip. "There is a red, blue and, as of yet, two undecided. Hanz would you to touch each one starting with this one?" I pointed to the one that was not Sam's or mine.

Hanz stuck out one finger and slowly moved it toward the grip. Just before he touched it, a spark jumped to his finger. He shook his hand, gave me a curious look, and moved toward the blue sword. He got within an inch of the grip before the spark jumped to his finger. From a foot away, the red sword sent out a popping spark. He jumped back and said, "Enough of the bullshit. That hurts. What the hell is going on?"

Mad briefly touched each grip. There were no sparks jumping to his finger.

Dee said, "Let me try." I pointed to the plain sword. She touched it with her finger and nothing happened, but a strange expression came over her face. She took hold of the grip, pulled the sword from its scabbard and said, "Oh! I like this. It's... Oh, my." She fell silent, staring into the blade.

Hanz asked, "What's going on with those things?"

I answered, "I don't know, but I believe they have something to do with my missing people."

Hanz asked, "What missing people?"

Mad spoke up. "Speaking of that, I've translated some of the journal and know some of what was on the obelisk. I'll get the book and meet you in the dining hall."

Dee was still holding the sword, staring into the blade.

Hanz asked, "Is she all right?"

I quipped, "She's just bonding" and walked out of the room.

Mad walked into the hall, holding the journal and a file folder. He placed them on the table and sat down. Opening the folder, he spread out pictures of the obelisk Sam had taken. "I think this may be a totem. There are fifteen groupings and each is a different language."

He spread out the enlarged pictures of each group. "I've only been able to find and translate seven so far. Each seems to be a prayer to a deity of one form or another. Two ask for guidance, strength, and wisdom, with an appeal for mercy. The other five have only one request and that is for absolution."

He slid four of the pictures to the side. "I used a dictionary to translate these and don't pretend to know or understand the intended inflections or subtle nuances of these languages."

He held up the last picture, one of a strange-looking block script. "This one, I can read and understand. After reading it, I realized these are not generic prayers given by a padre or shaman. These are personal prayers made directly to their god. Phrasings in this made me believe these people were being forced to do things which brought them shame and dishonor. This man was pleading with Odin, to forgive him for his actions. I reread each of the prayers." He waved his hand over the pictures. "I believe all fifteen of these people were being forced somehow, to do things they hated."

I asked, "Like what?"

"I don't know. At this point, it's another island mystery."

He picked up all the pictures, put them back into the folder and opened the journal. "This has also given me more questions than answers. From what I can gather, Jeremy, the person keeping this journal, started it in Latin. His handwriting is horrendous. Someone was correcting his spelling and making suggestions in the first part of the journal, but in looking ahead that stops."

Mad summarized, "He mainly talks about people on the island, like Big Nose Bob, who helped him cook and serve drinks. Everyone had a nickname, usually reference to a missing body part, No Nose Frenchy or Peg Leg Pete. Other than Big Nose Bob, few of them were ever mentioned more than once or twice.

"Sometimes weeks would pass without mentioning Bob, and then there would be an entry every day. There are times he doesn't write for months. Then he starts writing again, as if he had never stopped. If I hadn't been building a time line I might not have noticed."

Mad closed the journal and sat back in the chair. After a long moment, he said, "I think your demons..." He paused, looking to Hanz for a reaction, "were shuttling people on and off the island." He placed his hands on the journal and continued, "I believe you are going to find your pirate and demons in here."

Hanz said, "Don't tell me you are looking for a pirate's treasure? Mad, you should have learned by now, after all the empty holes you've dug. There is no pirate treasure. Arnold, you're screwed up enough without chasing fairytales."

"Call me Rick, please! Arnold is your Franz, a bad ass and I'm not feeling the part. Besides, Mad is just pulling your leg. We're not looking for treasure."

Hanz said, "Sorry, Rick, Sam told me you were mentally unstable and to watch for signs. You could go crazy at any moment and looking for pirate treasure is a sure sign of going crazy."

"No, it isn't. But according to my shrinks, an early indicator of craziness is hair on the middle knuckles of your left hand." Mad and Hanz both looked at their hands. "A sure sign, of course, is looking for it."

Each of them rolled their eyes. I smiled. "Hanz, take me on a tour and show me the island." He gave me a puzzled look. I pointed to my head. "Amnesia." Funny a few days ago I was embarrassed about having it, now I'm making jokes. I still can't remember anything, but I think I'm getting better.

Hanz stuttered, "Sure, what do you want to see?"

"Pretend I've never been here and show me around."

"Well, this is the dining hall where we sometimes eat and have meetings." Raising an eyebrow, I glared at him. "Hey, I'm adjusting to your forgetfulness. Franz and I still think you're faking just to get attention."

He smiled at Mad and gave him a wink; I sat there not saying a word. The silence finally broke. "OK, let's go up on the east wall, where we can get an overview of most of the island and I'll answer your questions."

As we got up from the table Mad said, "You boys have fun. I'm going to check on Dee. She really wants to apologize for missing the boat and I'm more than willing to let her."

We walked out of the dining hall, down a short hallway to a door that opened out to a small landing. To the left was the front of the monastery, to the right a set of stone steps led up to the top of the wall. Hanz took them two at a time. After a couple of steps, I started doing the same. They felt like they had been made for children or adults with much shorter legs and much smaller feet.

At the top of the wall was a walkway that seemed to circle around the entire island. A four-foot wall on each side enclosed the walkway. I leaned against the wall and looked down about thirty feet to the patchwork gardens divided by their own little stone walls. It looked like a cover off *Better Homes and Gardens.*

I stepped to the other side of the walkway and looked at the ocean. To my surprise, the man-made wall was at most ten feet high. Jagged rock and a sheer cliff face extended the rest of the way to the water. The view of crashing waves and turbulent water was a direct contrast to the peaceful gardens mere feet away.

Hanz started down the walkway, pointed to a building across the island from us. "That's our hospital, where you were taken when you fainted." I just smiled. "Those two buildings are where they do the research on Dad's little Garden of Eden. Those buildings are living quarters for the doctors and researchers; those over there are for supplies. That's our troubled desalinization plant, but now that we have a fresh water supply it's not as big a problem."

He stepped around a black cannon like you see on display in museums. After a closer look, something seemed out of place. Three large metal legs supported it. I stopped trying to make sense of what I was seeing.

Hanz came back and to my amazement, bent over and picked up the cannon, revealing a tripod, far newer than the hollow fiberglass cannon, he was holding.

I said. "A lot of metal to hold a toy canon don't you think."

Hanz looked puzzled and said. "Rick they're for..." Pain exploded behind my eyes and I fell against the wall.

"I'm sorry Rick, I didn't mean to."

I waved my hand to stop him. "It's OK. This is one of those things I need to find out about later. And from the way my head aches, I want it to be much later."

As I leaned on the wall looking down at the gardens, the pain started to subside. I noticed several small buildings at the far end of the island. Pointing at them, I asked, "What are those?"

"We were told the island was uninhabited and no one had live here for years. After arriving we found a small group of people living in those houses tending to the gardens. They're an odd bunch and stay to themselves. Franz and I think it's an old hippie commune that used way too much LSD and lost track of time. Dad likes them because one of them – his name is Bodo – knows a lot about the island's plants and trees."

The name Bodo gave me a déjà vu moment like I'd heard someone tell me that name while standing right here before, but the searing pain behind my eyes made me say, "I think it's time to go back to the monastery."

CHAPTER 45

My head had stopped hurting by the time we got to the steps. From the top of the wall, I noticed an ornate cross in the stonework of the monastery courtyard. "Very fancy," I said.

Hanz said, "Very fancy, considering the monks that ran this place took a vow of poverty."

"Can you take me through the gardens? My head has stopped hurting."

Hanz lead me across the courtyard and down some steps designed for a normal sized person. After a while he said, "Arnold…, I mean Rick, man that's going to take some getting used to, we've called you Arnold for three years."

"I know, give it time. Maybe I'll become Arnold again."

"Whichever you choose, cause, man, it's great to have you back. We were worried about you."

"So what's the deal with the two of you wanting to use Hanz and not Franz?"

He let out a huge laugh looked around to see if any one was close enough to hear "It's a twin thing; neither one of us cares. We just like to mess with people. We did the same thing with our real names Jim and Tim. I'm Jim by the way."

We followed the winding path through strange looking trees and plants for quite a while. "Anything in particular you want to see?"

I paused, rubbed my temples, "Yes, Bodo."

Hanz smiled, "You want to see Yoda."

"Yoda? I thought you said Bodo."

"His name is Bodo. We call him Yoda because he's a strange little dude."

After a long walk, we found the houses backing up to the wall. Built by the Spanish, there was a five-foot stone wall separating them from the rest of the island. An iron gate stood at the end of the path. Hanz took hold of my arm and stopped, looked up and down the path, in the trees and under the bushes. Then he whispered, "Don't move. And watch."

From directly behind us I heard, a nasal, oddly pitched voice with an accent I didn't recognize. "How may I help you Tim."

We both turned. Standing in the path where we had just looked was a thin man maybe four feet tall, with oddly colored skin. The Yoda comment must have influenced me, because the coloring of his skin did seem to be a light yellow-green. The fact he had a walking stick like Yoda didn't help. There was something else odd about him. It took a minute to realize, but he was hairless, with no hair on his head, no eyebrows, or eye lashes.

Hanz said, "I'm Jim."

"Of course you are, and who is this?" He stepped forward, then stopped and closed his eyes.

Hanz and I exchanged looks. Hanz mouthed, "May the force be with you." I gave a little chuckle and cleared my throat to cover it up, understanding the reference.

Bodo's eyes snapped open and I gave a little shiver. His unreadable expression didn't change, while he gave me a very unsettling stare. With quickness I hadn't expected, he stepped toward me and grabbed my left arm, twisting it until the black mark made by the sword was only an inch from his nose.

Not taking his eyes from the mark, he said, *"What are you called?"*

"My name is Rick Blane." I didn't know if he knew me as Arnold and didn't want to explain the saga if I didn't have to.

He let go of my arm stepped back, *"Have you heard the name Perdue."*

"Yes, doesn't he own some chicken farms?"

He raised the place where his eyebrows should be, leaned his head to the side and, very slowly, as if chewing each of the words, said, *"Chicken farm."*

He walked to the gate. Opening it he said, *"I have much to think about."* He looked me in the eyes and repeated, *"Chicken Farms."* Turning to Hanz he said, "Have a good day, Timothy." He closed the gate and disappeared behind the wall.

I smiled at Hanz and started down the path toward the monastery. "You were correct. That is one strange little man."

"Talk about strange. The last thing you said that I understood was Rick Blane."

"Really?"

"Yes, really. You and Yoda were babbling in some form of French. Unless there's another dead relative in there," he pointed to my head, "that speaks a different language, because whatever you were speaking wasn't English. It seemed to be French, but nothing I could understand."

CHAPTER 46

The sun was setting by the time we got back to the dining hall. Dee must have heard us because she stuck her head out of the door and said, "Boys, come here please."

We walked in the room to find Dee wearing some kind of a two-piece skintight black leather outfit holding her sword. Mad was relaxing in a chair against the wall and said, "Come in boys, and enjoy the show."

At some point, Dee had been shown how to handle a sword. She smoothly moved from one position to the next and it rapidly turned into a very sensual dance. After about twenty minutes she stopped, bowed to us, and said, "See what happens when all a young girl's friends are Lord of the Rings geeks?"

She looked at the blade. "There is something about this. It has energy." She glanced at Mad, cracked a wry grin and added, "Maybe it's battery-operated."

She placed the sword on the desk. "Enough of that. Now back to work. The timetable has been bumped up. Joey got a call and is on his way to meet the boat. He is handling this transfer in person and has a small armada escorting him. He plans on dividing up the shipment and sending boats directly to his safe houses. I tapped into his security system and can see everything in his safe houses. After we take the goodies, I'll run a generic loop until we drop the hammer on him."

I asked, "What can we do?"

Dee said, "Arnold, honey, you're going to be like Santa Claus. You'll be in four places at once taking Joey's bundles of drugs from some not so good but very cooperative little boys and girls."

I sat there trying to wrap my mind around what she was explaining. Dee saw my lack of understanding. "Sam and Hanz have arranged for multiple Arnolds, that way you can be in four places, none of the descriptions will match, and the legend of the mystical Arnold takes on a life of its own, striking fear in the hearts of evildoers throughout the universe."

"Universe."

"Hey, sci-fi and big boobs twisted my childhood," she winked at Mad, "but in interesting ways."

Mad smiled, "Oh, you're so right, baby!"

Dee looked at Hanz and me as she got up from the desk, walked over, straddling Mad and sat on his lap. "Boys, why don't you go outside and play until it's time for us to carry out our part of the plan? Me and daddy need to talk."

Mad smiled at us, "She can't help it."

Hanz and I walked into the dining hall and sat across from each other at the large wooden table. After a few minutes Hanz asked, "Rick, do you remember anything about living here?"

"No," I let out a sigh and continued, "After waking up in the hospital, as one of you said, my memories were reset to zero. It was scary at first, but the worst part was the looks on my friend's and family's faces. They would tell me what, at the time, seemed to be endless stories and I still could not remember"

"After a while they started acting like they had somehow failed. That made me start trying to force myself to remember, which gave me killer headaches and caused me to create false memories causing everyone to feel even worse. That part I couldn't tell them, because I didn't understand it myself. The memory loss didn't bother me as much as the other thing."

I stopped and looked down at my hands. "I knew beyond a shadow of a doubt, even though it was the home where I was raised, all of it was a horrible mistake. I didn't belong there."

"That all changed, when I cleared the harbor at St. Morgan on the *Alchemist*. It was where I belonged. As for these losses of memory; I haven't had time to miss them. I've been running on gut instinct and adrenaline since getting back."

"Rick, it's really nice you got that off your chest and all, but the reason I ask was you borrowed fifty dollars, just before the last memory reset and I was wondering if you remembered, because I'd like my money back."

"The way I remember it, you borrowed seventy-five from me."

"I knew you were faking, so you do remember some stuff?"

"Nope, just seemed like something a Franz would try."

Hanz laughed, "Shit, thought I had you."

CHAPTER 47

Mad appeared in the doorway. "Joey is back in range. Dee is tracking him on the big screen."

I got up from the big table and followed Mad back into Dee's computer room. For the first time, I saw a huge flat-screen TV covering almost the entire wall. In general, when a man walks into a room, if there is a TV he will notice it first, and then look for the Lay-Z-Boy. Dee's sword play had taken me to a more primal level, obviously, and I had missed this monster's beauty. In the lower left hand corner was an island, probably St. Morgan. There were four blinking dots of various colors, and one little happy face. They were all moving away from each other at a good clip. The happy face was traveling alone and in the general direction of St. Morgan.

Dee pointed to each of the multi-colored dots. "These bad boys are heading to a different island where Arnold is waiting."

She pointed to the happy face. "This is the asshole, and he's on his way back to his freezer."

Dee's phone rang. She answered, "Hey, baby, tell your people to expect company in the next couple of hours. Have fun. I'll be watching… OK, girl, be safe."

Dee changed the picture on the big screen from tracking the blinking dots to four separate pictures. "These are the security systems in Joey's safe houses. We can watch everything that goes on as Arnold takes the goodies. I have blocked Joey's phone so he won't know anything is going on till it's all over.

"Now we've got to get on the water and take care of our part of the plan."

I asked, "Our part of the plan?"

Hanz said, "This is what we came up with. Sam and Franz each have an Arnold, and are taking a house. I'm going to Shadow Bay, to meet my

Arnold and take Joey's drugs. You and Mad are going…" Dee cleared her throat. "And Dee is going to Bent Key."

Dee smiled and said. "We thought Rick needed to get his manhood back."

Hanz said, "We need to get going, I don't want these dirt bags to beat us there and get second thoughts."

Hanz walked out of the room. Without saying a word we each picked up our swords and followed him out of the monastery, down the steps and through the garden.

We walked through the gate and into the covered slips where Hanz got in a go fast boat and departed. Mad led us to a larger boat and said, "We get to use one of Gabriel's toys. Go with Dee, I'll play captain till we get there."

I noticed mounted on top of the cabin a heavy metal tripod, like the one holding up the fiber glass cannons on the wall. Part of a memory flashed just before that stabbing pain shot through my temple.

Dee took me by the hand and led the way into the cabin and turned on the lights. "Welcome to the Van Helsing mobile control center. Gabriel loves his toys." It was a mini version of Dee's computer room in the monastery.

Mad got us underway and Dee set to work pulling up the security systems in the four safe houses. She also pulled up the tracking screen and all the multi-colored dots. We watched the screens for a little more than an hour, with nothing happening.

Mad shouted down from the bridge, "We're about twenty minutes out, where's our guy,"

Dee answered, "We're good, he's out about an hour or so."

We saw movement in the lower left hand picture. Three men walked into the room each carrying bags. They placed the bags on the table and sat down. Just then, the screen went out of focus and stayed that way for a second or two. It cleared, as whatever was blocking the picture got further away.

Dee said, "Meet Arnold number one."

I asked, "How big is that guy?"

233

"Sam said he's around seven feet more or less. We put lift shoes on him."

We watched as Arnold pointed a gun at Joey's people. Two of his men taped Joey's boys to their chairs using good old duct tape. They also taped over their mouths and eyes. Then they picked up the bags and left, being very careful to not turn their faces toward the camera.

Something moved in the screen above that one. Two men walked into the room, and each threw a bag on the couch. One man went to the refrigerator and got each of them a beer. A flash of light filled the room with smoke. For a while, all we could see were shadows moving. Then nothing moved and all we could see was smoke.

Dee said, "I didn't know we were going to blow stuff up."

The smoke cleared and two men were lying on the floor. Their arms were pulled behind their backs and taped to their feet. Tape had been placed over their eyes and mouth.

I said, "Someone hogtied those boys."

"Don't worry, the cops are going to rescue them, after Joey sees what has happened. We don't want him to go nuts and take the loss out on them. It's part of the deal."

Mad shouted, "Rick come up and help me tie her off." After securing the boat, we both went into the cabin.

There was movement in the lower right screen. Six men filed past the camera all carrying bottles of beer. Two sat on the chairs, two on the couch, while the other two leaned against the wall. They all seemed to be laughing and having a good time.

Dee shrugged her shoulders. "I guess Arnold is running late."

Mad said, "Or, he's a party animal."

Dee's phone rang, "Its Sam. I'll put it on speaker... You're on speaker, how did things go?"

Sam said, "No problems on our end. What about yours?"

"Our company still hasn't arrived and there seems to be a party going on at one of the places."

Sam said, "A short, fat black guy with dreadlocks."

"How did you know?"

Sam said, "That damn Turtle, call you later."

We looked at the party screen and saw Turtle answer his phone. He jumped up, started pointing and shouting at the other people. Three men lay on the floor while the other two taped their hand and feet together. After placing tape over their eyes and mouth the two men, Turtle and his men grabbed the bags and left.

I looked at the tracking screen and said, "Our man will be here soon. What's the plan?"

Dee said, "It's simple, we go to the end of the dock and wait. They bring us the stuff; Rick introduces himself as Arnold; we tie them up and leave. After we are on our way home, I tell the cops there are three men tied up at the end of the dock."

Mad narrowed his eyes, "Something about this doesn't feel right."

Dee said, "Sam has talked to these guys and they're willing to go along."

I said, "I know Dee, but I agree with Mad, something is just off."

Mad opened a cabinet and said, "Better to be safe than sorry. Do you want a 9mm Glock or a .40 cal Beretta?"

"The .40, that 9mm may just piss them off."

"Not if you shoot them more than once. What about you Dee?"

Dee strapped on her sword and said, "Guns are like underwear, they just get in the way."

After buckling on my sword, I placed the Beretta in the small of my back. Mad did the same with his sword and Glock. We followed Dee out of the cabin, off the boat, and down the dock.

Dee stopped and asked, "Should we wait here?"

Mad put his arm around her and said, "Baby, let's go over to those two little houses and get out of the light, at least till the hair on the back of my neck stops tingling."

"Oh baby, you get me in the shadows and I'll make something else tingle."

We walked about three hundred feet down the roughly paved road and stood in the dark between the two leaning shacks that were as quiet and abandoned as the street.

Just as we got settled in, the sound of voices drifted out of the shadows from further down the street. Four men passed by each carrying a machete. I recognized them as the same men we had fought with the last time we were here.

Dee let out a blood-curdling scream causing me to jump away from her.

Then in an unworldly voice said, "I told you to never let me set eyes on you again."

The men turned and stared toward the sound of her voice. Dee spoke to them in that strange voice and langue as before. They froze as she talked, as if in a trance, each dropped his machete. She shouted something; the heavyset man fell over like a tree and the one she had sat on earlier pissed his pants. She went into a rhythmic chant. The three standing men shook violently like they were being shocked. Then turned and ran out of sight down the street away from the dock, leaving their friend lying in the street.

Just then, we heard the sound of a boat coming toward the dock.

Mad said, "Come on, we've got to get him out of the street."

We each grabbed a leg and started dragging him between the two shacks. I said, "Geez, Dee, next time pick on the skinny guy."

We watched as six men got out of the boat. Dee whispered, "There were only suppose to be two men."

We waited until the six men passed before stepping out into the street behind them. I said, "Excuse me gentlemen, but I think you are suppose to give me something."

The men all turned brandishing weapons. A tall dark-skinned man with a gravelly voice said, "Who du hell are you?"

That cold, calm feeling filled my chest and I said, "I'm Arnold!"

"Well it seems they be a lot of you, Mr. Arnold."

"So I've heard."

236

"I want to thank you Mr. Arnold for taking care of Joey, he was a real bastard, but I think with him gone, we keep the stuff and start our own little business. The odds of seven to three be in my favor. What you say?"

I heard a gasping sound and reached for the Beretta. I turned to see the fat man we had drug out of the street with his arm around Dee's neck. She winked, twirled her sword around, and stuck it into the man's gut. As his grip loosened, she spun free and removed his head with a single swipe.

I heard gunfire and saw movement out of the corner of my eye as Mad stepped forward. He severed the gun arm of the man closest to him, then plunged the blade into the center of the next man's chest.

The two men to my left were firing as they raised their weapons. I shot them both in the forehead before they could aim. The gravelly voiced man and the one next to him stood motionless, weapons still at their sides.

"Ok! Ok! Take the shit!"

Drop your weapons and get the hell out of my sight, while I'm still in a good mood.

The men ran down the street out of sight and Dee said, "Mad look at your arm, we've got our brands."

CHAPTER 48

After loading the boat and getting well away from Bent Key, Dee said, "I guess with all the gunfire there's no need in me calling the authorities. Now, we wait till Sam calls and tells us she has the goods, and then when she is safe and Joey is back at his home base."

She flipped the screen to tracking Joey. He was almost back to St. Morgan now. Dee's phone rang. Sam's voice came through the speaker. "We got the goods. See you soon," and hung-up.

Dee said, "OK, it's show time. The Lopez Cartel needs to be told little Joey Le Nau has ripped them off. I'm going to leave it on speaker, so don't say anything. They will be able to hear you."

Dee dialed a number and a voice said, "Who is this?"

Dee answered in a sexy voice, "Hey, big boy, I think you're cute. Can I tell you a secret?"

The voice lost its edge. "Who is this?"

"Just someone who wants to be a very good friend, if you know what I mean, but first, there's a secret about one of your new business partners I need to tell you. He is saying some bad things about you, baby, and bragging about ripping you off."

The edge returned to his voice. "I'm listening."

"Baby, those bundles your friend Little Joey Le Nau gave you are filled with shredded paper. He's telling everyone you're afraid of him and if there is a problem his big brother – well, you know about his big brother. Anyway, Joey thinks it will be days before you find out and by then he plans on being long gone."

The voice asked, "How do you know?"

"Joey's got a big mouth. What do you have to lose, baby? Make a call, have those red duct taped bundles checked. If I'm lying all you wasted was a phone call. If I'm telling the truth, and I am telling the truth, you can, well..." Dee paused for effect. "Joey will be staying in his bunker tonight, that is, if you're interested. Got to go, baby. Have fun."

As Dee ended the call, I looked up at the tracking screen. "Joey is back on St. Morgan." The computer speaker relayed the sound of a phone ringing. Joey answered, "What?"

"This is Ran Ran, man, you move your house?"

Joey said, "No, why?"

Ran Ran said, "Man, no one open door for Ran Ran. Got customers waiting, man!"

Joey said, "I'll give you a call."

Dee said, "No need in running, or fake tapes now. He gets 'live not Memorex'."

I shouted up at Mad, "You may want to come down here, things are about to get interesting."

She put the four rooms back on the screen, picked up the phone, dialed, and waited for an answer. "Sam, you need to call in the back up. Joey is about to see the real deal."

Mad said, "I would love to be a fly on the wall when Joey sees this."

We watched the cameras in silence. I almost felt sorry for Joey. His kingdom was falling apart around him. Dee's speakers started ringing again. "Joey's calling his boys." The ringing stopped and started several times as he called each house getting the same lack of response.

Mad said, "I bet he's bouncing off the walls."

Joey's phone rang and he answered. "Hello?"

A voice said, "You little fucking weasel, did you really thing you could rip me off and get away with it?"

Joey cried, "What! Rip *you* off? I've been ripped off!"

The voice said, "You and your brother are both dead. I'm going to rip your fucking heads off and feed them to my gators."

Joey asked, "Wait, what are you talking about? How did I rip you off?"

The voice said, "You know damn well those bundles were filled with paper. You're fucking dead!"

The line went silent. We watched as each of Joey's houses were entered by police. The men were untapped, questioned, and taken away. The speakers started ringing again. Dee said, "Joey is calling someone."

"What do you want, Joey?"

Dee said "That's Clarence."

Joey said, "I've got a big problem."

Clarence said, "So what's new about that?"

Joey said, "This is serious, man. Someone has ripped me off and I think it was that fucking Arnold."

Clarence said, "What is it with you and this Arnold? He's a ghost. No one has seen him but you, let it go."

Joey said, "Listen! I did a deal with the Lopez Cartel. Arnold somehow switched the money. Now they're going to kill both of us."

Clarence said, "You what? You fucking idiot!"

We heard gunshots and Joey screamed, "Fuck! They're already here. Fuck!"

The phone went dead and we looked at each other in stunned silence. I said, "Shit! That didn't take long."

We just looked at the screen for a while. Dee said, "Well, the excitement is over until morning." She looked at Mad, "Take me home I need to talk to you about making something tingle.

Mad said, "We're almost there."

CHAPTER 49

Hanz pulled into the slip as we finished tying off. He shouted, "Let's get some sleep; I'll unload this crap in the morning." Everyone agreed and after securing his boat, we followed him single file to the monastery.

Once in the dining hall I asked Hanz, "Where can I clean up?"

"In your room!" He paused when I gave him Sam's patented look, "Sorry, still getting used to this 'I don't remember crap' thing. Follow me," he mumbled. "I feel like a freaking tour guide."

I smacked him on the back of his head.

"See, I knew you were faking."

My room was a very nice suite, fully furnished with a kitchenette, dining area, even a living room with a great view of the gardens. The bedroom was large with nightstands, dressers, king-size bed, and a huge bathroom. I opened a dresser and found it filled with clothes all my size. I had been living on a boat for the last several weeks and a hot shower with some clean clothes sounded good.

After showering, I put on a robe that was hung on the back of the door, and lay across the bed. A little voice had been nagging me turned into a shouted warning, "You're missing something." I sat up and looked around the room. There were two night stands with lamps, two dressers, one on each side of the bed, and two separate closets. I opened one closet and found it filled with men's clothes. I casually opened the next one and stared for a long minute. It was filled to overflowing with women's clothes. I felt a little dizzy and staggered back a couple of steps, bumping into the dresser. I opened the top drawer; it was filled with women's panties, sexy women's panties. I sat down on the edge of the bed staring at a pair of black lace panties in my hand. That ice pick-like pain hit my temple.

Sam walked in and sat on the bed beside me. She took the panties from my hand, gave a shy little-girl grin and whispered, "You've been faking all along."

"Faking what? The Seurat painting of my life was begging to come into focus. "You...you said...you were in love with Arnold."

She stopped me, "No! I never said that, you assumed I was."

"You said... yes... you?"

She took my face in her hands forcing me to look in her eyes. "Arnold is a figment of Joey's imagination. I couldn't possibly be in love with a figment of someone's imagination." She pressed her lips to mine. A quick little dart from her warm, soft tongue parted my lips.

"But...I'm Arnold?"

"Yes, you are. I'm going to take a shower. We'll talk more after I'm all clean."

Knowing something and understanding it are two different things. I disliked Arnold almost from the beginning; some of it may have been jealously. I know I'm Arnold, but on some level, I haven't fully accepted it.

I heard the bathroom door open and saw her standing in the doorway wearing a matching robe. "How do you do that?"

"Do what?"

"Change, shower and look great in less time than it takes me to put on clean socks."

Looking me in the eyes as she walked toward me, "Mr. Blane, you think too much." She pulled me closer and gave me a long passionate kiss.

She sensed me trying to get my mind around this reality and said, "Rick, do you trust me?"

"Of course."

"Then relax…we've done this before." She untied my robe, put her arms around my waist, and pulled our bodies together, giving me another long kiss.

All my muddled thoughts vanished as her robe slid off her shoulders and dropped to the floor. I placed my hands on each side of her face and looked into her eyes. I ran my fingers through her hair and kissed her neck. My fingertips slowly caressed up and down her bare back as I lightly bit her neck and felt her nails dig into my buttocks.

Finding someone's likes or dislikes is a game of sorts. Most people are more guarded about their sexual desires, than any other part of their lives. It takes a lot of trust to let someone close enough to truly know the person between the sheets.

Being with someone for the first time who already knows all your secrets is unfair. No, it's better than that. It's freaking out of this world.

*****

I awoke to the smell of coffee and the sound of voices. Sam was lying beside me with her head on my arm, a leg and arm lying across me. It felt good. No... normal.

Her eyes opened as if she knew I was looking at her. After giving her a kiss, I said, "Good morning."

"Yes it is…it's great to finally have you back. I've missed you."

Her saying that seemed strange. My feeling for her probably returned when I saw her on the plane in Miami, but I had never missed her.

Sam got out of bed and I watched as she slipped on the robe. I thought Dee flaunted her sexuality to get attention, but Sam is truly a sexy lady with no need to flaunt anything. I watched her until the bathroom door closed.

Thinking of the night before, I was still in bed when Sam came out of the bathroom, hair dry and fully dressed. She bent over and gave me a kiss.

"I'll be having coffee with the boys."

242

"How does she do that?" I mumbled as I grabbed clean clothes and headed to the shower. I was fast, but not nearly that fast. The crew was waiting for me when I came out of the bedroom.

Dee chuckled and said, "Look, honey, our little boy is all grown up and has such a glow."

Sam gave me a wink. "The term 'little boy' doesn't really apply."

Dee let out a laugh. "Woo, Sam, talking smut. Go, girl."

CHAPTER 50

Dee said, "We've had some developments overnight, Grier and Bulza are missing."

I asked, "What do you mean missing?"

"The nurses checked on them this morning and they were gone."

Mad said, "I think Joey told them what happened and they packed their bags and got out of town."

Hanz stuck his head in the doorway. "Coffee, I forgot how good it smells." He poured himself a cup and looked at Sam. "Dad's back, and he wants to see you on St. Morgan."

"Why?"

"When he's like this I don't ask, but it's not good."

"Let's go." Hanz followed her out of the room.

I got some coffee and noticed Mad and Dee staring at me and smiling. "Is something wrong?"

Dee said, "No, we were beginning to wonder if you would ever realize you were 'The Arnold'."

I placed my hand to my forehead faked a groan and said, "I've been sick. I wonder why Gabriel didn't come to the island."

Mad laughed, "We're here, I don't know anyone who has ever seen him other than his family. He is spooky secretive."

"You never met him?"

"Not once in the thirty years I've worked for him."

Franz came in and I asked, "Why did Sam have to leave in such a hurry to meet Gabriel? She missed all the fun."

"Some German has been trying to claim he owns the island. Dad needed some papers brought to him on St. Morgan ASAP."

A loud moan came from the direction of Dee's computer room. She said, "It's Joey. He's crawled out from under his rock."

We ran to the room and saw Joey's icon blinking on the big screen.

Dee said, "He's left St. Morgan and is almost at Baneterra. He's going for the money."

Mad said, "Damn, I wish there was some popcorn because this is going to be a great show." He slid an old school desk around until it sat in front of the screen. He placed a control panel on the desk with around fifteen brightly colored buttons.

"Tell me when to activate it, baby," Dee said. Mad just shook his head in agreement. We all watched in silence as the icon moved closer and closer to the island.

"Do you want me to turn you on, baby?"

Mad didn't return the banter, just stared at the screen.

"I love a man who plays hard to get!"

Mad still didn't move or even make a sound. Dee stared at Mad with concern. She never took her eyes off him and the self-confident woman vanished, replaced by a troubled little girl.

Mad didn't move or take his eyes off the screen while saying, "I love you, Baby, This isn't just about what he did to Laura. It's about what I didn't do allowing this piece of shit to destroy countless families and lives with impunity for far too long. It's time to take a stand and bring this destruction to an end. He needs to feel hopeless and know what it's like to lose everything."

Mad took his eyes off the screen and turned toward Dee. "Baby, it's time. You want to turn me on?"

Confident Dee was back, a big smile flashing across her face. "Oh! Baby, I'll do more than turn you on, I'll put you in charge, then put it on the big screen so everyone can watch."

The box on Mad's desk lit up. He gave us a wink. "I don't want to kill him. I'm just trying to make him crap his pants. Too bad it's not dark. I think we could see the glow from here, when I light up his Fort Knox."

The big screen changed from the tracking map to six separate pictures. Dee explained, "I'm still using his signal for the top three shots. One is Fort Knox, two is the path, and three shows the planes and hangar. The next three are a new wider view of the Fort Knox area, the hangars and the runway. Baby, set them up for me the last time you were on the island."

"It's show time." Mad pushed one of the buttons. "I just ruptured the fuel lines on the planes. That way when we're ready, there will be a large fireball, then later, several huge explosions."

I saw something move on the wide view. "He's on the runway. Wait, there are three of them."

Dee reported, "The two in back are carrying guns."

Mad said, "They must be really scared. The way they're running, I'll have to be fast or I may accidentally blow someone up."

Dee said, "I'd hate it if that happened."

We watched as Joey and the men, ran the entire length of the runway. Mad said, "I'm going to blow Fort Knox when he starts down the path. It should knock them on their asses."

Joey appeared in the screen at the beginning of the path and stopped. He bent over as if trying to catch his breath. When he raised his head, Mad screamed, "Watch this, Mother Fucker!" and pushed a button.

A blinding light filled the screen. The wide view showed a huge fireball followed by a smaller explosion halfway down the path. Mad said, "I was afraid of that. The blast set off that damn land mine."

Smoke and dust blocked the camera showing the path. A shadow moved. It was Joey staggering to his feet. Mad chuckled, "I blew the bastard back about ten feet."

Joey stood there for a long minute trying to clear his head and understand what was happening. He turned and started toward the hangar.

Mad said, "Not so fast, asshole." He pushed another button and bright flashes filled the hangars.

Joey fell backward, staggered to his feet and started running down to the runway followed by the two men.

Mad said, "I bet this knocks them to the ground again." The hangar exploded, sending pieces of metal and wood flying in all directions. Joey and the others fell face first and tumbled forward. They slowly got to their feet and stumbled down the runway.

"I'm going to help get him off the island. The golf ball charges are on one and two-second delays. I scattered them from the hanger to the beach."

Small explosions started randomly popping up all over the strip. They panicked and looked like the Three Stooges as they tried to run from each blast.

Mad laughed, "Those things are just big firecrackers that make a lot of noise. But if you happened to be standing on one, it might blow off a toe or two."

At that moment, one man fell down, grabbed his foot and started rolling around on the runway. Joey and the other man kept running from the puffs of smoke never looking back and disappeared off the end of the runway. The third man got up and started hopping toward the boat until a cloud of dust appeared next to him. He broke into a run and dove off the runway out of sight.

Mad chuckled, "Now if he was a pirate. We could give him a funny name like in the journal. Something like Willy No Toes."

I said, "You're sick, but I like it."

Once they were off the island, Dee pointed to Joey's icon. "He's not going to St. Morgan."

We watched in silence until the icon blinked off the screen. Mad looked at the black control box for a long moment. "I'd like to have one more button to push and blow that son-of-a-bitch out of the water.

Dee said, "Baby, there's no place he can hide from the people looking for him."

CHAPTER 51

We worked on the journal for several hours until the door burst open and Hanz ran in the room almost out of breath. "Sam's been kidnapped, they took her and I couldn't do a damn thing to stop them!"

I asked, "Who took her, was it one of Joey's men?"

Hanz tried to catch his breath. "No…Just after we left St. Morgan a police boat came alongside, with six officers on board. They fired on us till we stopped, told Sam to get on their boat or they would kill me."

I asked, "Where did that asshole Clarence take her?"

"I don't think it was Clarence; I don't even think they were cops. They gave me this phone and said to have Arnold call or they will kill Sam."

"Give me the phone! If Sam hasn't killed them already I will!" There was one number in the phone and I pushed send.

A voice answered, "Arnold, is that you?"

"What've you done with Sam?"

"I didn't think you existed. I thought you were just part of this twisted freak's imagination."

"Who is this? Where is Sam?"

"Calm down. I don't want to hurt your lovely lady. Believe me; I want you to take her back. Two of my best men are going to need some serious medical attention. She's as dangerous as she is sexy."

"What do you want?"

"You Americans, You're always in such a hurry. No time for niceties. OK, just business. I don't want to hurt you or your lady. Some of my men on the other hand don't share my sentiment, so we need to make this quick. This little prick Joey has caused me a great deal of inconvenience."

I heard a dull thud in the background and the moan of someone in pain. "Whoops that may've broken a rib. Anyway, he said you took my last shipment and converted my payment into paper. Then you blew up his plane and took the rest of his money, good job by the way, you my friend are a man after my own heart. You know how to deal with assholes."

"What do you want?"

"I want my last shipment and that payment, and the rest of this asshole's money you took for my pain and suffering. I'll call you in two hours. Get a boat ready for a long trip. Nothing personal Arnold; just business." The phone went dead.

Hanz said, "We can load one of the go fast boats."

I said, "Give me a second, let me think."

I paced the floor for a moment and asked, "Where is the money?"

Hanz said, "In the vault."

We followed Hanz as he led us into another room, where he unlocked a heavy wooden door. That opened into a twenty by twenty storage room with no windows. The bundles of Joey's money were stacked next to the wall.

I said, "I may have the beginnings of a plan. James, get some help and put all the money and drugs on the boat, I was on last night and do something with that tripod." Stabbing pain shot through my temple and I staggered back leaning against the wall.

Mad asked, "Are you all right?"

"Yes but this headache thing is getting old. Mad get Timothy and meet me in Dee's office."

I looked at James and asked, "Have you got this."

He smiled and said, "I've more than got it."

CHAPTER 52

I got to the boat just as the tarp was being pulled over the stack of drugs and money on the bow of the boat. Hanz asked, "Where are Franz and Mad?"

"We're playing a hunch."

Hanz paused and looking past me said, "Holy shit!"

I turned to see Dee in a skintight black leather next-to-nothing outfit.

I said, "Damn it Dee! How are we supposed to concentrate with you wearing that?"

She smiled and said, "I could just take it off," and walked by us and disappeared into the cabin.

Hanz started the boat and pulled us out of the slip and to the end of the pier where we waited for the call. I glanced at the tarp and asked, "Is everything there?"

Hanz said, "Everything is ready for rapid delivery."

The phone rang and I answered; the voice gave me the coordinates.

Hanz plotted the course and said, "There's nothing out there but water."

I said, "They want to make sure we're alone. That's not where we're going."

Hanz said, "Let's get this show on the road."

"Don't be in a big hurry to get there; we need a little time for my plan to come together."

I went below and found Dee with every computer screen up and running. She looked at me, smiled, and said, "You're a smart little piggy, but first let's talk about Carlos Indigo Domingo Montoya Lopez, the undisputed leader of the Lopez Cartel."

She put his picture up on the screen. He had short cut dark hair, bushy eyebrows and a round face; not what you would picture as a major drug dealer.

"This is a nasty, nasty ruthless creature. He kills everyone that gets in his way and takes no prisoners. He has a reputation for mutilating his enemies and sending certain body parts to their families."

"He has a very bad temper, likes cigars, high stakes poker and loves card tricks. The sick bastard is into little girls. I mean eight or nine year old little girls, once they go into his house they never come out. The rumor is when he gets tired of them; he cuts them up and feeds them to his pet crocodiles. This bastard needs to die, and if I get a chance I'm going to kill him."

"I think you'll have to get in line."

She changed the big screen and said, "You were right about where they're taking us. Mad did a great job blowing up the place, but there are still a few cameras working. I think the man sitting in the lawn chair smoking that big ass cigar is Carlos. Now this is where it gets a little dicey, I'm not sure how many men he has on the island. There are two or three in the hangar with Sam. One man with a rifle went up the path at the end of the runway and disappeared into the brush."

I said, "Hiding people like that, he's not playing fair."

"Three or four men keep walking in and out of my view off the end of the runway toward the boat."

Hanz shouted down, "I see the boat; It's that police boat with six men on board."

I went up on deck and stood beside Hanz as we came along side. One of the men smiled and said, "Follow us."

Hanz said, "That's strange, they didn't ask about weapons or anything."

"With six men on the boat and at least that many on Baneterra, they're not worried."

"They've pissed Sam off, they should be worried."

"Tell me when we get close to the island. I'm going down in the cabin and get ready."

Dee was staring at the screen and said, "I've got their signal. The boat checked in, Carlos said not to kill anyone until he meets you, but when he gives the signal kill everyone and take the stuff to Bent Key."

CHAPTER 53

Dee said, "Carlos and two men are walking down the runway toward the boat."

Hanz called down, "We'll be there in ten."

I walked over to the bar and started looking through the cabinets and drawers until I found a deck of playing cards. After a good shuffle, I fanned them out and said, "Pick a card, any card, and I'll tell you what it is."

Dee gave me a grin, selected a card, looked at it, and then stuck it in her bra and said, "Now big boy, tell me what I've got."

Placing my fingers to my temples and closing my eyes. "I'm a little distracted by the location, but it's coming to me." I opened my eyes and stared at the back of the card. "The Ace of Hearts."

She pulled the card out and looked at it. "How the hell did you do that?"

I took the card from her hand and put it in my shirt pocked, gave her a wink and said, "Our friend likes card tricks, I hope to show him a disappearing heart."

Dee said, "That's going to be some trick."

"It may be the only chance we have."

I strapped on my sword and picked up Sam's as the phone rang, "How may I help you Carlos?"

There was no answer at first, "Very good, Arnold. When you get to the island, leave your man on the boat and walk up the path. I would like to meet you."

After the call ended Dee said, "The two brave men with Carlos, went to hide in the brush beside the runway, that's three out of sight. The odds keep getting better."

"Dee keep in touch, but when the time comes you may have to help Hanz."

"I know we'll be ready, I even dressed for the occasion."

I went up on deck and saw a boat with its nose on a little piece of sand. Two men were standing on the beach next to it. Hanz asked, "So, what's the plan?"

I answered, "Blow past these guys we've been following and let me jump off between those two big rocks."

"OK, then what?"

"Back out and don't let anyone on the boat till I give you the signal. If we can't come to an agreement and all hell breaks loose, kill them all, and let God sort them out!"

"Whoooo! Arnold's back!"

I raised an eyebrow and looked at Hanz. This is the second time I've met my alter ego and I'm not sure if I like him, but I'm glad he's here. Two men standing on the beach were surprised when our boat came to a stop and I jumped down.

One of the men ran over and got in front of me as I started up the bank. He put his hand on my shoulder and said, "You're not going up there with those swords."

"You may need that arm to unload the boat; I suggest you get out of my way."

He placed his other hand to his ear, listened for a second, then stepped back. "Go on, we're going to follow you."

When I got to the top of the bank Carlos said, "Really bringing knives to a gun fight, I thought you were smarter than that."

"It's all I need."

CHAPTER 54

Carlos looked down and saw my boat backing away from the island and said, "What do you think you are doing, get that boat back here so we can get it unloaded."

"You don't get a damn thing till I see Sam!"

He turned toward the hangar, placed his hand to his ear, and said something to his men.

Turning back to me, he smiled and said, "Arnold, you really fucked Joey over."

Dee's voice whispered in my ear, "Baby, they've put bags over Sam and Joey's heads and are bringing them to you. He told the sniper to blow the head off the bitch when he removed the hood, and then kill everyone."

Carlos continued, "But you see, I've got a problem. You're a dangerous man. After seeing how you messed Joey up without him even knowing it was happening. How do I know you're not going to try and mess with me?"

"You don't."

"I could just kill you now."

"You could, but I've heard you like card tricks and I've got one you've never seen before."

He glanced at the Rolex on his wrist. "Make it quick."

Pulling the card from my pocket, "If you don't mind I would like for you to take a close look at this card and give it back to me."

Carlos looked at the men standing behind me and said, "If he tries anything shoot him."

We each took a couple of steps toward each other and I handed him the card, "It's the Ace of Hearts."

I went back to where I had been standing and watched as the men leading Sam and Joey stopped next to Carlos.

Someone had tied their hands in front with yellow rope. The man with Sam had been limping and there was a bandage on his foot. The other man had two black eyes and tape over his nose, and was all but dragging Joey.

Dee whispered in my ear peace, "Mad wants you to know all the hidden assets are neutralized."

I said to Carlos, "I want to make sure she's all right." I walked around her and whispered, "Sam, do you trust me?"

"Of course."

"Don't move when he takes the hood off."

I walked back from her about ten feet. I placed the card between my thumb and index finger and said, "I'm going to raise this card over my head while you remove the hood from her head."

Carlos gave me a twisted smile and said, "I like this trick so far."

I raised my hand as he removed the bag and quickly stepped back. Sam blinked her eyes trying to adjust to the light.

I felt the card shake and showed it to Carlos. A hole replaced the heart in the center of the card. "This is from a fifty-caliber sniper rifle, which is aimed at your head. Your boys shouldn't have gone into the brush alone. This island doesn't like strangers."

Carlos said, "You don't know who you're fuckin' with!" as his men nervously looked at every tree and bush trying to decide where the shot came from.

Ice cold resolve filled my chest as our gazes locked. "Oh, I know exactly what I am dealing with; a child molesting, drug pushing, murdering degenerate. Now, untie Sam."

The man with the bandaged foot stepped back and said, "You untie the bitch."

Sam walked toward me with a smirk on her face and I said, "Still not playing well with others I see."

She added, "Untie my hands and give me my sword and I'll show you not playing well with others. He plans on killing us you know."

I answered, "Right now he's more interested in your brother not blowing his head off." I showed her the card.

Giving me a big kiss, as I untied her hands and passed her the sword, she said, "I love it when a plan comes together."

Carlos gave me an angry look. "This little shit Joey tried to intimidate me; by having his new boys kill my cousins. My ancestors learned how to deal with their enemies hundreds of years ago. I gutted and skinned them like pigs and sent their body parts back to their families.

Sam whispered, "He's going to send Joey's parts to Clarence."

Carlos said, "Take that bag off his head so he can say goodbye to his friends."

The man I saw in person was not what I expected. He had a gaunt hatchet face, dark beady rat like eyes and short nappy hair. He blinked as his eyes adjusted to the light. Our eyes locked and his face filled with rage.

A primal sound came from deep in his throat. He swung his hands wildly hitting the man's already broken nose; with his hands still tied he grabbed a pistol from his belt before kicking him in the knee. Still making that guttural sound, he raised the pistol toward me. Sam shouted, "Look out."

I ducked to the side and heard a shot; crimson, mixed with pink fluffy wet cotton candy exploded from the side of Joey's head. With his eyes still locked on me, he dropped to his knees and crumpled face first into the runway arms still extended.

Carlos shouted 'kill them all' and dove to the ground pulling a pistol and aiming at me as he fell. In that instant, his gaze and aim changed from me to Sam. The expression on his face went from anger to something far more sinister.

I shouted, "Sam, move!"

Everything went into slow motion. He fired as I threw my sword like a Bowie Knife and watched as the blade buried itself to the hilt in the center of his chest. His eyes never blinked or closed as the gun dropped from his grip.

I turned toward Sam and saw a blur as she lunged toward the bandaged man, cutting him across his mid-section. Then, faster than I thought humanly possible she spun and plunged the blade through the neck of the man with two black eyes. Both men dropped to the ground.

Automatic weapon fire erupted from the brush behind me. There was also some kind of a loud hissing growl. I turned and saw Mad stepping out of the brush firing on the men who had followed me up from the boat. A black dot appeared in the forehead of one man and several crimson sprays erupted from the chest of the man next to him.

A quick glance of the area showed the bad guys on the ground bleeding and all the good guys still standing. I walked over retrieved my sword and bent down to pick up the Desert Eagle pistol Carlos had used. Not a practical weapon because it was way too big and heavy, but having one pointed at you does leave a lasting impression. Out of the corner of my eye, I saw something move. The man behind Sam sat up holding his throat with one hand and pointed a pistol at her with the other.

I fired the Desert Eagle just as Sam bent over toward Joey. The impact of the round flatted the man instantly; Sam jumped, placing a hand on her backside, and shouted, "Ouch! What are you doing?"

Pointing to the man lying on his back still holding the pistol, "He was going to shoot you."

I heard that loud hissing growl again, but this time it was followed by an explosion. I looked in the direction of the explosion and saw parts of the police boat rise into the air.

Dee was standing on the bow of our boat behind a huge weapon spraying smoke and fire... The weapon growled again and pieces of fiberglass ripped from the boat nosed up on the beach. Dee let out a peculiar almost hysterical laugh

Mad asked, "What the hell is she firing?"

I said, "I don't know, but it makes her look good."

"It makes her look hotter than hell."

Sam walked up behind me, smacked the back of my head and said, "That's one of Father's toys, a Gatling gun off an A-10 Warthog."

Mad said, "That man does like his toys."

I tried to give her a kiss and she pulled away saying. "Don't try that after what you did."

"What are you talking about?"

Hanz stepped out of the brush and asked, "What's up?'

She turned around and pointed at her butt. There was a hole in her shorts and a spot of blood.

Hanz said, "Rick as big as that is and you still almost missed it; you should be ashamed."

Sam glared at Hanz. "Sis, I'm just saying."

I said, "It was an accident."

Looking at Hanz while twirling the necklace in her fingers she said, "He accidentally shot me while trying to save my life."

They both looked at me and Hanz said "It happens."

Rubbing the side where the piece of rib was missing, "I guess it does."

Sam smiled, "I guess we're even."

Dee fired another burst and Mad clicked his headset and said, "Baby you need to stop firing, you might hit one of us."

Dee said, "Baby this has got me so turned on, oh baby I'm so freakin hot."

"We'll be back to the island soon, but for now just go to the cabin and have a glass of wine."

Hanz said, "May we go now, this place gives me the creeps."

Mad looked at Hanz and said, "Let's go."

Sam said, "You can ride with us."

"Hell no! That girl needs to calm down a little; I'm not as young as I used to be."

Sam placed her hand over the spot of blood on her shorts and said, "My butt hurts."

I smiled at her and said, "You want me to kiss it and make it better."

She looked at me narrowing her eyes and mumbled, "Men!" with a grin she continued, "We'll talk about that when we get home."

That's when I realized this is what I have been looking for; this is home.

*****

After getting back to the monastery, I took Sam by the hand and led her out to the patio and looked down into the garden. Holding her tight, I thought, I still don't remember a lot about myself, but I think I'm one of the good guys. The rest of my past will bubble to the surface eventually. I have great friends and I'm in love with a wonderful woman.

Staring at the Garden of Eden, I said, "This island was named for Saint Giles, the Patron Saint of the poor, lepers, and cripples. Maybe they should have named it for Saint Roman, the Patron Saint of silence and secrets."

Epilogue: The Twelfth Ship

One week later

Sam and I went to Dee's office where we found Mad trying to solve more of the journal's secret code.

I asked, "Have you found anything?"

Mad answered, "Nothing on the numbers, but I feel all these blank pages are some how significant."

Hanz walked in, gave me a big smile and said, "Yoda said he wants to see you. He's down in the garden."

"I wonder what he wants?"

The sun was beginning to set as I followed the path through the perfectly manicured garden. I got to the north end of the island where I had met Bodo earlier. He was not there, but the gate was open. I went through the gate and followed a narrow path to a small building.

I asked, "Bodo, are you here?" He appeared in the doorway, stared at me, and then motioned for me to come inside.

The house was one room, very clean but small. There was a bed, a table, two chairs, and two small tables. One wall had shelves with plates, cups, bowls, and cooking pots. Assorted herbs hung on strings dangling from the ceiling. On the wall next to the bed were shelves covered in old books and rolled up papers. The room was cool and well ventilated. Even with the small windows and door, the room seemed well lit.

Bodo said, *"Not have many visitors, so social skills lacking, please sit."* I sat down in one of the chairs next to the bigger table. *"This not my language. Not spoke long time. Hope can understand."*

259

I saw a faded mark of the sword on his left arm. He noticed me looking. *"Faded over time, hope not to return."*

He walked up to me and placed his hand on my chest. *"Must guard, from ones who gave you scars, not to let curse be yours."*

He held my gaze intensely. *"Enigma, you speak his voice, his language.* He paused *"Blood, yes his blood, but how."*

"I speak in whose voice and have whose blood?"

"Perdue, much must to explain, this Perdue." He pointed to me. *"A thief, other Perdue was a cruel Captain."*

Bodo had asked me earlier if I had heard the name Perdue, but I hadn't. Is he trying to tell me this guy in my head was a thief? Most people say they are channeling kings, queens or important people; I get stuck with a freaking thief. I knew we were not speaking English but it didn't seem to matter.

Bodo continued, *"Perdue stole food and medicines for the sick on ship. The Captain caught him taking supplies to the sick and had him flogged. Thinking he was near death, the captain dropped him off on this island with the others to die. He took the captain's name, learned his language and swear to never forget."*

Well, at least I was channeling a Good Samaritan thief.

"With Perdue came doctor, her name was Maya. She used Incantations, herbs, elixirs and some bad things, to make the people better.

"A ship arrived from Europe with the black death and other death." He dropped his head and paused for a long moment. *"Maya tried many things, strange things to stop Death. Most die, others pray for death. She became ill and out of desperation used black magic to save lives. People took the cure gladly, because she did not tell them the price that must be paid."* He walked to the door and stood for a long time, looking out at the garden.

Continuing to look at the garden he said, *"Demons you are looking for, did not start as demons, they were good men. Maya, terrible deal became a cursed. Revenge changed them to what you seek.*

Blood Memory: Eye for an Eye

Evil is like age, it changes, a hair at time, until one day. The mirror reflects truth." Bodo walked over to the bed; from under it, he pulled out a box and brought it to the table. The box was made of woven metal straps and could hold a healthy stack of legal size documents. On the top was the word *Annani.*

He went to the shelves filled with books and papers. From the bottom of one of the stacks, he pulled out something and brought it to the table. He sat down and pushed a small leather bag and parchment letter toward me. It had an elaborate cross imbedded in the wax seal.

"What is this?" I asked.

He let out a deep breath like he had been holding it for a long time *"Their reflection!"* He gave me a strange far away look. *"And mine!"*

Bodo walked to the door and stared out at the garden. *"Read the letter, I think it was written for you."*

I carefully broke the seal and started reading. *"My name doesn't matter. I took the name Perdue to remind me of his cruelty. I keep the name to remind me of what I became."*

This is weird; I'm reading a letter from the man I'm evidently channeling.

"People on this island were starving and dying from the lack of the simplest medicines. I found a way with Maya's help to get the food and supplies we needed. As more people came and survived, our needs grow. I had to take more and more chances to get what we needed. Our luck ran out and Captain McBride killed three of the monks.

"While mourning our loss, a ship came with the Black Death, but it also brought the means to take what we needed. On board was one who practiced Alchemy. Maya used his mixtures in ways never intended and cursed us all.

"The monks became blinded by revenge and justifying what they did to McBride by saying eye for an eye. It's God's will.

"At first we would only take from those who had harmed us. We soon found excuses to take what we wanted. Pirates feared our vengeance and ran at the sight of our flag.

"When the Annani arrived at our doorstep, with Perdue and the monk's tormentor, they thought God had sent them a sign. Filled with anger and revenge, we did nothing that could be called God-like.

"Our actions revealed the price of Maya's cure; hate turned our hearts to stone. Our act of revenge sealed the curse.

"I leave my confession with the only one who did not seek revenge. Whose curse is to live with the knowledge his creations were used in ways he never imagined. The only one who didn't seek a cure, my mentor, the Alchemist, maker of swords, keeper of secrets, and friend, Bodo."

I read the name again Bodo! It couldn't be this Bodo! I glanced at the doorway and he was gone. I looked back at the letter. The page was blank; the words had vanished.

I walked to the monastery and into the office carrying the letter, bag and box, still digesting what I had read. Sam her brothers Mad and Dee had all gathered wanting to hear what Bodo had said.

Mad asked, "What do you have?"

"Don't know. I've never seen anything like this. Have you?" I set the box on the desk next to him.

"Never in person. They're very rare. This is a document box and would have been used to carry contracts, deeds, treaties, important papers." He read the name on top of the box. "Annani could be the name of a ship or a person."

"How do you get them open? There is no place to put a key."

"It's just hidden." After about ten minutes he said, "Here it is." He moved a piece of the strapping to the side. "Now if we only had the key."

Mad covered the keyhole with the metal strap. I asked, "Don't you want to open it?"

Mad answered, "Yes, but there is a trick. Put a key in wrong and turn, glass vials inside break, dumping acid and destroying the papers inside."

I said, "That'll have to wait, but we can see what's in the bag." I pulled the leather bag open and looked inside.

Mad and Dee asked at the same time. "What's in there?"

I smiled, "A monk's mirror!"

Mad asked, "What?"

"You told me about a bishop that worked in this area, before going to get Queen Ann shiny things."

Mad said, "Yes, a real bad ass. He had the swords made."

"What happened to him?"

"He went down with the treasure fleet in 1715."

I opened the bag. "You showed me a picture of the fancy cross he wore around his neck. It looks a lot like this one." I pulled out the cross, a long gold chain, and several pieces of eight stamped 1715 and placed them on the table.

Mad's eyebrows went up. "Looks like someone found the shipwreck."

I pulled out a mummified white-gloved hand wearing a ring that matched the cross. "The monks took their revenge and it cursed them."

Dee said, "I looked up Annani. She is the Aztec deity for Karma, destiny, fate, you know, all that stuff."

Mad asked, "Then what do you think is in this box?"

I answered, "I suspect it has to do with Captain Perdue and your twelfth treasure ship."

Ordering Information

To order this book and other books by Skip Clark please visit our website:

www.BentKeyPress.com

About the Author

Skip Clark grew up in a small town of Eastern Kentucky. After a couple of bouts with higher education, he moved to Florida. While he worked for a major retail chain, he moved around the South collecting stories and characters for his books.

After the death of his wife Maria, he moved to the Orlando area with their 5-year-old son. He became a successful real estate investor, which allowed him to spend time with his son and pursue his hobbies. He likes collecting antiques, flying his small plane, and riding his Harley. Taking long road trips leads him to new adventures and gives him time to think up great stories.

When the real estate market went south and his son left for college, he found the time to pursue his true love of writing. He has written many short stories and poems through the years but has now started the *Blood Memory* series of books; a project he has been thinking of for years.